TORN FROM
THE NEST

TORN FROM
THE NEST

CLORINDA MATTO DE TURNER

Translated from the Spanish by
JOHN H. R. POLT

EDITED AND WITH A FOREWORD AND CHRONOLOGY BY
ANTONIO CORNEJO POLAR

New York   Oxford
Oxford University Press
1998

Oxford University Press

Oxford New York
Athens Auckland Bangkok Bogotá Buenos Aires Calcutta
Cape Town Chennai Dar es Salaam Delhi Florence Hong Kong Istanbul
Karachi Kuala Lumpur Madrid Melbourne Mexico City Mumbai
Nairobi Paris São Paulo Singapore Taipei Tokyo Toronto Warsaw
and associated companies in

Berlin Ibadan

Published by Oxford University Press, Inc.
198 Madison Avenue, New York, New York 10016

Oxford is a registered trademark of Oxford University Press, Inc.

Library of Congress Cataloging-in-Publication Data
Matto de Turner, Clorinda, 1852–1909.
[Aves sin nido. English]
Torn from the nest / Clorinda Matto de Turner ;
edited and with a foreword and chronology by Antonio Cornejo Polar :
translated from the Spanish by John H.R. Polt.
p. cm. — (Library of Latin America)
Includes bibliographical references
ISBN 0-19-511005-6
ISBN 0-19-511006-4 (pbk.)
I. Cornejo Polar, Antonio.
II. Polt, John Herman Richard, 1929–
III. Title.
IV. Series
PQ8497.M3A913 1998 863—dc21 97-40726

1 3 5 7 9 8 6 4 2

Printed in the United States of America
on acid-free paper

Contents

Series Editors'
General Introduction

The Library of Latin America series makes available in translation major nineteenth-century authors whose work has been neglected in the English-speaking world. The titles for the translations from the Spanish and Portuguese were suggested by an editorial committee that included Jean Franco (general editor responsible for works in Spanish), Richard Graham (series editor responsible for works in Portuguese), Tulio Halperín Donghi (at the University of California, Berkeley), Iván Jaksić (at the University of Notre Dame), Naomi Lindstrom (at the University of Texas at Austin), Francine Masiello (at the University of California, Berkeley), and Eduardo Lozano of the Library at the University of Pittsburgh. The late Antonio Cornejo Polar of the University of California, Berkeley, was also one of the founding members of the committee. The translations have been funded thanks to the generosity of the Lampadia Foundation and the Andrew W. Mellon Foundation.

During the period of national formation between 1810 and into the early years of the twentieth century, the new nations of Latin America fashioned their identities, drew up constitutions, engaged in bitter struggles over territory, and debated questions of education, government, ethnicity, and culture. This was a unique period unlike the process of nation formation in Europe and one which should be more familiar than it is to students of comparative politics, history, and literature.

The image of the nation was envisioned by the lettered classes—a minority in countries in which indigenous, mestizo, black, or mulatto peasants and slaves predominated—although there were also alternative nationalisms at the grassroots level. The cultural elite were well educated in European thought and letters, but as statesmen, journalists, poets, and academics, they confronted the problem of the racial and linguistic heterogeneity of the continent and the difficulties of integrating the population into a modern nation-state. Some of the writers whose works will be translated in the Library of Latin America series played leading roles in politics. Fray Servando Teresa de Mier, a friar who translated Rousseau's *The Social Contract* and was one of the most colorful characters of the independence period, was faced with imprisonment and expulsion from Mexico for his heterodox beliefs; on his return, after independence, he was elected to the congress. Domingo Faustino Sarmiento, exiled from his native Argentina under the presidency of Rosas, wrote *Facundo: Civilización y barbarie,* a stinging denunciation of that government. He returned after Rosas' overthrow and was elected president in 1868. Andrés Bello was born in Venezuela, lived in London where he published poetry during the independence period, settled in Chile where he founded the University, wrote his grammar of the Spanish language, and drew up the country's legal code.

These post-independence intelligentsia were not simply dreaming castles in the air, but vitally contributed to the founding of nations and the shaping of culture. The advantage of hindsight may make us aware of problems they themselves did not foresee, but this should not affect our assessment of their truly astonishing energies and achievements. It is still surprising that the writing of Andrés Bello, who contributed fundamental works to so many different fields, has never been translated into English. Although there is a recent translation of Sarmiento's celebrated *Facundo,* there is no translation of his memoirs, *Recuerdos de provincia (Provincial Recollections).* The predominance of memoirs in the Library of Latin America series is no accident—many of these offer entertaining insights into a vast and complex continent.

Nor have we neglected the novel. The series includes new translations of the outstanding Brazilian writer Joaquim Maria Machado de Assis' work, including *Dom Casmurro* and *The Posthumous Memoirs of Brás Cubas.* There is no reason why other novels and writers who are not so well known outside Latin America—the Peruvian novelist Clorinda Matto de Turner's *Aves sin nido,* Nataniel Aguirre's *Juan de la Rosa,* José de Alencar's *Iracema,* Juana Manuela Gorriti's short stories—should not be read with as much interest as the political novels of Anthony Trollope.

A series on nineteenth-century Latin America cannot, however, be limited to literary genres such as the novel, the poem, and the short story. The literature of independent Latin America was eclectic and strongly influenced by the periodical press newly liberated from scrutiny by colonial authorities and the Inquisition. Newspapers were miscellanies of fiction, essays, poems, and translations from all manner of European writing. The novels written on the eve of Mexican Independence by José Joaquín Fernández de Lizardi included disquisitions on secular education and law, and denunciations of the evils of gaming and idleness. Other works, such as a well-known poem by Andrés Bello, "Ode to Tropical Agriculture," and novels such as *Amalia* by José Mármol and the Bolivian Nataniel Aguirre's *Juan de la Rosa*, were openly partisan. By the end of the century, sophisticated scholars were beginning to address the history of their countries, as did João Capistrano de Abreu in his *Capítulos de história colonial.*

It is often in memoirs such as those by Fray Servando Teresa de Mier or Sarmiento that we find the descriptions of everyday life that in Europe were incorporated into the realist novel. Latin American literature at this time was seen largely as a pedagogical tool, a "light" alternative to speeches, sermons, and philosophical tracts—though, in fact, especially in the early part of the century, even the readership for novels was quite small because of the high rate of illiteracy. Nevertheless, the vigorous orally transmitted culture of the gaucho and the urban underclasses became the linguistic repertoire of some of the most interesting nineteenth-century writers—most notably José Hernández, author of the "gauchesque" poem "Martín Fierro," which enjoyed an unparalleled popularity. But for many writers the task was not to appropriate popular language but to civilize, and their literary works were strongly influenced by the high style of political oratory.

The editorial committee has not attempted to limit its selection to the better-known writers such as Machado de Assis; it has also selected many works that have never appeared in translation or writers whose work has not been translated recently. The series now makes these works available to the English-speaking public.

Because of the preferences of funding organizations, the series initially focuses on writing from Brazil, the Southern Cone, the Andean region, and Mexico. Each of our editions will have an introduction that places the work in its appropriate context and includes explanatory notes.

We owe special thanks to Robert Glynn of the Lampadia Foundation, whose initiative gave the project a jump start, and to Richard Ekman of the Andrew W. Mellon Foundation, which also generously supported the project. We also thank the Rockefeller Foundation for funding the 1996 symposium "Culture and Nation in Iberoamerica," organized by the editorial board of the Library of Latin America. We received substantial institutional support and personal encouragement from the Institute of Latin American Studies of the University of Texas at Austin. The support of Edward Barry of Oxford University Press has been crucial, as has the advice and help of Ellen Chodosh of Oxford University Press. The first volumes of the series were published after the untimely death, on July 3, 1997, of Maria C. Bulle, who, as an associate of the Lampadia Foundation, supported the idea from its beginning.

—*Jean Franco*
—*Richard Graham*

Translator's Note

In translating this novel I have received help from my friend and colleague at Berkeley, the late Antonio Cornejo Polar, editor of this volume, Cristina Enríquez de Salamanca (Barcelona), Susan Kirkpatrick (University of California, San Diego), Naomi Lindstrom (a colleague at the University of Texas in Austin who has published an emended version of the 1904 translation, *Birds Without a Nest*), and, above all, Beverley Hastings Polt, my wife, always a source of useful criticism and information. Such blunders and infelicities as may mar these pages I achieved on my own.

—*John H. R. Polt*

Foreword

by ANTONIO CORNEJO POLAR

The novel emerged late in Latin America; in fact, a relatively steady production of novels began only with the years of the struggle for independence (1810–1824), and especially after the wars that culminated in the destruction of the Spanish colonial system. This is not the occasion to examine the many attempts to explain this fact; two obvious considerations will suffice. In the first place, the novel was the literary genre most persecuted by the censors of church and state. As an example, we might recall the instructions that Queen Juana sent to the Casa de Contratación in Seville on April 4, 1531:

> I have been informed that many books of useless and irreligious tales written in Spanish, such as *Amadís* and others of that sort, are being shipped to the Indies; and since this is not suitable reading for the Indians nor something that should concern them, therefore do I command you that henceforth you not permit or allow any person to ship to the Indies any book of tales and irreligious matters. . . .[1]

Second, the novel is a genre whose existence depends to some extent on factors typical of modernity, factors that obviously did not exist during the three colonial centuries. This aspect of the problem holds particular interest. In the process of forming national identity in Spanish America, the chief aim was quickly to achieve the modernity blocked by the colonial regime, especially in regions that, like the Viceroyalty of Peru, had been the seats of Spanish power. This was a many-sided effort that affected the entire social and cultural life of each country. Everything, from the economy to the mores, was to be modernized, though sometimes — in fact, all too often — the changes were no more than skin-deep. There are dozens of texts that satirize this situation; and even many years later, minds as perspicacious as that of the Cuban José Martí (1853–1895) were to express their concern, declaring that "the colony lived on in the republic."[2]

Of course culture was not left on the sidelines in this effort to modernize. On the contrary, it often served as the engine for what were considered the most desirable social changes. We must not forget that this was a period of remarkable growth for journalism, which often became the conduit for new trends in science and literature, or that many nineteenth-century novels, following the European fashion, were published as supplements to the newspapers and magazines of the time.

This relationship between journalism and the novel as two typical manifestations of modernity that awakened much the same enthusiastic response is profoundly significant. If we add public oratory, we have the principal cultural instruments with which the educated elite attempted the process of modernization. After all, journalism, oratory, and the novel made a powerful impact on the various classes of society, even overcoming the limitations imposed by widespread illiteracy. We know that newspapers and novels were read aloud in public places for those unable to read for themselves.

We also know that the problem of modernization in nineteenth-century Latin America was extraordinarily complex and gave rise to passionate polemics. In greatly simplified terms we could say that the two poles of the discussion were Europeanism, which struggled to assimilate the Spanish American republics to the nations of Europe (and, later, to the United States), and Americanism, which sought distinct forms of modernization that would take account of the uniqueness of this part of the New World. Domingo Faustino Sarmiento (Argentina, 1811–1888) and José Martí (Cuba, 1853–1895) could symbolize these two tendencies; yet we must remember that there were numerous intermediate positions between these two extremes, and that beyond the limits of this debate were to be found the most conservative orders, which strove to restore, in one way or another, the colonial regime.

The problem was a great deal more complex and contentious in the countries where indigenous societies and cultures, though transformed, had not disappeared and constituted a substantial demographic majority dominated by the Creole elite. With more or less visible variations, the same is true of those societies in which slavery had produced a sizable population of African origin. In these cases the problem of national modernization naturally involved that of suppressing or culturally integrating the Indian and black masses. The nineteenth century saw the education of these masses and their corresponding Westernization as the necessary condition for beginning a genuine process of modernization.

Significantly, republican ideals did not by themselves suffice to effect the immediate abolition of slavery or the feudal obligations imposed on the Indians. In some countries the model of a rigidly stratified society based on slavery and forced labor actually survived for several decades after independence. This is why in a good many cases the indigenous and African masses felt no involvement in the process of emancipation and sometimes adopted a rather pro-Spanish position. To complicate matters even more, the legislation of the first decades of independence favored the excessive growth of the landed property of the Creoles. Ironically, the great estates, both cultivated and grazing lands, were the products not of the colonial regime but of political decisions by the new republics.

In the case of the Andean republics, Bolivia and Peru, we must add the traumatic experience of the war with Chile, begun in 1879, which dramatically displayed their military weakness, and the deep moral crisis and, indeed, profound disintegration of both nations. We know that many Indian soldiers had no clear idea of why they were fighting. Paradoxically, the indigenous guerrilla units organized on the high plateau to struggle against the Chilean invasion were models of self-sacrifice and heroism.

At the time that concerns us, there were, as we have noted, segments of society that in one way or another advocated the disappearance of the indigenous and African masses. They based themselves on the most conservative tenets of Positivism and did not hesitate to affirm the innate inferiority of these races. As we have also noted, from this point of view the modernization of countries with an indigenous or African majority was inconceivable. There is no need to quote here the profoundly negative opinions on which this position rested; suffice it to say that Indians and blacks were considered barbarians, savages, or simply animals. There are hundreds of affirmations in this sense. In the case of the indigenous peoples, those who denied their civilized status had to deal with the evidence to the contrary provided by the advanced development of the indigenous cultures of the past. The usual solution was to recognize the greatness of these civilizations, while at the same time pointing out that three centuries of oppression had debased the race to the point where its degeneracy was irreversible.

Obviously not everyone held to such an ideology, but there was certainly consensus about the inferiority of indigenous men and women. The most progressive intellectuals thought that this situation was indeed the product of the abuses of colonialism, but that precisely because its causes were historical and social, not biological, it could be overcome through education. Surprisingly enough, throughout the nineteenth century people believed passionately in the power of education yet at the same time did not examine the real, socioeconomic situation of the indigenous population.

The most radical intellectual of the period, the Peruvian Manuel González Prada (1844–1918), exemplifies what we have been saying. González Prada is absolutely opposed to any biological interpretation that might attempt to offer racial reasons for the decline of the indigenous peoples. He considers their situation the result of the exploitation and terrible living conditions to which they were subjected during the colonial period and the first years of independence, blames the excessive consumption of coca and alcohol on the great landowners who used these products to "pay" for the labor of their peons, and, finally, points out that these great landowners are precisely the ones who impose their interests and determine the policies of the state. Oddly enough, the only remedy that he proposes concerns the education of the Indians, an education conceived in terms of their gradual Westernization. He writes, for example:

> For three hundred years the Indian has dragged along on the lower levels of civilization, a hybrid possessing the vices of the barbarian and lacking the virtues of the European. Teach him at least to read and write, and you will see whether or not, in a quarter of a century, he rises to the dignity of being human. You schoolteachers are called on to galvanize a race sleeping beneath the tyranny of the justice of the peace, the governor, and the priest, that trinity that stultifies the Indian.[3]

González Prada firmly maintained this position for many years. Only in 1904 did he come to understand that the problem was not pedagogical but economic, and that its only real solution would be the return of the land to its former and legitimate owners.

It is odd that González Prada, in spite of his negative view of the indigenous people as long as it lacked suitable education, should, ever since 1888, affirm categorically:

The true Peru does not consist of the groups of Creoles and foreigners who inhabit the strip of land between the Pacific and the Andes; the nation is made up of the masses of Indians scattered along the eastern slope of the mountains.[4]

González Prada's polemical statement could be seen as an effort to stir a drowsy national consciousness by setting before its eyes the fact that the country had a largely indigenous population. At any rate it must have had a profound effect on the society of its time, especially on the young people and workers who were the impassioned students of the master's lessons. Years later González Prada would adopt the creed of anarchism and become the precursor of a good part of progressive thought in the Andean zone.

Clorinda Matto: The Writer and Modernization

González Prada clearly exercised a guiding influence on Clorinda Matto de Turner (1854–1909). She had been born in Cuzco and had an intimate knowledge of life in the Andean highlands. Furthermore, although by birth and by her marriage in 1871 to a British subject (Joseph Turner, who died in 1881) she was certainly far removed from the daily struggles of the life of the Indians, ever since her earliest youth she felt that the indigenous race was constantly mistreated and that its exploitation was morally unacceptable. The words of González Prada must have enlightened this as yet vague consciousness as to the injustice at the base of Peruvian society.

She began her literary career with the *Tradiciones cuzqueñas* (*Tales of Old Cuzco*) (1884)[5] in which, with enthusiasm and an inquiring mind, she recounted legends of the pre-Hispanic past and modern customs of the Indians. No clear signs of protest against the unjust plight of the Indians appear in these *Tales.* They lead to the development of a more critical and committed mode of literary production, which was to take form especially in Matto's novels but which does not affect her other texts.

Before we examine some aspects of the author's novels, and specifically of *Aves sin nido* (*Torn from the Nest*), we must examine her journalistic activities. As a very young woman she contributed articles on various subjects to newspapers in Peru and Argentina, and on the death of her husband she decided to become a professional journalist. As such she served from 1883 to 1885 on the editorial staff of *La Bolsa* (*The Ex-*

change), a newspaper published in Arequipa and one of the most prestigious in southern Peru. Far more important, in 1889 she became editor of the Lima weekly *El Perú Ilustrado* (*Modern Peru*), which was unquestionably the most important of the time, as it systematically disseminated new developments in science and literature in addition to providing thorough coverage of Lima's high society. The efficacy of her direction of this journal was impaired by the publication in 1890 of a translation of "Magdala," a story by the Brazilian writer Henrique Coelho Netto that deals with a possible romance between Jesus and Mary Magdalene. This translation produced a scandal and, of course, the indignation of the Church, which on occasion managed physically to block the distribution of the paper. The next year Clorinda Matto was forced to resign her editorship.

We must emphasize not only Clorinda Matto's religious heterodoxy but also the courage with which she faced the most powerful forces of her time. As in the case of *Torn from the Nest*, she stressed her adherence to "pure Christianity"; and there is evidence of her being on very good terms with the first Protestant missionaries to reach Peru. Her religiosity is further evidenced by her translation into Quechua of parts of the Bible.

What is more important than all this is that Clorinda Matto's dedication to journalism and the novel show her to be a woman with clear ideas about the cultural vehicles of modernity. It is true that in her own novels and in the newspapers and magazines she edited, not everything by any means conforms to the spirit of modernity; yet here and there we find ideas and attitudes that reinforce our image of her as a woman who, in spite of her traditional upbringing, sufficiently understood the time in which she lived. And to be fair we should add that modernization in nineteenth-century Peru had limitations similar to, or more severe than, those we find in Clorinda Matto.

Let us now examine some general attributes of her fiction.

Representation and Thesis: Two Levels of Narrative Discourse

Torn from the Nest, Índole (*His Natural Bent*), *and Herencia* (*Birthright*) follow the same basic narrative system. In each case we find what amounts to a twofold level of discourse. On the one hand it seeks to represent referents in reality (life in the Peruvian mountains, both in hamlets, as in *Torn from the Nest*, and on landed estates, as in *His Natural Bent*, and life in Lima, in *Birthright*); but on the other hand it also seeks to demonstrate one or more theses in each novel. A necessary consequence of this duality is the application, within a single text, of two narrative strategies, since the purpose is to achieve two not always congruous aims; likewise implied is a twofold creative impulse. This duality of aims, clearly embodied in a two-level narrative system, is perhaps the most distinctive feature of Clorinda Matto's fiction.

The Level of Representation: Showing, Judging, Explaining

Beginning with her first novel, and very explicitly, Matto stresses the realistic nature of her fiction; indeed, by using such terms as "photograph" or "copy" she assigns to it an almost absolute evidentiary value. In the preface to *Torn from the Nest* she declares that she has "sketched from nature, offering [her] copies to the reader so that he may judge and decide"; and this idea is twice repeated in her last novel, *Birthright*, where she points out that "the novelist copies and does not invent" (139),[6] and, speaking of society's hidden vices, stresses that "the novelist copies with true coloring and ascertains their true character" (153). This is, then, a realism understood in terms of absolute fidelity to truth.

This extreme realism seems in general to operate with landscapes, milieus, and customs, while the reproduction of characters and situations reflects certain stereotypes of Romantic fiction. In fact none of Clorinda Matto's novels produced social scandals such as those that arose from the personal allusions contained in novels like *Blanca Sol*, by Mercedes Cabello de Carbonera,[7] which may be the target at which Emilio Gutiérrez de Quintanilla aims deprecatory remarks in the "Juicio Crítico" ("Critical Remarks") introducing the second edition of *Torn from the Nest.*[8] Limiting our examples only to matters of landscape, however, Kíllac is clearly, as Manuel E. Cuadros has shown, a fairly faithful reproduction of the environs of Tinta;[9] and the Lima reflected in *Birthright* hews so close to reality that its author is forced to falsify some details of the cityscape, explicitly announcing the fact in footnotes, precisely to avoid any troublesome identification of persons. In their very naiveness these notes are most revealing: "The propensity to find similarities with real persons in works like the present one forces us to give imaginary names to some streets" (43). Or again: "There is no tenement house on this street, but the reader will understand the reasons that have moved the author to change the setting in this and other cases" (53).

Her insistence on explaining the reasons for such petty deviations from fact only emphasizes how strongly Clorinda Matto ties her narrative to referents in reality. Oddly enough, this obsession with realism does not preclude the appearance, on the level of action, of elements bordering on the inverisimilar, such as the late discovery of the incestuous relationship between the leading characters in *Torn from the Nest*, the finding of the compromising letter in *His Natural Bent*, and the masking of Aquilino's identity under a false title of nobility in *Birthright*. When we come to study the taxonomy of Matto's fiction we shall find the explanation for this obvious contradiction.

At no time, however, is realistic representation in the work of Clorinda Matto a neutral and objective representation; on the contrary, the level of simple showing is always accompanied by a kind of second voice making judgments or offering explanations. Consequently, while the narrative as a whole is divided between a level of representation and one of thesis, the former is in turn divided to serve the function of showing reality and a second function that is sometimes merely evaluative and sometimes also explanatory. The language of *Torn from the Nest*, *His Natural Bent*, and *Birthright* shows and judges/explains its referents; it is thus a multipurpose language that merits careful analysis.

The level of representation postulates a system of evaluative interpretation that operates on what is being shown realistically to the reader. One might almost say that each story is a sequence that alternates, mixes, and blends a chain of existential statements ("Reality is thus") and another chain of value judgments ("It is good/bad that reality should be thus"). In this sense the narrator is not only omniscient with regard to the world of his story; he is equally omniscient in his function of teacher addressing the reader. In the model of communication imposed by Matto's novels, the reader must accept the double requirement of recognizing, on the one hand, that the text is "copying and not inventing," and, on the other hand, that it is being enriched by means of a moral lesson.

On the level of representation, the narrative system of Clorinda Matto de Turner's fiction contains still other alternatives: as we have seen, the showing of the referent may be followed by a value judgment or by reflections designed to explain the represented realities. The constant of showing is thus accompanied by two variants, judgment and explanation, the latter appearing timidly in *Torn from the Nest*, becoming more noticeable in *His Natural Bent*, and developing rather freely in *Birthright*. Judgment does not disappear in the last two texts, but its position in the system of novelistic representation is different.

A Complex and Contradictory Taxonomy

The novels of Clorinda Matto de Turner actualize two narrative models: their manner of representation is indebted to realism, and they thereby fall within the mainstream of the Western, and especially the French novel; but it is also *costumbrista*, that is, intent on portraying manners, mores, and typical figures, and this connects Matto's novels with a literary vein that, though not indigenous (for Peruvian *costumbrismo* is obviously linked to that of Spain), had undergone long and exhaustive development in Peru. Thanks to this abundant production and the consequent appearance of certain characteristic traits, Peruvian costumbrismo displays a degree of authenticity that the imitative output of Peru's Romantics, for example, could not approach. In this sense the affiliation of Matto's novels with costumbrista prose creates within the process of Peruvian literature a dynamic whose study allows us to glimpse the existence of a national tradition,[10] even as we appreciate the relationship between her work, and Peruvian realism in general, and the French model.

The taxonomic complexity of Clorinda Matto de Turner's fiction does not end with this twofold relationship; indeed, her method of "physiological–moral observation" unquestionably recalls, especially at first, the Naturalistic novel, specifically, Zola's ideas on the "experimental novel."[11] Analysis of her last two novels shows that the insertion of the Naturalist model, though quite open and even boastful, is never anything but partial and ambiguous. The weaknesses of Matto's Naturalism exactly parallel the limitations of the Positivist movement in Peru, a movement that, a few personal exceptions notwithstanding, was never able fully to implement its own principles.

At any rate, the sharpest clash is evidently the one between the Romantic substratum that never disappears in any of Clorinda Matto's three novels and is strikingly obvious in her first, and this added element derived from Naturalism. In this regard we have already noted that the faithfully realistic representation of landscapes, milieus, and customs is not repeated at the level of characters and action, which are rather informed by stereotypes clearly derived from Romanticism and indicate an equivocal idealist position on the part of the narrator. To the cases of inverisimilitude mentioned above, which show the survival of a system very remote from that of Naturalism, we could add some further examples, such as the characterization of Father Peñas or the recourse to the redeeming "sound nature" of some characters uncontaminated by the errors of a false civilization, not to mention the obvious contradiction in alternately calling on the concept of heredity and physiological causality, on the one hand, and that of Providence on the other. Romanticism and Naturalism thus appear side by side in every text, generating insoluble contradictions, with no sufficient level of harmonization or synthesis in sight.

The "National Scene" and the Recourse to Lived Experience

In this multiple, heterogeneous, and contradictory fashion, Clorinda Matto de Turner's fiction reflects two spaces that constitute the essence of the country: in her first novels, *Torn from the Nest* and *His Natural Bent*, the Peruvian highlands, life in hamlets and on landed estates; and in her last novel, *Birthright*, life in Lima. In this manner her work tries to represent (i.e., show, judge, explain) what could well be considered the most significant poles of Peruvian nationhood. In the rural world of the Andes she depicts the smallest units, which reflect the neglect, backwardness, and poverty characteristic of that region, and in the urban world of the coastal region she focuses on what is clearly emblematic of it: Lima, the capital.

This choice of spaces does not seem to be the result of chance; on the contrary, it suggests the existence of a firm resolution to make the "national scene" known in its essential aspects, those which, precisely because of their disparity, form the basic opposition that constitutes Peruvian nationhood. It is truly symptomatic that many years later, almost at the close of the process initiated by Clorinda Matto, Ciro Alegría and José María Arguedas should also feel obliged to leave behind the Andean space of their first novels to plunge into the problems of the coastal region. Allowance made for all their obvious differences, *Lázaro (Lazarus)* and *El zorro de arriba y el zorro de abajo (The Highland Fox and the Lowland Fox)* repeat, within the creative trajectories to which they belong, the position that *Birthright* occupies in relation to the series of works that it concludes.[12] Seen from this point of view, the novels of Clorinda Matto anticipate the integrative drive that marks the course of the best Peruvian fiction, the desire to make the novel an instrument for the interpretation of national reality as a heterogeneous yet coherent whole.

There is, as yet, no integrating vision here, no order that interprets the vast universe being represented; yet even lacking these, *Torn from the Nest*, *His Natural Bent*, and *Birthright* constitute a laudable effort to elucidate our national problems and to establish certain values that were to guide the course of Peruvian society. It is true that Clorinda Matto's novels allow their social message to be diffused in a moralizing idealism; but it is equally true that their irate denunciation of poverty and exploitation lays out the path that our critical fiction will follow and, on the personal level, implies a spirit of bold nonconformity.

Clorinda Matto's decision to represent the two most important spaces of Peruvian reality in her fiction and the critical manner in which she carries out this task are related to another important intention, that of contributing "to the creation of our national literature," as is explicitly stressed in *Torn from the Nest* and implied in the subtitle, *Novela peruana (Peruvian Novel)*, of all her longer fiction. Clorinda Matto does not seem to have reached any profound understanding of what is meant by the term "Peruvian literature," which she interprets as having to do with the description of spaces and the discussion of national problems; but even so, and with this obvious limitation, her effort deserves to be recognized. In this connection we should note that Clorinda Matto rather quickly departs from the line of the "tradition" in the manner of Ricardo Palma, which she had cultivated without much success in her *Tales of Old Cuzco*, and that in general she went beyond the superficial approach to reality practiced by our costumbrista writers. While the aim of the "traditions" was to strengthen a sense of being part of a historical process, distorted at times, and not without a touch of irony,[13] into the myth of a "golden age," and while our early costumbrismo led no farther than mockery of certain collective habits that were only the most visible surface of much deeper conflicts, Matto's fiction suggests more profound levels of Peru's national problems and makes it possible to meditate on the future of the country. Her treatment of the theme of the Indian is certainly Clorinda Matto's most memorable achievement in her effort to construct a Peruvian literature. The system of representation can thus be enriched with a new dimension, that of leading to the discovery of some areas of reality of which the reader is unaware and which the narrator strives to project into the national consciousness.

The Level of the Thesis: A Constant Ethical Perspective

As we have seen above, each of Matto's novels overlays the already heterogeneous level of representation with a second stratum designed to demonstrate one or more theses. To the functions specific to the level of representation, taxonomically diverse and even contradictory, we must thus add another function, which attempts to produce conviction in the minds of the readers—in effect, a plea. This is the final function in the complex narrative framework of Matto's novels.

In some instances her theses are explicitly propounded, whether in preliminary texts or in expository interpolations that arrest the course of the narrative; in others, they implicitly underlie the narration of events, though their discovery never demands much effort on the reader's part. Sometimes these two modalities coincide with respect to a single point: *His Natural Bent*, for example, explicitly declares confession to be inappropriate for married women, while implicitly challenging the sacrament of penitence in general. In most cases it is easy to explain this play of disclosure and concealment (only a relative concealment, as we have noted) by taking account of the degree to which the thesis advanced may be socially controversial—in other words, of the repressive reaction that some of the theses defended by Clorinda Matto, especially those having to do with the Church and with religious life, might encounter and in fact did encounter.

From another point of view, the theses propagated by Matto's novels differ in how they are linked to the narrative development of the representational level. As we should expect, there is always an effort to establish a substantive connection between the two levels so that the conviction aimed for might flow from the narrative itself; but sometimes the thesis rests, even if not exclusively, on a kind of discourse not integrated in the narrative, thereby offering an extreme example of the duality that defines the narrative system of *Torn from the Nest*, *His Natural Bent*, and *Birthright*, while at the same time showing how the textual space of each novel can comprehend various forms of the essay and of oratory. Such is the case, for example, in the first novel: while the attack on clerical celibacy is embodied in the representation, through characterization and the development of the action, the affirmation of the saving power of education for the condition of the Indians, which is another of the novel's theses, lacks any representative correlate and is formulated rhetorically in the speeches of some characters or directly in the discourse of the narrator. It is precisely here that non-novelistic forms enter the work.

In the analysis of each of Matto's novels it is easy to determine and categorize the theses propounded; yet even before this analysis we need to know that they concern a vast range of problems whose central points are of a religious, sociopolitical, and scientific nature. Clorinda Matto wants to convince her readers of the validity of certain ideas about religion (e.g., that priestly celibacy is unnatural), as well as to propose solutions to such very specific sociopolitical problems as the selection of provincial administrators. With regard to both areas, however, there is always an underlying moral intent, so that the system of theses advanced, whatever they may concern specifically, always corresponds to an ethical point of view, whose permanence, moreover, defines all of Clorinda Matto's work. Even the theses of a scientific nature (the determining role of heredity, for instance) are always developed from, and toward, an unequivocally moral stance. In this sense, the novels of Clorinda Matto de Turner, no matter how much they may differ in some respects, make up a constant course of ethical thought and invite the reader to take part in something of an exercise in the discernment of values.

The Reception of Torn from the Nest

The three novels that Clorinda Matto wrote met with strikingly different fates. The second, *His Natural Bent* (1891), and the third, *Birthright* (1895), were quickly forgotten by the public and by critics, who practically ignored them from the time of their publication until a few years ago. The first novel, on the other hand, *Torn from the Nest* (1889), was received with a mixture of enthusiasm and outrage, which may explain the speed with which it appeared in a second (1889) and third (1906) edition and in a relatively early, though incomplete, translation into English with the title *Birds Without a Nest: A Story of Indian Life and Priestly Oppression in Peru* (1904).

The first editions of *Torn from the Nest* appear with the subtitle *Peruvian Novel*, intended to show the effort to reflect differing aspects of national life. Indeed, in her preface the author has recourse to the typical metaphor of realism, the photograph: ". . . the task of the novel is to be the photograph that captures the vices and virtues of a people, censuring the former with the appropriate moral lesson and paying its homage of admiration to the latter." With these words the author describes her narrative project in terms of an extreme realism that for her is also one of the values of her novel.

It is quite clear that this photograph is focused on life in the small villages of the Peruvian mountains and on the conflicts between Creoles and Indians that daily take place in them. I suppose this was one of the factors that drew the attention of the public and that explains the novel's initial success. The other factor has to do with the novel's thesis: the very sharp criticism of the moral behavior of the Catholic clergy, which in the novel seems to arise from the issue of priestly celibacy but which actually challenges almost every aspect of the priests' conduct. This challenge does not keep Clorinda Matto from repeatedly declaring herself in favor of "pure Christianity." The strongly anticlerical tone of the novel certainly had a strong impact on the Catholic public and especially on the Church hierarchy, which immediately condemned the book and considered it irreverent and heretical, setting in motion an extended persecution of its author.

By the second decade of this century readers had forgotten the novel, and the attacks of critics on its obvious technical flaws were becoming ever harsher, even employing racist satire to ridicule the author's Andean (but not indigenous) origins. For a critical revival we must wait until 1934, when Concha Meléndez, in her famous book *La novela indianista en Hispanoamérica (1832–1889)* (*The Spanish American Novel on Indian Themes, 1832–1889*), [14] emphatically defends the value of *Torn from the Nest*, a defense continued decades later by Aída Cometta Manzoni.[15] From that point on, Clorinda Matto's novel receives more attention from critics and is considered an essential element in the evolution of "indigenism" in Latin America and in the transition from Romanticism to Realism. It is of course Peruvian critics who have been most interested in this work, whose obvious defects do not detract from its extraordinary historical value. Today it is considered a classic of Spanish American literature.[16]

Killac: Reality and Symbol

The novel begins with the description of Killac, an Andean hamlet that lives by commerce (especially the trade in alpaca wool) and from mining activities in the surrounding area. Its geographical location is ambivalent. Within the southern mountains it occupies a privileged position and is considered "centrally located for commerce with the capital cities of the departments into which Peru is divided"; but with respect to the coast its isolation is extreme: it lies "five days on horseback" from the nearest railroad station, and the train only reaches that "every two weeks." The derailment of the train that is carrying the protagonists away from Killac, in a somewhat unnecessary episode,[17] serves to emphasize this isolation: distance is enhanced with a sign of difficulty and danger (Part II, Chapter 27). Apart from how rigorously realistic the portrayal of Kíllac may be, bearing in mind that it can be considered something like the "poetic name" of Tinta, [18] what is truly important is that this dual position of integration and isolation permits, through the former, the adaptation of the specific details of Kíllac to a type, that of small Andean towns, and, through the latter, the creation of an ideal perspective on the coastal space and its paradigm of civilization, obviously centered on Lima.

Torn from the Nest thus offers two spaces: that of Kíllac, directly represented and occupying the foreground of the narrative, and that of Lima, whose ideal image, composed more of conjecture than of direct knowledge, ever haunts the characters. As we shall see, the narrator constantly contrasts these two spaces, either in his own discourse or through the speech of the characters, so that the entire novel rests on this permanent comparison and the values that underlie it.

Kíllac is the symbol of mountain hamlets. The narrator and the characters repeatedly concur in pointing out this quality and occasionally do so explicitly (e.g., "what happens in Kíllac, as in every small town of the Peruvian hinterland"). This is why what is true of Kíllac can easily be applied to any other Andean village, and why throughout the narrative we find a constant tendency toward the most obvious generalizations: "the deadening stream of depravation that runs through our minor towns, rightly called major hells." Even though, as we have noted, Kíllac alludes to a very concrete referent, which entails some degree of specificity, *Torn from the Nest* gradually slips toward a degree of abstraction, as the world it represents is far more a *type* than a specific and distinct reality. What happens in Kíllac would actually be irrelevant if it did not exemplify a far greater and more important reality, life in the small towns of the Peruvian mountains. This, at bottom, is the true referent of *Torn from the Nest* and what really interests the narrator.

The "Gentry": Denunciation and Elusiveness

Kíllac (that is, what Kíllac represents) is seen in the novel in markedly negative terms. Except for the landscape, always praised, and for a few features of the simplicity of village life, which the narrator regards sympathetically, the image of Kíllac offered to us is almost frightening: "a major hell," as the preceding quotation puts it. Nonetheless it must be noted that Kíllac is not a homogeneous space; on the contrary, from the beginning it is shown to contain two orders of reality, that of the town's "gentry" and that corresponding to the indigenous masses. Though the image offered in both cases is deplorable, and that of the town as a whole consequently deplorable as well, each of these spaces has its own character and its own structure, beginning with the fact that the relationship between the "gentry" and the Indians is one of exploiters and exploited—in other words, one of class conflict.

Torn from the Nest shows the "gentry" in the abusive exercise of their power, whether to obtain direct and immediate economic gain or to consolidate and defend the group's favored social status. Except for the priest Vargas, who uses power to satisfy his sexuality, repressed by celibacy, the other "gentry" are mainly dedicated to obtaining more or less direct economic benefits. It is curious, however, that in no case do we find a clear explanation of the ruling group's situation on the level of economic production; the specific nature of their activities in this respect remains a mystery. Although we may suppose them to be landowners and/or cattlemen, or merchants on a less important scale, the novel never focuses on them in terms of these activities but only insofar as they hold power, whether executive (Pancorbo as governor), judicial (Verdejo as judge), or ecclesiastical (Vargas as priest).

There is at any rate no doubt that *Torn from the Nest* gives priority to the administrative—"political," so to speak—side of the Andean world, or, more specifically, of life in the small mountain towns. The preface declares that one of the novel's aims is to call for "taking great care with whom we send to govern the destinies, civil and ecclesiastical, of the remote villages of the Peruvian hinterland." In this sense its probe, though cognizant, with the limitations already pointed out, of underlying economic conditions, is essentially directed at the juridico–political superstructure, especially and quite insistently at very concrete aspects of the organization of the state. That is why, as we read *Torn from the Nest*, we may at times get the impression that the dreadful condition of the Indians and the problems that crush the hamlets of the hinterland could be resolved if the governor, the judge, and the priest complied with their obligations.

This ideal of efficiency and morality in public administration is not complied with in *Torn from the Nest* . Governor Pancorbo, after a short-lived repentance, goes back to his corrupt ways, and the new subprefect, whose term in office begins with the rightful jailing of some of the "gentry," is soon imitating the vices of his predecessors. Fernando Marín, one of the characters who serve as spokesmen for the narrator, takes a sorrowfully skeptical view of this relapse: "Obviously there's no solution," he declares.

The distinguishing characteristic of the "gentry" of Kíllac is, then, their obstinate immorality: all of them, including the priest, are drunkards, womanizers, and thieves. Since this class is depicted in connection with the exploitation suffered by the Indians, the novel lays special stress on the many means employed by the "gentry" to fleece the Indians, whether these means are to some extent institutionalized, like unpaid personal service, or openly criminal, like seizure of the property of accused persons (Part II, Chapter 17) and the high-handed refusal to refund an excess payment (Part I, Chapter 12). The fact that "amazingly, there's no comparison between the conduct of the men and that of the women," for which the novel accounts in terms of a vague Romantic feminism, is better explained by a social structure that excludes women from economic life.[19] Dedicated to their function of "poeticizing the home" and to the exercise of "the domestic virtues," the women of Kíllac take no part in their husbands' depredations; on the contrary, motivated by their natural goodness, they try to restrain the men's lust for pillage.

The radical immorality of the "gentry" is explained by their lack of education. In presenting each of the characters from this class, the narrator insists on pointing out the defects in his education. Thus, for example, Pancorbo "received as elementary an education as the three years he spent at a city school allowed," Verdejo is almost illiterate (Part II, Chapter 1), and the best educated of them all, Estéfano Benítez, simply has "good handwriting." The narrator is so determined to stress this defect that when presenting Father Pascual he notes the "serious doubts as to his having studied or learned, while at the seminary, either theology or Latin"; and when speaking of the subprefect, Colonel Paredes, he immediately informs us that "he had never received any instruction in matters military" and that in general "his education had been minimal." As we shall see presently, the positive characters, who come from outside Kíllac, are characterized by possessing an excellent education. The words of Manuel, a character who also serves as the narrator's spokesman, might epitomize the relation between morality and education that the novel proposes: "[I]t's ignorance that digs the grave of Good." It is thus clear that *Torn from the Nest* attributes great importance to education and marks it as the highest social value. Its functioning or its absence determine the very nature of communal life.[20]

The Indians: Between Indigence and Extinction

Beneath the level of the "gentry" there appears in Kíllac the world of the Indians. Although the novel generalizes its references by speaking of "the race" and of "brothers born in adversity," thereby making plain that its discourse applies to the entire Indian people, novelistic representation focuses on only two families, that of Juan Yupanqui in Part I, and that of Isidro Champi in Part II. Their economic condition differs: the Yupanquis live in poverty, even though they are "Indians who own alpacas," while the Champis enjoy a certain affluence—Isidro's position as sexton of the village church confers a special status on him within Kíllac, and with his wife he is said to own "a lot of cattle," though it is made clear that these cattle "represented a lifetime of indescribable sacrifices on [Isidro's] part and that of his family." This difference of fortunes is of no consequence when the arrogant power of the "gentry" falls upon the two families. They are equally defenseless before it. It seems clear that the similarity of destinies that unites Yupanqui and Champi, despite the difference in their economic status, is designed to express one of the central ideas of the novel, the conviction that it is the entire "indigenous race" that finds itself in a desperate situation because of the exploitation by the "gentry."

In spite of this situation, *Torn from the Nest* offers a remarkably favorable image of the Indians. Contrary to the consensus of the times, when even the defenders of the Indian considered him degenerate—the fault, of course, lay with his exploiters[21]—*Torn from the Nest* strives to reveal not only individual values, like bravery or gratitude, but also, though very cursorily, cultural values, as can be seen in the admiration that the elegance of a pre-Hispanic artifact evokes in Manuel. We are also struck by the novel's appreciation of the beauty of Indian women, not only that of Margarita, whose mestizo ancestry is immediately revealed ("her loveliness reflected that mixture of the Spaniard and the Indian that has produced stunning beauties in Peru") but also that of the Indian Marcela ("a woman in the full flower of her years, striking for her typically Peruvian beauty").

All the values assigned to the Indians seem to be concentrated in their "way of life, charming in its simplicity," diametrically opposed to the "corrupt customs" of the powerful. The ingenuousness of their feelings, the spontaneity of their behavior, even their defenseless passivity, impregnate the representation of the Indians with a bucolic quality that connotes the survival, in spite of their exploitation, of natural goodness and an ever-possible happiness.

The Indians' misfortunes begin with the interference of the "gentry." The novel extols the natural goodness of the indigenous people, whose simple customs could make it happy; and it correspondingly condemns the potentates who defile that original goodness. There is an obvious Romantic perspective in this way of looking at things, which may contain a remote echo of the "noble savage" happy in his primitive state were it not for the depredations of his oppressors.

Torn from the Nest shows a different pattern, however, when in place of the relation between Indians and "gentry" it concerns itself with that between Indians and outsiders, that is, characters from beyond the confines of Kíllac. In this case the educational ideal so characteristic of this novel reappears. Indigenous values, for all the praise bestowed on them, turn out, in effect, to be clearly inferior to those of the civilization brought by the outsiders; and one can consequently envision a gradual educational process that will lead the Indians to the superior level occupied by truly civilized men, by those in possession of genuine "modernity." As the narrative makes explicit, the task of education takes precedence over any other measure that might favor the development and progress of the Indians; what is more, improving the life of the Indians without first raising their consciousness through education would be dangerous and harmful for society as a whole.

We see, then, that the novel incorporates an ideological system of a positivistic bent, a system that as it affirms the value of progress through education is negating the praises of the primitivism of the indigenous people. This second conceptual framework yields yet another version, with some variants, of the well-known contrast between civilization and barbarism. The elemental innocence of the Indians, which appears as a positive value in contrast with the wickedness and ignorance of the "gentry," loses a good deal of its merit when compared with the civilized paradigm. From this new perspective, whose emphasis ultimately dilutes the other one, there is obviously no reason to preserve the Indian's way of life; on the contrary, it becomes urgent to modify it in keeping precisely with an ideal of civilization, modernity, and progress.

The Preeminence of the Outsiders

In the overall structure of the novel, outsiders, specifically Fernando and Lucía Marín, hold an important position. In fact, as we have seen in the preceding paragraphs, the action of *Torn from the Nest* is the result of the personification in typical characters of the social groups that inhabit Killac and of the conflictive relationship that links them and opposes them one to another. The destinies of the "gentry," the Indians, and the outsiders are interwoven in a web of relationships that is as dense as the space in which they coexist is narrow. The whole novel is actually organized as a sequence that follows the threads of the different relationships that the characters establish in representation of the social groups to which they belong. Analysis of this system of relationships shows that the outsiders occupy the axiological summit of the novel: they directly oppose the immorality and ignorance of the "gentry" and generously support the helpless Indians who implore their assistance. To use the language of the novel, the outsiders are the main figures in "the bloody battle of the good against the wicked." The assault against the Maríns is the narrative climax of this struggle.

The family of Fernando and Lucía Marín is presented in the text by means of an accumulation of virtues that are set, in what can come to be a very meticulous comparison, against the vices of the "gentry." What emerges from this process is an extremely idealized image: ever untainted by even the slightest fault, the Maríns are cultured, generous, brave, amiable, thoroughly decent. Although the greatest emphasis clearly falls on moral qualities (they themselves say that they are "on the side of virtue"), whereby the narrative merely confirms the defining note of all of Clorinda Matto de Turner's fiction, one can also glimpse a certain sociopolitical significance in the background. Products of a careful upbringing on the coast, members of a liberal and modernizing bourgeoisie whose ideals could coincide with those of the "practical republic" of President Pardo, who is acclaimed in the novel,[22] the Maríns see the destiny of Peru in terms of a degree of industrialization, in the area of mining, and of a flourishing foreign trade, naturally linked to the sale of minerals. It is truly symptomatic that Fernando Marín is presented as a major stockholder in a mining company, of which he is at the same time manager, for these particulars distinguish him from the traditional miner and inscribe him in a modern economic order.

We can thus see why the Maríns clash head-on with the "gentry": while the former seek the modernization of the country in the framework of a nascent capitalism, the latter, linked to more traditional sectors of society, defend a static social order and the consolidation of a basically feudal social structure. Although the novel says nothing in this regard, the defense of the Indians could well be interpreted in connection with the need for a labor force that the Andean feudal system is by nature not willing to furnish. We have, then, two antagonistic concepts of society, one conservative and the other modernizing, which compete with each other in defense of their interests. It is obvious that the narrative perspective unconditionally privileges the modernizing concept. If in terms of reality Kíllac appears as the concrete representation of the retrograde concept of society, Lima, the Lima evoked by the characters, clearly corresponds to the modernizing concept; it is its emblem. The narrative perspective of *Torn from the Nest* causes Lima to appear in a crudely idealized version.

Torn from the Nest is, then, a harsh denunciation of the "gentry" and of the social order that they impose; but at the same time it is an extravagant acclamation of what the group of outsiders signifies, of the vision of society that they embody. This preeminence of the outsiders also manifests itself, and very powerfully, in the novel's narrative system: in effect, without the intervention of the Maríns, without their resolute interference in the hamlet's social code, life in Kíllac would lack the dynamic that converts it into the stuff of fiction. In this respect it is clear that the relationship simply between the Indians and the "gentry" appears in the novel as a normalized situation, unchanging and in no way productive of action; it is precisely its stability that imprints a sense of tragedy on the description of the life of the Indian people. On the most immediate textual level, the action that generates narrative content is situated in Lucía Marín's efforts to prevent the sufferings of the Yupanquis. Without this effort there would be no action and the text might evolve in the direction of the costumbrista sketch or the elegy. Hence we see not only that the outsiders occupy the highest point in the appreciation of the narrator, whose attitude and perspective, whose world view, they share, but also that they are the indispensable element for the realization of *Torn from the Nest* as a novel.

From what we have seen we can easily deduce the wholly external character of the perspective that governs the overall construction of Clorinda Matto's first novel. In this sense *Torn from the Nest* must be considered the literary result of the critical contemplation of the Andean world from a radically extraneous and distant point of view, in spite of the fact that the preface suggests the operation of another, rather internal, point of view, derived from the author's personal experience.[23] The perspective of novelistic concretion therefore demands that the Andean world change substantially so that it may be incorporated into a specific concept of nationhood, a concept made in the image of the ideals of civilization and progress that the bourgeoisie believes it represents. Although Clorinda Matto obviously adopts a generous attitude toward the Indian and a valiantly combative one toward his exploiters, it would be naive to explain this position in its totality merely as the result of a noble character in search of justice. There is no doubt that Clorinda Matto was that; but her attitude toward the world of the highlands also reflects very concrete interests of a segment—the most progressive segment—of the Peruvian bourgeoisie of her day. This is the central perspective of the novel, even if at times it hides behind an apparently timeless and unqualified morality.

The Love Plot: From the Personal to the Social

The subsequent development of the indigenist novel has led critics to concern themselves primarily with the explicitly social dimensions embodied in *Torn from the Nest*, neglecting and even forgetting other elements that in spite of appearances to the contrary also have a quite precise social significance. This is especially the case of the love plot developed in this novel. According to its preface, the plot of *Torn from the Nest* differs from "the love story or the mere pastime." This notion must be understood, in the light of what the text shows us, in two complementary senses: on the one hand, the love plot occupies a secondary place within the story, which is more intent on developing other narrative lines; on the other hand, even as we follow the romantic vein we find significance of another, more "transcendental," so to speak, kind: specifically, social significance. This second sense is particularly interesting.[24]

Torn from the Nest touches on the love theme in different tones: in general and, to be sure, symptomatically, the treatment of love episodes is in keeping with the value system of the novel as a whole. Thus, for example, the conjugal relationship of the Maríns is perfect, as is the social group to which they belong, while Sebastián Pancorbo, the governor, causes nothing but worry and suffering for his wife, Doña Petronila, who as a woman is exempt from the inevitable faults of the "gentry." As we shall see, the theme of celibacy is also treated in terms of this system.

There is, however, one special case, that of the relationship between Manuel and Margarita. To begin with, this line of action is privileged by the narrator in that the title of the novel is derived from it. Although in Part I the term "torn from the nest" refers to Margarita and Rosalía, the daughters of Juan and Marcela Yupanqui, adopted by the Maríns after the death of their parents, in Part II it is applied to Manuel and Margarita and alludes to the despair into which they are plunged by the discovery that their love bears the stigma of incest. Regardless of some problems that might arise from this twofold meaning of "torn from the nest,"[25] it is the second version of the title that in fact remains impressed on the reader's memory. Margarita and Manuel are the "fledgling birds torn from the nest" (174) who must pay with their ineffable suffering for the sin of their common and secret father, Bishop Miranda y Claro.[26] Of course the tragic denouement of this story, besides repeating certain patterns typical of the Romantic novel,[27] functions in direct relation to the novel's thesis: that priests should not be bound to celibacy. In this sense the plot, as the preface declares, is not a mere love story. Considerations of another kind underlie its development, and it expresses problems that go well beyond the limits of personal experience. From this point of view the story of Manuel and Margarita is, to be sure, the story of two unhappy lovers; but it is at the same time a novelistic protest against an institution of the Roman Catholic Church.

There is a second and more significant dimension to the relationship between Margarita and Manuel. They are offspring of the two opposing strata that make up the primary social structure of Kíllac; in the chronology of the novel they belong to a second generation and thus share a common trait from the first moment of their characterization. This resemblance grows as the reader discovers that both are exceptional: Margarita and her sister are the only young Indians (they are almost children) who become genuine personages in the novel, and they are at once shown to be remarkable for their beauty, while Manuel is clearly different from the other young "gentry" of Kíllac. While these are characterized by the same vices that mark their elders, Manuel, in permanent opposition to his stepfather, Governor Pancorbo, appears as a figure abounding in virtues, as a rare example to the young people already entrapped in the deplorable habits of the citizens of Kíllac. Margarita and Manuel are thus an exceptional couple.

Beginning with this exceptional nature, the narrative will show the gradual rise of both characters to the superior level occupied by the outsiders. *Torn from the Nest* does not adequately analyze this development in the case of Margarita: once she is adopted by the Maríns as their daughter, her new situation is all it takes to modify everything about her. She will live by the rules of the Marín family; and her feelings will soon harmonize with what this family stands for, as can be seen, more than in this novel, in *Birthright*, the sequel to it.[28] What is emphasized in this context is obviously the education that Margarita and her sister will receive: they have to be "brought up with every care," Fernando Marín declares. Farther on, when the clash between the outsiders and the "gentry" is more violent, the Maríns decide to "have the girls brought up somewhere else ... [i]n Lima, of course."

The development of the characterization of Manuel is not particularly complex, either. He first appears in the narrative when he has just returned to Kíllac, which he left as "a boy," the bearer now of an excellent education: he is "a second-year student of law," feels quite at ease with the Maríns, uses a language as refined as theirs, and fully shares their view of things. Although his origin lies in the "gentry," he is in a way one more outsider. In fact his relation with the village "gentry" is extremely conflictive, as can be seen in his relationship with Governor Pancorbo, his stepfather, and his opinion of that class is as negative as that expressed by the Maríns. At best the "gentry" evoke only pity in the young student's mind. The system of values and ideas that Manuel expresses in his frequently pompous language repeats practically all the commonplaces of the outsiders' thinking: he, too, believes in civilization and progress, in education, in justice, and so on. It is natural, therefore, that his most urgent concern should be getting out of Kíllac: "four to six months" seems to him too long a time to spend in his home town.

It is most significant that the relationship between Margarita and Manuel should begin with the latter's effort to teach reading to a girl who at that point seems to be nothing more than the Maríns' adoptive daughter. Although the episode (see Part II, Chapter 2) is developed in terms of extreme Romanticism, the mere fact that Manuel and Margarita should be joined in this learning process clearly proclaims that the narrator wishes to endow the story of his characters with an undertone that goes beyond the personal. In the minds of both characters the fullness of love is also the fullness of a civilizing education; it is therefore no accident that for Manuel the "happiness of society" should be "a natural consequence" of "the happiness of our families" and that the latter, in turn, should be possible only within the precepts of civilization, which, as we are repeatedly told, can be reached only by the path of education.

Margarita and Manuel are the examples that *Torn from the Nest* uses to demonstrate that through education it becomes possible for the Indians and the "gentry" of the highlands to enter the world of the outsiders, or perhaps, more broadly, that the world of the Andes can and must adapt to the principles and values that within Peru guide its polar opposite. This is more of an exemplary display than a socially feasible proposal. In fact, Manuel and Margarita, since they are presented as exceptional, do not depict the destiny of the groups from which they spring, which must disappear as groups in the course of the country's development, but evince in their personal trajectory the possibility of escaping from an outmoded world and becoming part of another, better one, modern and civilized. In neither case is the group saved; these are individuals capable of rising to the only social stratum that seems to justify their existence, that of the outsiders. The social significance that underlies the story of Manuel and Margarita must therefore be understood in terms of insisting once more on the superiority of the outsiders: the fact that the pick of the two Andean strata should join the modern world is to the credit of the kind of redeeming force that the Maríns represent in Kíllac.

From "Pure Christianity" to the Conflicts of Father Pascual

Clorinda Matto's relation with the Church never ceased to be conflictive. Although she repeatedly insisted on her total adhesion to Christianity and even overrated its virtues and ideals, the fact is that she also repeatedly, and with almost the same insistence, attacked the vices of the Church and especially the immorality of its ministers. Manuel E. Cuadros is right when he rejects the image of Clorinda Matto as an antireligious and anti-Christian woman, but unfortunately he does not sufficiently analyze her persistent accusations against the corrupt clergy, which are unquestionably one of the most recurrent features of her work.[29] The theme already appears in some of the *Tales of Old Cuzco*, is developed in *Torn from the Nest*, and culminates in *His Natural Bent*. Robert Bazin, contrasting Clorinda Matto's adherence to Christian principles with her permanent criticism of religious practices, correctly points out that Matto "had created her own idiosyncratic form of Christianity because her country's Church was unacceptable."[30]

In *Torn from the Nest* the religious theme appears precisely in the form of an endless series of acclamations of "pure Christianity" and an also extensive elucidation of the vices that make the activities of the highland priests wholly ineffective. Its starting point, in terms of explaining why the treatment of this theme is important, is summarized thus:

The influence that priests have in these places is so great that their word almost becomes a divine command; and the Indians are so docile that although in the intimacy of their huts there may be veiled criticism of cer-

tain acts of the clergy, the superstition that the priests maintain is powerful enough to crush all discussion and make their voice the law of their
parishioners. (38)

The power wielded by the priests unquestionably makes even their
private life crucially important for society. That is why *Torn from the
Nest*, in its effort to judge life in the hamlets of the Andes, gives special
weight to the activities of the parish priests and their disastrous consequences. Although the paragraph quoted stresses the power of superstition, in a context whose ambiguity might suggest a critical intent that
goes well beyond what the novel actually develops, the fact is that on the
level of plot *Torn from the Nest* particularly emphasizes the problem of
priestly celibacy.

Two priests play a role in the novel: one who is only remembered but
whose past actions will set in motion the conflict of the novel—Don Pedro Miranda y Claro, secret father of Manuel and Margarita—and one
who is actively present in the novel, Father Pascual Vargas, Miranda's
successor in the parish and in his vices. The figure of Father Vargas is un-
doubtedly odious; and the narrator stresses his physical and moral traits
to the point of caricature: a slave to every vice, a drunkard, womanizer,
thief, and gambler, Father Vargas, along with the other "gentry" of the
village, mercilessly exploits the Indians.[31] Like González Prada, *Torn from
the Nest* makes the priest part of "that frightful trinity that embodied a
single injustice" (47).[32] Although in his depredations the priest violates
every right of the Indian people, turning his ministry into ignominious
commerce, the novel especially focuses on his sexual licentiousness and
relates it to the requirement of celibacy. In effect, the novel tries to show
that the unnatural single state in which Father Pascual is obliged to live
conditions this category of his faults, both abundant and very grave.
Speaking of himself in a moment of repentance, he says:

> Pity the man cast into the wasteland of the priesthood without the sup-
> port of a family! . . . I've been more unfortunate than depraved. It's folly
> to spin a flimsy theory and then expect a priest to be virtuous removed
> from family. . . . Alone, in this remote parish, I am the bad father of chil-
> dren who will never know me, I am only a memory for women who never
> loved me, I am a sad example for my parishioners. (71, 73)

The vices of Father Pascual are seen in the text to a large extent as
consequences of the celibacy imposed on him; the always negative assessment of this character therefore spills over onto the Church that

maintains so unnatural a requirement and in effect forces its ministers constantly to transgress it. In this sense Father Vargas appears as the victim of an institution that takes no account of the human nature of its priests. The question is raised, rhetorically, in the preface: "Who knows but what after turning the last page of this book the reader . . . may recognize society's urgent need for a married clergy?"

The answer given by the text, in the story of the parish priest of Killac and also through references to the earlier conduct of Miranda y Claro, who ironically is rewarded by the Church with a bishopric, is resoundingly affirmative. The interests of society are more important than the rules of the Church, and in the name of those interests celibacy should be abolished. This thesis naturally produced a great scandal. We know that in some cities the ecclesiastical authorities had copies of *Torn from the Nest* publicly burned, along with the portrait of its author.

The Limits of Torn from the Nest: *Perspectives*

Without disparaging its early and valuable reflections on the problem of the indigenous people, it is easy to see that the limitations of *Torn from the Nest* are linked, on the one hand, to its inability to understand that not every process of national integration must involve the elimination of regional differences, and, on the other hand, to the inappropriateness of overlaying the indigenous world, and the Andean world as a whole, with the principles, values, and interests of other sectors of the country. Although *Torn from the Nest* acknowledges some values in the Indians, derived from their oft-mentioned "charming simplicity," the truth is that it also calls for the dilution of the indigenous world in a new order conceived in the terms of the then modernizing bourgeoisie. There is thus in *Torn from the Nest* no real movement toward reassertion and reassessment; what there is, is a complaint and a protest against injustice and abuses, and a determination to homogenize Peruvian society according to the model whose emblem is a paradisiacal Lima. In this respect we can find differences between this novel and later indigenist fiction, in which protest against abuses and accusations against local tyrants and their practices are not the only concern of the narrative; on the contrary, these works always add, as a basic dimension, a new appreciation of the indigenous people, which of course means a respectful attitude toward its unique ways.

Furthermore, *Torn from the Nest* does not grasp the socioeconomic meaning of the indigenous problem, for which it proposes solutions that never go beyond a vague and ill-defined morality, a position that leads it to overrate the process of education and the consequent change in "harmful customs." In this regard we must remember that it was 1904 before even González Prada managed to understand the indigenous problem as a basically economic one;[33] it is consequently not surprising that Clorinda Matto, who was certainly less radical than González Prada, should in 1889 ignore this fundamental aspect, which later on will be the essential nucleus of the modern indigenist novel.

The limitations of *Torn from the Nest* result to a great extent from the state of development of Peruvian national consciousness at the end of the nineteenth century. The defeat by Chile fostered both a radicalization of moral demands and an obsessive concern with modernity and progress seen from an ultimately bourgeois point of view. When Clorinda Matto, in *Torn from the Nest*, draws up the paradigm of the Maríns and points out the urgent need to adapt Peruvian society to the ideas represented by this family, and when she imparts a moral significance to all her discourse, she is in reality acting in obedience to the conditions of her time. In consonance with it, embracing both its possibilities and its limitations, Clorinda Matto produces an as yet incipient and incomplete vision of Andean life, interpreted in terms alien to it; yet at the same time she awakens the national consciousness to a new set of problems and a new interpretive approach. After *Torn from the Nest* the wretched condition of the Indian, his unjustifiable sufferings, cannot be forgotten: later novels rise to the challenge offered by Clorinda Matto and, as they correct, deepen, and radicalize her vision of this complex world, confirm the permanent relevance and value of that first and in more than one sense foundational effort.

(*Translated by John H. R. Polt*)

Notes to the Foreword

1. Quoted in Irving Leonard, *Los libros del conquistador (The Books of the Conquistadors)* (Mexico: Fondo de Cultura Económica, 1953), 81.

2. "Nuestra América" ("Our America"), 96. I quote from the Martí *Antología* (Madrid: Editora Nacional, 1975).

3. "Discurso en el Politeama," 73–74. I quote from *Pájinas libres* (Lima: Universo, 1976).

4. Ibid., 73.

5. A second volume of *Tradiciones cuzqueñas* appeared in 1886 (Lima: Imprenta de Torres Aguirre). There are several later editions. The first truly complete edition of the different *Tradiciones cuzqueñas* was published by Estuardo Núñez in *Tradiciones cuzqueñas completas* (Lima: Peisa (Biblioteca Peruana), 1976).

6. I quote from the 1974 edition (Lima: Instituto Nacional de Cultura).

7. *Blanca Sol: Novela social (Blanca Sol: A Social Novel)* (Lima: Universo, 1889). See also Augusto Tamayo Vargas, *Perú en trance de novela (Peru as a Novel)* (Lima: Baluarte, 1940). This is a study of the works of M. Cabello.

8. These "Critical Remarks" are reprinted in the edition published by the Universidad del Cuzco, 1948. In them the author condemns novels that "live off scandal" (12).

9. *Paisaje y obra, mujer e historia: Clorinda Matto de Turner (Landscape and Work, Woman and History)* (Cuzco: Rozas, 1949).

10. A thorough investigation of the inner developmental process of Peruvian literature and, within it, of the costumbrista tradition, probably coming as far as our own time with some aspects of the fiction of Alfredo Bryce, is an urgent and important task.

11. Cf. Émile Zola, *El naturalismo*, ed. Laureano Bonet (Barcelona: Península, 1972), and Guillermo Ara, *La novela naturalista en hispanoamérica* (Buenos Aires: Eudeba, 1965).

12. In this respect it is interesting to observe that *Birthright* serves as a kind of self-criticism in relation to the two earlier novels. In these, Lima is seen as an example of civilized perfection, an image that in *Birthright* is diluted to the point of becoming quite negative.

13. Cf. Sebastián Salazar Bondy, *Lima, la horrible (Lima the Horrible)* (Lima: Populibros, 1964).

14. Madrid, Hernando. Second edition: Río Piedras: Universidad de Puerto Rico, 1961.

15. *El indio en la novela de América (The Indian in the Novel of the Americas)* (Buenos Aires: Editorial Futuro, 1961).

16. Some Peruvian bibliography on Clorinda Matto and *Torn from the Nest:* Francisco Carrillo, *Clorinda Matto de Turner y su indigenismo literario (C. M. de T. and Her Literary Treatment of the Indian)* (Lima: Biblioteca Universitaria, 1967); Alberto Tauro, *Clorinda Matto de Turner y la novela indigenista (C. M. de T. and the Novel on Indian Themes)* (Lima: Universidad de San Marcos, 1976); Tomás Escajadillo, *"Aves sin nido, ¿novela 'indigenista'?"* ("Is *Torn from the Nest* an 'Indigenist' Novel?") (in press; this is Chapter 2 of the author's doctoral dissertation, "La narrativa indigenista: un planteamiento y ocho incisiones" ("Indigenist Fiction: General Approach and Eight Incisions"), Universidad de San Marcos, Lima, 1971, pp. 66–92). See also my studies collected in *Clorinda Matto de Turner, novelista* (Lima: Lluvia Editores, 1992).

17. The episode only serves to create a certain suspense in the development of Part II, matching that created in Part I by the episode of the assault. On this

point see my prologue to the Cuban edition of *Aves sin nido* (Havana: Casa de las Américas, 1974).

18. See Cuadros.

19. Carrillo shows that Abelardo Gamarra in "La mamacha" ("Holy Mother") presents a "realistic contrast to Clorinda Matto's idealization" (34).

20. Recall the words of González Prada quoted above, from his famous 1888 "Discurso en el Politeama."

21. The quotation from González Prada recalled in the previous note allows us to glimpse these ideas.

22. See Jorge Basadre, *Historia de la República del Perú* (Lima: Ed. Universitaria, 1969), vols. 6 and 7.

23. Cf. the studies by Cuadros and Carrillo cited in notes 9 and 16, as well as Alfredo Yépez Miranda, "Clorinda Matto de Turner," prologue to an edition of *Aves sin nido* in a testimonial volume of the II Congreso Indigenista Interamericano (Cuzco: Universidad Nacional del Cuzco, 1948).

24. This is a general characteristic of Matto's fiction: the characters and their personal adventures always suggest a broader significance.

25. It would be worth studying to what extent Part II of the novel is an unnecessary addition that entails new episodes and a changed interpretation of the title rather than something that grows organically out of Part I. On this point see my prologue to the Cuban edition and the study by Carrillo.

26. Presently we shall discuss the problem of celibacy. The elevation of Father Miranda to the rank of bishop obviously implies an open criticism of the Church.

27. Suffice it to recall that the Ecuadorean Juan León Mera also includes the theme of incest in his novel *Cumandá* (1879).

28. In *Birthright*, whose action is set in Lima, Margarita is almost indistinguishable from the other young women of the capital. She has been assimilated into the Marín family.

29. Cuadros, *Paisaje y obra*, 26, 32, 41, etc.

30. *Historia de la literatura americana en lengua española (History of Spanish-Language Literature in the Americas)* (Buenos Aires: Nova, 1963), 319.

31. The first and, until recently, little studied Peruvian novel *El padre Horán (Father Horán)* by Narciso Aréstegui also includes clearly anticlerical elements and especially emphasizes its opposition to priestly celibacy. Oddly enough, one aspect of this novel has been confused by Rudolf Grossmann with the plot of *Torn from the Nest (Historia y problemas de la literatura latinoamericana* (Madrid: Revista de Occidente, 1972), 343).

32. González Prada's expression, reflected in Matto's novel, is "trinity that stultifies the Indian."

33. The article "Nuestros indios" ("Our Indians"), which explains the socioeconomic nature of the problem of the Indian, appeared with the date 1904 in the second edition. of *Horas de lucha (A Time of Struggle)* (Lima: Luz, 1924), 311 ff.

Chronology of Clorinda Matto de Turner

1854   Clorinda Matto is born in Cuzco Peru on November 11. Her parents are Ramón Matto Torres and Grimanesa Concepción Usandivaras. Manuel E. Cuadros affirmed that she was born on November 11, 1852, the date on a birth certificate in the name of Grimanesa Martina Mato Usandivares, whom Cuadros identifies with Clorinda Matto. Later scholars, such as Alberto Tauro, have not accepted this assertion.

1862   Clorinda's mother dies on September 22. Clorinda becomes a boarding student at the Colegio de Nuestra Señora de las Mercedes, later called Colegio Nacional de Educandas, in Cuzco. In her childhood she spends much time at her father's estate in the village of Paullu.

1868   Clorinda completes her schooling. She is eager to continue with higher education but cannot obtain her father's permission. Her father is appointed subprefect of the Province of Calca. Clorinda settles in the family home in Paullu, where she cares for her two younger brothers, Ramón Segundo David and Ramón Daniel.

1871   On July 27 Clorinda marries Joseph Turner, an Englishman. The couple settles in Tinta, a village 120 kilometers from Cuzco and the model for the Kíllac of *Torn from the Nest*.

Clorinda, using various pseudonyms, begins to publish her first writings, especially "traditions" of the Cuzco region in the manner of Ricardo Palma. At the outset she publishes in small regional newspapers, such as *El Heraldo del Cuzco, El Ferrocarril, El Eco de los Andes, El Rodadero,* and *El Mercurio.* Subsequently her texts are accepted by important national and foreign publications, such as *El Correo del Perú, La Ley, La Bolsa, El Correo de Ultramar, La Alborada del Plata,* and *La Ondina del Plata.*

1876   With the support of her husband, she begins to publish the literary weekly *El Recreo* in Cuzco.

1877   Accompanied by her husband, Clorinda Matto makes her first visit to Lima. She is very well received in the literary circles of the capital. On February 28, Juana Manuela Gorriti offers one of her celebrated soirees in her honor. Among the prominent guests are Ricardo Palma, Abelardo Gamarra, the Ecuadorean Numa Pompilio Llona, and Mercedes Cabello de Carbonera.

1879   The outbreak of the Pacific War pits Peru and Bolivia against Chile. Clorinda Matto contributes in various ways to the war effort. She writes patriotic articles, organizes the collection of funds for equipping the army, especially the battalion "Libres del Cuzco" ("Cuzco Volunteers"), and sets up a military hospital for the wounded in her house in Tinta.

1881   Joseph Turner dies on March 3. After a deep depression, Clorinda Matto makes an effort to take charge of her husband's business affairs. The course of the war goes badly for Peru. Lima is occupied by Chilean troops on January 17. Resistance continues in the Andes, led by Andrés Avelino Cáceres, whom Clorinda Matto will always support enthusiastically.

1883   The victim of unscrupulous individuals, she sees her business ruined. She decides to leave Tinta and settles in Arequipa. The war ends in a Chilean victory. The army of occupation begins to evacuate Peruvian territory.

1884   She is named editor in chief of *La Bolsa (The Exchange),* an important newspaper in Arequipa. She publishes her first book, *Tradiciones cuzqueñas (Tales of Old Cuzco),* with a prologue by Ricardo Palma. Her play *Hima-Súmac* is performed in Arequipa.

1886   She moves to Lima, and joins the Círculo Literario, then presided over by Manuel González Prada, whose ideas were to have an important influence on her. She also joins the Ateneo de Lima. Andrés Avelino Cáceres becomes President of the Republic.

1887   She launches a series of cultural gatherings in her home, somewhat in the manner of Juana Manuela Gorriti's famous soirees.

1889   She becomes editor of *El Perú Ilustrado (Modern Peru)*, one of the most important Peruvian papers of the time, which introduces the work of Rubén Darío to Peru and carries that of the nation's leading writers, such as Ricardo Palma and Manuel González Prada. She publishes her first and most important novel, *Aves sin nido (Torn from the Nest)*.

1890   A serious scandal arises when *El Perú Ilustrado*, on August 23, publishes the short story "Magdala," by the Brazilian author Henrique Coelho Netto, which depicts Christ momentarily attracted by the charms of Mary Magdalene. The Catholic hierarchy launches a campaign against the paper and its editor. Oddly enough, the story had been published shortly before (June 19, 1890) in the daily *La Razón* without provoking the least scandal.

1891   On July 11 she is forced to resign from the editorship of *El Perú Ilustrado*. She publishes her second novel, *Índole (His Natural Bent)*, in which she again attacks delinquent priests.

1892   With the help of her brothers she founds and manages a press, La Equitativa, which employs only women. There she publishes several of her works, including *Hima-Súmac*, as well as a semiweekly political and literary paper, *Los Andes* (September 1892 to May 1893).

1894   Andrés Avelino Cáceres again becomes president of the Republic. Clorinda Matto supports him and criticizes his opponent, Nicolás de Piérola.

1895   She publishes *Herencia (Birthright)*, her third novel, in which some of the characters of *Torn from the Nest* reappear. A violent conflict breaks out between Cáceres and Piérola. Piérola, with the support of his guerrilla bands, seizes Lima on March 17. Cáceres is overthrown and goes into exile. Clorinda Matto, known as a Cáceres supporter, is attacked by mobs of Piérola supporters that sack her house and her press. She decides to go into exile (April 25) and settles in Buenos Aires.

1896   In Buenos Aires she launches the publication of *Búcaro Americano*, "a family magazine," which printed sixty-seven issues between February 1, 1896, and August 15, 1909. She is favorably received in the intellectual circles of Buenos Aires and publishes frequent articles in the Argentine press *(La Prensa, La Nación, La Razón, El Tiempo)* and abroad *(Revista Nacional de Literatura y Ciencias Sociales* (Montevideo), *El Cojo Ilustrado* (Caracas), *Las Tres Américas* (New York). She is also active as a teacher.

1901   At the request of the American Bible Society she begins to publish Quechua translations of the Gospels and other New Testament texts.

1908   She travels in Europe for eight months, visiting Spain, France, England, Italy, Switzerland, and Germany. Her health fails, and she returns to Buenos Aires.

1909   Clorinda Matto dies in Buenos Aires on October 25. Her book *Viaje de recreo: España, Francia, Inglaterra, Italia, Suiza y Alemania,* an account of her European voyage, is published posthumously. We know that she was preparing two other books, never finished: *Apuntes sobre historia contemporánea del Perú (Notes on Contemporary Peruvian History)* and a novel, *Comprado (Bought),* probably on a political theme.

1924   By order of President Augusto Leguía, Clorinda Matto de Turner's remains are conveyed to Peru.

Bibliography

Works by Clorinda Matto de Turner

Tradiciones cuzqueñas. Prologue by Ricardo Palma. Biographical notes by Julio F. Sandoval. Arequipa: Imprenta de La Bolsa, 1884. Vol. 2: Prologues by José Antonio de Lavalle and Ricardo Palma. Lima: Imprenta de Torres Aguirre, 1886.

Elementos de literatura según el Reglamento de Instrucción Pública, para uso del bello sexo. Arequipa: Imprenta de La Bolsa, 1884.

Don Juan de Espinosa Medrano o El Doctor Lunarejo: Estudio biográfico. Lima, 1887.

Aves sin nido: Novela peruana. Lima: Imprenta del Universo de Carlos Prince, 1889.

Aves sin nido: Novela peruana. Buenos Aires: Félix Lajouane Editor, 1889.

Bocetos al lápiz de americanos célebres. Lima: Bacigalupi, 1890.

Índole: Novela peruana. Lima: Bacigalupi, 1891.

Hima-Súmac: Drama en tres actos y en prosa. Lima: Imprenta "La Equitativa," 1892.

Leyendas y recortes. Lima: Imprenta "La Equitativa," 1893.

Herencia: Novela peruana. Lima: Imprenta Masías, 1895.

Analogía: Segundo año de Gramática Castellana en las escuelas normales, según el programa oficial. Buenos Aires: Imprenta de Juan A. Alsina, 1897.

Apostolcunac ruraskancuna pananchis Clorinda Matto de Turnerpa castellanomanta runa simiman tticrasccan. Translation into Quechua of the Gospel According to St. Luke and the Acts of the Apostles. Buenos Aires, 1901.

Apunchis Jesucristoc Evangelion San Juanpa qqelkascan. Pananchis Clorinda Matto de Turnerpa runa simiman, castellanomanta thicrascan. New York: Sociedad Bíblica Americana, n.d.

Apunchis Jesucristoc Evangelion San Lucaspa qqelkascan. Pananchis Clorinda Matto de Turnerpa runa simiman, castellanomanta thicrascan. New York: Sociedad Bíblica Americana, n.d.

San Pablo Apostolpa romanocunaman qquelkascan. Pananchis Clorinda Matto de Turnerpa runa simiman, castellanomanta thicrascan. Translation into Quechua of St. Paul's Epistle to the Romans. New York: Sociedad Bíblica Americana, n.d.

Boreales, miniaturas y porcelanas. Buenos Aires: Imprenta de Juan A. Alsina, 1902.

Apunchis Jesucristoc Evangelion San Marcospa qqelkascan. Pananchis Clorinda Matto de Turnerpa runa simiman, castellanomanta thicrascan. Buenos Aires, 1903.

Apunchis Jesucristoc Evangelion San Mateoc qqelkascan. Pananchis Clorinda Matto de Turnerpa runa simiman, castellanomanta thicrascan. Buenos Aires, 1904.

Birds Without a Nest: A Story of Indian Life and Priestly Oppression in Peru. Translated from the Spanish by J. G. Hudson. Preface by Andrew M. Milne. London: Charles J. Thynne, 1904.

Aves sin nido: Novela peruana. Valencia: F. Sempere y Compañía, 1908.

Cuatro conferencias sobre América del Sur. Buenos Aires: Imprenta de Juan A. Alsina, 1909.

Viaje de recreo: España, Francia, Inglaterra, Italia, Suiza, Alemania. Valencia: F. Sempere y Compañía, 1909.

Aves sin nido. Cuzco: Universidad Nacional del Cuzco, 1948.

Aves sin nido. Prologue by Antonio Cornejo Polar. Havana: Casa de las Américas, 1974.

Índole. Prologue by Antonio Cornejo Polar. Lima: Instituto Nacional de Cultura, 1974.

Herencia. Prologue by Antonio Cornejo Polar. Lima: Instituto Nacional de Cultura, 1974.

Tradiciones cuzqueñas completas. Prologue and selection by Estuardo Nuñez. Lima: Peisa, 1976.

Aves sin nido. Prologue by Antonio Cornejo Polar. Notes by Efraín Kristal and Carlos García-Bedoya. Chronology and Bibliography by Efraín Kristal. Caracas: Biblioteca Ayacucho, 1994.

Birds Without a Nest: A Story of Indian Life and Priestly Oppression in Peru. Translation by J. G. Hudson (1904), emended by Naomi Lindstrom. Austin: University of Texas Press, 1996.

Secondary Sources

Carrillo, Francisco. *Clorinda Matto de Turner y su indigenismo literario.* Lima: Biblioteca Universitaria, 1967.

Cometta Manzoni, Aída. *El indio en la novela de América.* Buenos Aires: Editorial Futuro, 1961.

Cornejo Polar, Antonio. *Clorinda Matto de Turner, novelista.* Lima: Lluvia Editores, 1992.

Cuadros, Manuel E. *Paisaje y obra, mujer e historia: Clorinda Matto de Turner.* Cuzco: Rozas, 1949.

De Mello, George. "The Writings of Clorinda Matto de Turner." Ph. D. dissertation, University of Colorado, Boulder, 1968.

Franco, Jean. *An Introduction to Spanish American Literature.* London: Cambridge University Press, 1969.

Kristal, Efraín. "The political dimension of Clorinda Matto de Turner's Indigenismo." *The Andes Viewed from the City: Literary and Political Discourse on the Indian in Peru, 1848-1930.* New York: Peter Lang, 1987.

Meléndez, Concha. *La novela indianista en Hispanoamérica (1832-1889).* Madrid: Hernando, 1934.

Miller, John C. "Clorinda Matto de Turner and Mercedes Cabello de Carbonera: Societal Criticism and Morality." In *Latin American Women Writers: Yesterday and Today.* Ed. Ivette E. Miller and Charles M. Tatum. Pittsburgh: Latin American Literary Review, 1977. Pp. 25-32.

Swaine, Joyce R. "An Analysis of *Aves sin nido.*" *Neohelicon* 1-2 (1974): 217-25.

Tauro, Alberto. *Clorinda Matto de Turner y la novela indigenista.* Lima: Universidad de San Marcos, 1976.

TORN FROM
THE NEST

Author's Preface

If history is the mirror where future generations are to contemplate the image of generations past, the task of the novel is to be the photograph that captures the vices and virtues of a people, censuring the former with the appropriate moral lesson and paying its homage of admiration to the latter. The importance of the novel of manners is therefore such that its pages often hold the secret of how to reform, if not eliminate, certain social types. In those countries where, as in ours, Literature is in its infancy, the novel must exercise greater influence in the refinement of mores; consequently, when a work appears that seeks to rise above the sphere of the love story or the mere pastime, well may it beg its readers to receive it attentively and stretch out their hands to pass it on to the people.

Who knows but what after turning the last page of this book the reader will understand the importance of taking great care with whom we send to govern the destinies, civil and ecclesiastical, of the remote villages of the Peruvian hinterland? Who knows but what he may recognize society's urgent need for a married clergy? I express this hope encouraged by the faithfulness with which I have sketched from nature, offering my copies to the reader so that he may judge and decide.

I feel a tender love for our native race, precisely because I have closely observed its way of life, charming in its simplicity, and the degradation to which it is subjected by those backwoods despots who, while their names may differ, are ever worthy of the title of tyrants. And that, in general, is what our priests, our governors, our local headmen, and our mayors are. This love has led me for fifteen years to observe many an episode that, had it occurred in Switzerland, Provence, or Savoy, would have found a poet, a novelist, or a historian to immortalize it with the lyre or the pen, but that in the remote areas of my country can barely aspire to the dull pencil of a sister spirit.

I repeat that as I submit my work to the judgment of the reader, I do so hoping he may conclude that we must better the condition of the small towns of Peru, but even if these pages evoke no more than common sympathy, their author will have achieved her aim: While pointing out that we have brothers who suffer, exploited in the night of their ignorance, tormented in that darkness that cries out for light, she will have raised points of no small importance for our country's progress and contributed to the creation of our national literature.

PART I

1

S miling happily on that cloudless morning, Nature offered her hymn of adoration to the Creator of her beauty; and the heart, peaceful as the nest of the dove, was rapt in contemplation of the magnificent scene.

The single square of the village of Kíllac covers less than a tenth of an acre, and around it roofs of red terracotta tiles are scattered among plain thatched ones with eaves of rough timber. These different roofs serve to classify the inhabitants and to distinguish the *houses* of the *gentry* from the *huts* of the Indians.

On the left side of the square, within a stone enclosure, stands the common home of all Christians, the church; and its old adobe tower, where the bronze of the bells weeps for the dead and laughs with joy for the newly born, is also the nesting place of those little gray doves with ruby eyes known by the pretty name *cullcu*. On Sundays you can meet all the inhabitants of the village in the church cemetery after their faithful attendance at mass, while they gossip and tell tales about the lives of their neighbors just as they do in their little shops or on the threshing floor, where the work of the harvest proceeds amidst shouts and an occasional drink.

If you walk south a scant half-mile you come upon a fine country house remarkable for its elegance, which contrasts with the simplicity that prevails in the village. Its name is "Manzanares"; and it once belonged to Don Pedro de Miranda y Claro, the former village priest and then bishop, about whom loose tongues, speaking of things that happened during the twenty years that he headed the parish, spread some not very edifying gossip. It was during those years that Don Pedro built "Manzanares," which later served as His Excellency's summer residence.

Kíllac's cheerful setting amidst small plots of fruits and vegetables, its flumes of bright bubbling water, its outlying cultivated fields, and the river that bathes it, all make this a most poetic spot.

The previous night had been stormy, with rain, hail, and lightning; and the freshly cleansed air bore that special aroma that evaporation draws from the moist earth. The golden sun peeked over the horizon with renewed radiance and aimed its slanting rays at the quivering plants adorned with crystal drops still clinging to their leaves. Sparrows and thrushes, those merry inhabitants of every cold clime, hopped from the branches onto the roofs, singing their varied tunes and showing off their shimmering feathers.

December mornings such as this, bright and cheerful invitations to life, inspire the painter and the poet of our Peruvian fatherland.

2

No sooner had the sun, on that day, risen from its dusky bed while birds and flowers leapt to meet it, bearing the homage of their love and gratitude, than a peasant, carrying his implements and his food for the day, drove his pair of oxen across the square. A goad and a yoke with its leather straps would serve for his work; and the traditional brightly woven pouch or *chuspa*, holding coca leaves and balls of *llipta*,[1] would provide his breakfast. As he passed the portal of the church, he reverently removed his fringed hat and mumbled something like a prayer; then he went on his way, turning around from time to time to cast a mournful glance at the hut he was leaving behind.

---

1. *Llipta*, a mixture of quinoa ashes and mashed potato, for chewing with coca leaves.

What stirred his soul at those moments: fear or doubt, love or hope? Something, at any rate, that moved him deeply. A head peeked out over the stone wall that marks the southern edge of the square. Quick as a fox it hid once more behind the stones, but not without revealing itself to be a woman's, well-shaped, with two braids of long straight black hair framing a lovely face against whose rather copper-colored complexion the cheeks stood out with a red hue, contrasting even more with the heavy hair.

The peasant had barely disappeared on the distant slopes of Cañas when the head hiding behind the wall jumped forward and thus acquired a body, that of a woman in the full flower of her years, striking for her typically Peruvian beauty. She might have been thirty years old, but the freshness of her bloom was that of twenty-eight at the most. She wore a flowing skirt of dark blue baize and a jacket of coffee-colored corduroy with bone buttons and with silvery trim at the neckline and the wrists. As best she could she brushed off the mud that had adhered to her clothes as she jumped over the wall, and then headed toward a small whitish house with a tile roof. In its doorway stood a young woman in a pretty gray wool dress with mother-of-pearl buttons and lace trim; and this was none other than Lucía, who with her husband Don Fernando Marín had taken up temporary residence in the village.

When she reached the house, Lucía's visitor wasted no time in preliminaries and said, "For Our Lady's sake, *señoracha*,[2] help a family in distress, help us today! That man who just passed by you and went off into the fields carrying his *cacharpas*[3] is Juan Yupanqui, my husband and the father of two little girls. Ay, señoracha! His heart was half dead as he left our home, because he knows that today is the day they'll come by with the advance payment; and since the headman is sowing barley now, my Juan can't hide because on top of being locked up he'd be fined eight *reales* for missing work, and we don't have any money. There I was crying next to Rosacha, who sleeps by the hearth in our hut, and suddenly my heart told me that you're good; and although Juan doesn't know anything about it I've come to beg you to help us, for Our Lady's sake, señoracha, ay, ay!"

This plea, ending in tears, puzzled Lucía, who had only lived in the village a few months and therefore knew nothing of its customs and could not appreciate the seriousness of what the unfortunate woman,

---

2. *Señoracha*, equivalent of *señorita*, "young lady."
3. *Cacharpas*, tools.

who certainly piqued her curiosity, was telling her. One must see these poor abandoned creatures from up close and hear the story of how they live from their own lips and in their own expressive language in order to understand how a noble heart comes spontaneously to sympathize with them and to share their suffering, even if it is mere intellectual curiosity that first draws us to observe customs unknown to most Peruvians and lamented by a few. Lucía's kindness was unbounded; and since the words she had just heard had instantly aroused her growing concern, she asked, "And who are you?"

"I am Marcela, señoracha, Juan Yupanqui's wife, and I'm poor and helpless," answered the woman, drying her eyes on the sleeve of her jacket.

Lucía laid a kindly hand on her shoulder and asked her to come in and sit down on the stone bench in the garden of the white house. "Sit down, Marcela, dry the tears that cloud your lovely eyes, and let's talk calmly," she said, eager to gain a thorough knowledge of the customs of the Indians.

Marcela composed herself and, impelled perhaps by the hope of finding relief, answered Lucía's questions readily and in full detail; and she came to feel so at ease with her that she would have told her even her transgressions, even those wicked thoughts that rise like vapors from the corrupt seeds within us. It was thus with a comforting sense of release that she said, "You're not from here, *niñay*, [4] and so you don't know the tortures we go through with the collection agent, the headman, and the priest. Ay! Why didn't the plague carry us all off so that by now we'd be sleeping in the earth?"

"And why are you so troubled, poor Marcela?" Lucía interrupted. "There must be a way out; but you are a mother, and a mother's heart lives in a single lifetime as many lives as she has children."

"Yes, niñay," Marcela answered, "your face is the face of the Virgin to whom we pray, and that's why I've come to ask for your help. I want to save my husband. He told me as he was leaving, 'One of these days I'll throw myself in the river because I can't bear this life any longer, and I'd want to kill you before I give my body to the water.' You can see this is madness, señoracha."

---

4. The Indians call a lady of the upper class *niña*. The -y attached to this and other words (e.g., curay) denotes possession and affection, e.g., "my dear lady," "Father" (said to a priest), etc.

"It's a sinful thought, a demented thought; poor Juan!" Lucía said sorrowfully; and fixing a penetrating look on her interlocutor, she added, "And what is most pressing right now? Tell me, Marcela, just as if you were talking to yourself."

"Last year," the Indian replied, speaking freely, "they left ten pesos in our hut as advance payment for two *quintales* of wool, two hundred pounds. We spent that money at the fair to buy these things I'm wearing, because Juan said we'd be collecting the wool in the course of the year; but we haven't been able to do that because of the work he's forced to do, without any pay, for the people in charge here, and because when my mother-in-law died last Christmas, Father Pascual attached our potato harvest to pay for the burial and the masses. Now it's my turn for the *mita*;[5] I'll have to serve in the rectory and leave my hut and my daughters, and while I'm doing that, who knows whether Juan will go mad and die? And who knows what fate is in store for me, because the women who go in there to serve come out . . . looking down at the ground!"

"That's enough! Tell me no more," Lucía interrupted, shocked by the turn Marcela's tale was taking. Its concluding words had frightened that innocent dove, who was learning that civilized beings were nothing but monsters of greed and even of lust. "This very day I'll speak to the governor[6] and to the priest, and perhaps by tomorrow your worries will be over," she promised; and, as though to send Marcela on her way, she added, "Now go take care of your daughters; and as soon as Juan is back, try to calm him, tell him that you've spoken with me, and ask him to come here."

In reply, the Indian sighed with satisfaction for the first time in her life.

Finding a generous hand that offers help in our supreme distress is an experience so solemn that the heart does not know whether to bathe that outstretched hand in tears or cover it with kisses, or simply to call out blessings upon it. Such was the state of Marcela's heart at that moment. Those who do good to the unfortunate can never gauge the power of a single kind word, a single sweet smile that for the fallen, the wretched, is like the ray of sunshine that brings new life to limbs numbed by the frost of misery.

5. *Mita*, unpaid service to the civil and ecclesiastical authorities required of the Andean Indians.
6. Administrative head of a town appointed by the central government; in addition, a mayor is chosen by the local citizens.

3

In almost every province where alpacas are raised and the wool trade is the chief source of wealth, the principal merchants, some of the richest men in town, practice the custom of advance payment. They force money on the Indians; and they appraise the wool the Indians must deliver to repay these advances at so low a price that the capital they invest yields them in excess of five hundred percent, a degree of usury so extreme, and obtained with such extortion, that there almost has to be a hell to punish the savages who practice it.

The Indians who own alpacas leave their huts when the time for these advances comes, so as not to receive money that is as accursed for them as the silver coins of Judas. But can they find safety by leaving their homes and roaming the solitary peaks? No. The collection agent, who also distributes the advances, breaks into the hut, whose flimsy lock and leather door offer no resistance; he deposits the coins on top of the corn mill and leaves at once. A year later he returns to collect, armed with a list that for the unhappy and unwilling debtor is the sole witness and judge, and accompanied by an escort of ten or twelve mestizos, sometimes masquerading as soldiers. Using a special scale with stone weights, he extracts fifty pounds of wool for every twenty-five pounds owed; and if the Indian hides his only property, if he protests and curses, he is subjected to tortures that the pen is loath to recount, even if granted a special dispensation for the more shocking cases.

One of the Peruvian Church's most enlightened bishops speaks of these excesses in a pastoral letter but does not dare to mention the cold-water enemas used in some places to make the Indians declare the property they have hidden. The Indian fears them even more than the lash of the whip, while the brutes who confuse the letter of the law with its spirit claim that flogging is prohibited in Peru, but not the barbaric treatment they mete out to their brothers born in adversity.

Would that God, in the exercise of His goodness, might one day ordain the extinction of the native race, which, resplendent once in imperial greatness, now drinks the fetid cup of degradation! God grant it extinction, since it can never recover its dignity or exercise its rights!

Marcela's bitter tears and her desperation at the thought of the impending arrival of the collection agent were thus the anguished and understandable outburst of one who saw all around her a world of poverty and ignominious suffering.

4

Lucía was no ordinary sort of woman. She had received quite a good education, and her keen intelligence was able to reach the light of truth by observing the world around her and making comparisons. She was tall and of that darkish complexion that in Peru we call "pearl color." Her lovely eyes looked out from under thick lashes and soft eyebrows; and she possessed that special womanly charm, heavy long hair that, when loosened, cascaded over her back like a cloak of wavy and shining tortoise-shell. She had yet to reach the age of twenty, but marriage had stamped her features with that mark of the great lady so becoming to the young woman who knows how to couple an amiable character with a serious manner. Since coming to Kíllac with her husband a year earlier, she had lived in "the white house," which also served as the headquarters for the silver mining operations in the adjoining province. Don Fernando Marín was the chief shareholder in this enterprise and its current manager.

For the miner and the inland merchant, Kíllac has the advantage of being centrally located for commerce with the capital cities of the departments into which Peru is divided; and its good roads lighten the task of the laborers carrying hampers of ore and of the llamas used for slow transport.

After her conversation with Marcela, Lucía began to search for a way to remedy the poor woman's plight, which, to judge by her revelations, was grave indeed. The first thing she thought of was to speak with the priest and the governor, and to accomplish this she sent each of them a brief note requesting that he call on her. The intervention of Don Fernando might have sufficed to accomplish those measures that had to be taken immediately, but Don Fernando had gone to visit the mines and would return only many weeks later.

Once Lucía had decided to summon the persons whose help she needed, she began to brood about how she might speak persuasively to these provincial dignitaries. "What if they don't come? In that case I'll go to them," she asked and answered simultaneously, with the speed of a mind that no sooner sets its aims than it decides how to achieve them; and she began dusting the furniture, taking on first one chair and then another, until she reached a sofa, where she sat down and went back to thinking how she might speak most persuasively, though without the rhetorical flourishes she would have needed for a city gentleman.

Time weighed heavily on her as she first formed and then rejected one thought after another, until someone knocked and the glass-paneled door opened softly to admit the priest and the governor of the poetic village of Kíllac.

5

Short stature, a flattened head, dark complexion, a massive nose with widely flaring nostrils, thick lips, dark little eyes, a short neck protruding from a collar adorned with small black and white beads, a sparse but ill-shaved beard; for clothing a kind of imitation cassock of black cloth, shiny, badly cut, and worse kept; a Panama hat in his right hand: such was the appearance of the first visitor to step forward, whom Lucía made haste to greet with a clear show of respect, saying, "A very good afternoon to you, Father Pascual."

Anyone meeting Father Pascual Vargas, successor to Don Pedro Miranda y Claro as parish priest of Kíllac, would immediately feel serious doubts as to his having studied or learned, while at the seminary, either theology or Latin, a language that was ill at home in his mouth, defended by two ramparts of large, very large, white teeth. He was approaching the age of fifty; and his manner provided strong justification for the fears that Marcela had expressed when she had spoken of going to serve in the rectory, which, as the Indians say, women leave "looking down at the ground." A penetrating observer would have recognized in

Father Pascual a nest of lustful vipers, ready to awaken at the least sound of a woman's voice.

Lucía's mind was instantly vexed by the question of how so ill-favored an individual could have risen to the most exalted of offices, for among her religious convictions was belief in the sublimity of the priesthood, which watches over man on this earth, receiving him in his cradle with the waters of baptism, depositing his remains in the grave with the waters of purification, and sweetening the bitterness of his pilgrimage through this vale of tears with words of sound counsel and with the gentle voice of hope. She forgot that the priestly mission depends on the will of man, which is inclined to err; and she knew nothing of what sort of priest generally serves our remote parishes.

The individual who followed Father Pascual, wrapped in a flowing Spanish cape that is mentioned in fourteen last wills and testaments, which might be taken as proof of its antiquity, if not of the family tree of its owners, was Don Sebastián Pancorbo, which name His Excellency had received in a solemn baptismal ceremony celebrated three days after his birth with a great cross, new vestments, a silver saltcellar, and organ music.

Don Sebastián, to judge from the first impression produced by his dress, is a quaint personage. He is tall and bony; no trace of beard or mustache, so bothersome to his sex, ever appears on his face; his lively and covetous black eyes show in their sideways glances that he is not indifferent to the sound of silver or to a woman's silvery voice. In his youth he twisted the little finger of his right hand while slapping a friend of his, and since then he wears a half-glove of vicuña, although he moves that hand with a special elegance. There is not a trace of dynamite in the man's blood; he seems to have been created for a peaceful life, but the weakness of his character often leads him into ridiculous scenes that his companions manipulate to their advantage. He strums the guitar with an outstandingly poor ear and equally bad technique, though he drinks like a member of an army band.

Don Sebastián received as elementary an education as the three years he spent at a city school allowed; and after he returned to his village, he played an important part in the processions of Holy Week, he married Doña Petronila Hinojosa, the daughter of one of the local gentry, and right after that they made him governor, which means that he reached the highest position known and aspired to in a village.

The two visitors pulled up the easy chairs that Lucía had pointed out to them and made themselves comfortable. Their hostess blended logic and amiability in her effort to awaken their sympathy for Marcela; and directing her words especially to the priest, she said, "In the name of the Christian religion, which is nothing if not love, tenderness, and hope; in the name of your Master, Who ordered us to give all our goods to the poor, I ask you, Father, to cancel this debt that weighs on the family of Juan Yupanqui. In return you shall have twofold treasure in Heaven."

"My dear young lady," replied Father Pascual, leaning back in his chair and placing both hands on its arms, "this is all a lot of pretty-sounding nonsense; but when we get down to facts, for Heaven's sake, who can live without income? Nowadays, what with higher taxes on the Church and all that civilization that will come with the railroad, our stipends will dry up, and . . . and . . . I'll come right out with it, Doña Lucía, that'll be the end of us priests; we'll starve to death!"

"So that Indian Yupanqui came to you for that, did he?" the governor added in support of the priest; and with a note of triumph he concluded emphatically, "Frankly, ma'am, you have to realize that custom has the force of law, and nobody's going to tamper with our customs, do you understand?"

"Gentlemen, charity is also a law, a law of the heart," Lucía interrupted in reply.

"So Juan . . . hmm . . . Frankly, we'll see whether that tricky Indian tries to work any more angles," Don Sebastián continued, disregarding what Lucía had said, and with an ominous sort of slyness that Don Fernando's wife could not but notice, even as her heart trembled with fear. The brief conversation had exposed the moral nature of these men, from whom nothing was to be hoped for and everything to be feared.

Her plan lay in shambles; yet her heart still felt for Marcela's family, and she was determined to protect it against any abuse. Her gentle heart had been wounded in its self-esteem, and she blanched. She had to make a decisive move right then, and so she answered energetically, "A sad situation, gentlemen! Well, I now realize that vile selfishness has withered even the fairest flowers of humane sentiments in this part of the world, where I'd expected to find patriarchal families united by brotherly love. Forget our conversation. The family of the Indian Juan will never ask you for favors or protection." As she spoke these heated words, Lucía's lovely eyes glanced imperiously at the door.

The two village potentates were startled by so unexpected a tone; and seeing no chance of resuming a discussion from which it was at any rate in their interest to escape, they picked up their hats.

"Señora Lucía, don't take offense at all this, and rest assured that I am always at your service," said the priest, turning the straw hat he was holding; and Don Sebastián added a hurried and curt "Good afternoon, Señora Lucía."

For her part, Lucía dismissed her visitors with a nod of her head; and as she saw these men depart, leaving the deepest impression on her angelic soul, she trembled and emphatically said to herself, "No, that man's an insult to the Catholic priesthood. In the city I've seen superior beings, their heads hoary with age, go silently and covertly to seek out the poor and the orphan in order to help and console them. I've observed the Catholic priest at the bedside of the dying, standing pure before the sacrificial altar, weeping humbly in the home of the widow and the orphan. I've seen him take his only loaf of bread from his table and hold it out to the poor, depriving himself of nourishment and praising God for His gift. And is Father Pascual anything like that? Ah, these backwoods priests . . . ! As for the other one, the governor, that soul formed in the mold of the miser, he no more deserves the respect due to an honorable man than does the priest. Good riddance to them; I don't need them to plead with my Fernando and fill our home with the sweet perfume of doing good."

Five strokes of the household bell told Lucía the time and informed her that dinner was served. Her cheeks glowing from the excitement of her recent impressions, she walked down several corridors and reached the dining room, where she sat down at her usual place.

The ceiling and walls of the dining room were painted to imitate oak paneling. An elegant print showed a half-plucked partridge; another, a rabbit ready for the stew-pot. On the left, the mirrors of a cedar sideboard reflected the symmetrically placed dishes. Two small tables stood on the right, holding a chess-board and a roulette wheel, for this was the room the employees of the mining company used for their recreation. On the central dining table, covered with a spotlessly white ironed tablecloth, lay a simple place setting of red-rimmed blue china.

Dense steam rose from the soup, whose aroma proclaimed it to be the hearty *cuajada de carne*, made with ground meat, spices, walnuts, and biscuit. After the soup came three delicious courses, among them a tasty stew, the traditional *locro colorado*. A servant was just bringing a small porcelain cup that emitted the stimulating fragrance of hot and strong black Carabaya coffee when a messenger delivered a letter for Lucía, who seized it eagerly and, recognizing Don Fernando's handwriting, opened the envelope and quickly scanned the lines within. An observer of the changing expressions on her face could have guessed the contents of that message, in which her husband told her that he would return home the following morning, since the avalanches caused by the heavy snowfall in the Andes had put a temporary halt to work at the mines. He also asked for a new horse, as his had lost its shoes.

6

W hen Marcela, her heart filled with hope, returned to her hut, she found her daughters awake, and the younger one crying disconsolately at the absence of her mother. A few maternal caresses and a handful of *mote*[7] sufficed to calm that innocent victim of fate who, though born amid the rags of a hut, wept the same clear and bitter tears as do the children of kings.

Eagerly Marcela took hold of the poles supporting the portable loom that with her older daughter's help she set up in the middle of the room, preparing the woof and the threads of the ground to continue weaving a pretty poncho striped with all the colors the Indians produce from the combination of brazilwood, cochineal, anatta, and the flowers of the *quico*. Never had she taken up her daily work more cheerfully, and never had the poor woman spun more dreams about how to share her good news with Juan.

For that very reason, time passed slowly; but at last evening fell, spreading its delicate shadows over the valley and the village and sending the tuneful doves fluttering off in different directions as they abandoned the fields in search of their treetop shelter. Juan returned with them; and as soon as she heard her husband's footsteps, Marcela came out to meet him, helped him to tether his oxen at the fence, poured corn into the manger, and, once he had sat down on a stone bench inside, began to speak to him somewhat timidly, thereby betraying her doubts as to whether Juan would be pleased by her news.

"Do you know the señoracha Lucía, Juanuco?" she asked.

---

7. *Mote*, boiled corn, part of the basic diet of the people of the highlands.

"I go to mass, Marluca, and so I'm bound to; you get to know everybody there," Juan replied apathetically.

"Well, I talked to her today."

"You talked to her? What for?" the Indian asked with surprise, looking intently at his wife.

"I'm troubled by all that's happening to us, and you've shown me very clearly that you're in despair about our life . . ."

"Did the collection agent come?" Juan interrupted, and Marcela replied calmly and confidently, "Thank Heaven he hasn't come; but listen, Juanuco, I think this señoracha will be able to help us. She told me she will, and that you should go see her."

"Ah, Marluca, poor desert flower," the Indian said, shaking his head and picking up little Rosalía, who was about to put her arms around his knees, "your heart is like the fruit of the *penca:* you break one off, and without any effort on your part another grows to take its place. But I'm older than you, and I've wept in despair."

"Well, I haven't; and although you say I'm like the *tuna,* ay!, that's better than being like you, a poor flower of the cress that wilts as soon as you touch it and never recovers. Some evil sorcerer has touched you, but I've seen the face of the Virgin just as surely as I've seen the face of Señora Lucía," said the wife, laughing like a little girl.

"That may be," Juan answered sadly, "but here I come exhausted from my work and without a single loaf of bread for you, who are my wife, and for these little chicks," and he pointed to the two girls.

"Now, now, things aren't as bad as all that. Aren't you forgetting that when the priest gets home with his pockets stuffed with money from praying for the dead on All Saints' Day, there's nobody waiting for him with open arms the way I wait for you or with loving kisses like these two little angels? What an ingrate! You talk about bread; here we've got cold *mote* and cooked *chuño*[8] that smells so appetizing on the hearth. You won't go hungry, you ingrate!"

Marcela was a changed woman, thanks to the hopes instilled in her by Lucía. Her arguments, in concert with the voice that springs naturally from the heart of woman, were irresistible. Won over, Juan drew his two daughters toward him along with Marcela, who at that moment was picking up two black earthenware pots from the hearth; and the four of them shared a frugal but pleasant supper.

---

8. *Chuño,* a preparation of potatoes.

After supper, with the gloomy shades of night that enfolded the hut broken only by the dim flame that rose now and then from the sticks of *molle* on the hearth, they rested on a common bed placed atop a broad platform of adobes, a hard bed that for the love and modest wants of Juan and Marcela was as soft and comfortable as the feathers that Cupid sheds from his white wings, a bed of roses where love, like primordial tenderness, lives without the uncertainties and the midnight mysteries that the city tries in vain to hide even as it makes them food for its gossip.

Once our narrative comes to recount our characters' experiences in Peru's wealthiest city, we may have occasion to compare the fresh awakening of the countryside with the all-night revels of the capital.

Punctually at the appropriate time, Juan's family rose from their humble blanket of flowered flannel, said their morning prayers, crossed themselves, and set about the tasks of the new day.

Marcela, her mind astir with ideas, was the first to speak: "Juanico, after a bit I'm going to Señora Lucía's. You're not saying anything or expecting anything, but ever since yesterday my heart's been speaking to me."

"Go on, then, Marcela, go, because today the collection agent will come for sure. I dreamt it, and she's our only hope," the Indian replied. His mood, influenced by his wife's words and by the superstition kindled by his dream, seemed to have undergone a marked change.

7

Happiness pervaded the white house that morning, because Don Fernando's return brought infinite joy to the home where he was loved and respected.

Lucía, intent on finding a practical way to carry out her aim of helping the family of Juan Yupanqui, naturally thought of taking advantage of the sweetness and poetry that the first meeting after an absence holds for husband and wife. A few hours earlier she had seemed languid and sad like a flower deprived of the sunshine and the dew; yet now she regained her vigor and her freshness in the arms of the man who, when he made her his wife, had entrusted to her the sanctuary of his home and name, the holy ark of his honor. The chain of flowers with which the god of love bound Don Fernando and Lucía was now renewed, fusing two wills into one.

"Fernando, my dearest darling," Lucía said, placing her hands on her husband's shoulders and resting her forehead, not without coquettishness, against his chin, "I'm going to collect a debt from you, and . . . with all deliberate speed."

"My, my, such learned language! Speak up, sweetheart; but bear in mind that if there's no legal proof of this debt you'll pay me . . . a fine," answered Don Fernando with an expressive smile.

"A fine! If it's the one you always collect, greedy, I'll pay it. But I have to remind you of a solemn promise you made me for the 28th of July."

"For Independence Day?"

"Now you're pretending not to remember? Don't you recall that you promised me a velvet dress to wear in the city?"

"Right you are, sweetheart; and I'll keep my promise, because I'll order it by the next mail. Ah, how pretty you'll be in that dress!"

"No, Fernando, no. What I want is for you to let me have what that dress would cost, provided I appear on the 28th more elegant than you've ever seen me since our wedding."

"But what . . . ?"

"No, sweetheart, no questions allowed! Say yes or no," and Lucía's lips sealed those of Don Fernando, who, satisfied and happy, replied, "You do know how to wheedle and coax! If you're going to talk to me like that, how can I say no? How much do you need for that whim of yours?"

"Not much: two hundred *soles.*"

"All right," said Don Fernando, drawing out his billfold, tearing a sheet of paper from a pad, and writing a few lines with a pencil, "here's an order for the company cashier to send you the two hundred *soles.* And now let me go to work to make up for the days I missed while traveling."

"Thank you, Fernando, thank you," she replied, taking the paper, happy as a little child.

As Don Fernando left Lucía's room on his way to his office, his mind was awash in a sea of sweet thoughts, born of his wife's request, childlike in comparison with the exorbitant outlays that other women inflict on their husbands in their passion for luxury; and this comparison was bound to confirm his belief in the power of the habits that Peruvian women, who as a rule are docile and virtuous, acquire in their childhood home.

A few moments after these scenes, Marcela was crossing the courtyard of the white house, followed by a young girl, a marvel of beauty and
liveliness who at once intrigued Lucía and made her eager to know her
father, for her loveliness reflected that mixture of the Spaniard and the
Indian that has produced stunning beauties in Peru. As she watched the
girl approach, Don Fernando's wife said to herself, "This child will no
doubt be Marcela's guardian angel, because God puts the mark of a special glow on the face that mirrors a superior soul."

8

Once the priest and the governor had left Lucía's house after the interview to which she had summoned them to plead for the Yupanqui family, an interview whose details we learned in Chapter 5, these
two worthies walked down the street chatting as follows:

"What an idea! What do you say to the demands of this high and
mighty lady, my dear Don Sebastián?" said the priest, taking a cheap
cigarette from his case and smoothing out its ends.

"Frankly, dear Father, that's all we needed, having outsiders come
here to set rules for us and, frankly, change customs handed down from
our ancestors," the governor replied, stopping for a moment to wrap
himself in his great cape.

"That's right, you get these Indians all worked up, and pretty soon
there'll be nobody to so much as draw the water for washing our dishes."

"Frankly, Father, we've got to get rid of these outsiders, because once
the Indians get any backing they become, frankly, well, unbearable," said
Don Sebastián, tripping on a protruding cobblestone.

"Bless you!" the priest quickly said, before continuing in a confidential tone, "That's just what I was going to suggest to you, my dear governor. We lead a good life here, just the family, so to speak; and these
outsiders just come to keep track even of how we eat and whether our
tablecloth is clean and whether we eat with a spoon or with *topos.*"[9] And
Father Pascual concluded by blowing a great cloud of smoke.

9. *Topo,* a spoon-shaped brooch.

"Frankly, my dear Father, don't fret about it. We'll stick together, and we'll soon get the chance to chase them out of our town," Pancorbo replied calmly.

"But let's keep all this quiet, my dear Don Sebastián. We've got to be careful; these people have connections, and we might miss our mark."

"You're right, Father, because, frankly, they're just looking for trouble. Do you remember what Don Fernando said one day?"

"You bet I do! We should get rid of the advance payments, he says, because they're not right and fair. Ha, ha, ha!" the priest answered, laughing sardonically and throwing away the butt of his cigarette, which he had consumed with a few deep draughts.

"We should offer free burials, he says, because the families are poor, and we should even cancel their debts. Free burials, just what these times call for! Frankly, dear Father!" said Don Sebastián, whose eternal refrain of "frankly" showed him to be a hypocrite or a fool. Since the two friends had now reached the door of the town hall, the governor invited the priest to come in; and as they entered one of the public rooms they found some of the local gentry gathered there, emitting their several opinions about the summoning of the priest and the governor to Don Fernando's house, for the news had already spread throughout the town.

Everyone rose to exchange greetings with the newcomers, and the governor immediately asked for a bottle of Majes liquor. "Frankly, dear Father, we'd better have a little drink to help us over this annoyance," he said slyly, taking off his cape and folding it twice before depositing it on a bench.

"Right you are, my dear Don Sebastián, and you've got the right stuff for it," the priest answered, rubbing his hands.

"Yes, my dear Father, frankly, it's good stuff, because Doña Rufa sends it to me without first baptizing it with water."

"So it's a little heathen you're offering us?"

"A little heathen!" they all repeated laughing, and at that moment a *pongo*[10] appeared with a green bottle of liquor and a small glass of etched crystal.

The room was furnished, in the style typical of the place, with two sofas upholstered in black oilcloth with round-headed brass tacks; a few chairs made of wood from Paucartambo, their backs painted with bouquets of flowers and bunches of fruit; a table in the middle, covered with

---

10. *Pongo,* a male Indian performing unpaid obligatory service to the authorities.

a long light-green plush-like flannel cloth, and on it, boasting an air of civilization, a tin-plate tray bearing an inkwell, a pen, and a pewter container for blotting sand. The walls, papered with pages from illustrated magazines, displayed an odd assortment of persons, animals, and European landscapes. Espartero and King Umberto were posted there alongside the heron that listened to the sermons of Saint Francis; next came Pius IX and the Swiss countryside, where the merry peasant girl and the cow with its cowbell around its neck join in rustic revels. The floor pleased the eye with the color of fresh straw mats from Ccapana and Capachica.

Eight persons made up the gathering: the priest and the governor; Estéfano Benites, a quick-witted youth with good handwriting who, having profited somewhat more from his classroom hours than did his fellow-students, is already an important figure on this rustic stage; and five others, members of distinguished local families, solid citizens all, since they had married at nineteen, which is the usual age at marriage in these villages.

Estéfano first saw the light of day twenty-two years ago. He is tall; and his extraordinary thinness, along with the waxen pallor of his face, so unusual in his part of the world, calls to mind the consumption that destroys the bodies of those living in tropical valleys.

Estéfano took the bottle that the *pongo* had left on the table and served a glass of liquor in turn to each of those present. There was enough for two glasses per stomach; but after the second one their thirst had been stimulated, and on Don Sebastián's orders one bottle after another made its appearance.

The priest and the governor, sitting next to each other on the sofa on the right, were speaking confidentially, to the accompaniment of Pancorbo's eternal refrain, which was heard frequently, while the others conversed in a second group. But since the bottle is a great loosener of tongues, and these had now been steeped in Majes liquor, the time soon came to lay the cards on the table and speak clearly.

"Frankly, Father, we shouldn't put up with it; just ask these gentlemen!" said Don Sebastián, raising his voice and pounding the table with the bottom of the glass he had just emptied.

"Hush!" the priest replied, drawing a black and white checked madras handkerchief and blowing his nose, more to cover up his warning than to obey any dictate of nature.

"What's all this, gentlemen?" Estéfano asked, and they all turned toward the priest.

At this point Father Pascual adopted a rather solemn air and replied, "It's that . . . Señora Lucía has summoned us to hear a plea for some sly tricky Indians who don't want to pay their debts; and she's done it with words that once the Indians hear them, frankly, as Don Sebastián says, will in effect put an end to *our* customs, the advance payment, the *mitas*, the *pongos*, and all the rest of it."

"What the devil, we won't put up with that!" shouted Estéfano and the others; and Don Sebastián added with refined cunning, "And she's even suggested we should bury the poor for nothing; and frankly, what's to become of the father here once he's been left penniless that way?"

These words did not produce the same effect on the public as had Father Pascual's speech, which is quite understandable when we recall that there were strong and pressing personal interests at stake. Nonetheless Estéfano spoke for them all with a terse, "What won't these outsiders be asking next!"

"We've got to put a stop to this pernicious talk once and for all. Any outsider who comes here and doesn't want to follow our customs must be thrown out, because, frankly, it's we who are the true citizens of our town," said Don Sebastián, raising his voice arrogantly and approaching the table to pour another glass for the priest.

"Yes, sir, it's our town."

"Right you are!"

"We were born here."

"It belongs to us."

"We're genuine Peruvians."

And on they talked, but no one thought of asking whether the Maríns were less Peruvian for having been born in the capital.

"Just let's be careful, very careful; let's not make any noise, but get to work," the priest added, with a show of that hypocrisy that deceives a brother and misleads a father.

And that afternoon, in the chambers of the civil authorities and in the presence of the religious authorities, a bond of hatred was forged, a hatred that would engulf our upstanding Don Fernando in the tide of blood brought on by his wife's friendly and charitable request.

9

A s soon as she saw Marcela by her side, Lucía could not keep from asking her in surprise, "Is this your daughter?"

"Yes, niñay," the Indian replied, "she's fourteen years old and her name is Margarita and you're going to be her godmother."

This reply was marked by a gratified air that would have clearly told any observer, "This woman is relishing the sweetness of the legitimate pride that a mother feels when she knows that her daughter is admired—a mother's blessed vanity that is a woman's ornament, whether in the city with its electric lights or in the village bathed in the rays of the melancholy traveler of the nocturnal skies."

"Good, Marcela; it was a good idea to bring along this pretty girl. I love children. They're so innocent, so pure," added Lucía.

"That's because your soul is a flower born for heaven, niñay," Marcela replied, ever more delighted at having found the protection of a kind angel.

"Have you talked to Juan? How much money do you need to pay off all your debts and live in peace?" Lucía asked eagerly.

"Ay, señoracha, I can't even count it! But it must be a lot of money, lots and lots, because the collection agent, if he's willing to take back money for the advance, will want sixty pesos instead of each *quintal* of wool, and times two . . ." and she began to count on her fingers; but Lucía helped her mathematical operations along by suggesting, "Let's say a hundred twenty."

"All right, señoracha, a hundred twenty. Ah, what a lot of money!"

"And how much did you say they advanced you?"

"Ten pesos, niñay."

"And for those ten pesos they now want to collect a hundred twenty? That's outrageous!"

As Lucía spoke, Marcela's husband arrived, dazed and perspiring, and without pausing for any formalities threw himself at Lucía's feet. Startled at seeing him, Marcela left the seat she had just taken, while Lucía, forgetting her, asked, "What's the matter? What happened? Tell me!"

And the poor Indian's sobs and fatigue barely allowed him to bring forth, "My daughter, niñay . . . ! The collection agent . . . !"

At this point Marcela, beside herself, burst into almost savage cries and also threw herself at Lucía's feet, saying, "Have pity on us, niñay!

The agent's carried off my daughter, the little one, because he didn't find any wool. Ay, ay!"

"How dare they!" Lucía exclaimed, unable to understand the degree of inhumanity reached by those rapacious lackeys of usury; and stretching out her hands to the unfortunate parents, she tried to calm them by telling them in a kindly voice, "But if all they've done is carry off your girl, why all this despair? They'll soon bring her back. You'll take them the money and everything will be settled, and we'll praise God Who allows evil so that we can better appreciate good. Be calm!"

"No, señoracha, no," the Indian replied, somewhat recovered from his perturbation, "if we waste any time we'll never see my daughter again. There are men who come here from Majes to buy girls and take them to Arequipa."

"Good Lord, is that possible?" Lucía exclaimed, raising her clasped hands toward heaven, just as Don Fernando made a welcome appearance in the doorway, where he heard his wife's words and stood still for a moment as he caught sight of the Indians' faces. Lucía no sooner saw him than she threw herself into his arms and said, "My dearest Fernando! We can't live here! And if you say we must, then we'll live here waging the bloody battle of the good against the wicked. Ah, let us save them! Look at these unfortunate parents! It was to help them that I asked you for the two hundred *soles;* but even before they could put this money to use, their younger daughter's been kidnapped and is going to be *sold!* Ah, Fernando, help me, because you believe in God, and God demands of us charity above all things."

"Señor!" "*Wiracocha!*"[11] Juan and Marcela called out simultaneously, wringing their hands while Margarita wept in silence.

"Do you know where the collection agent took your daughter?" Don Fernando asked of Juan, trying to hide the emotions that were mirrored in his face, for he knew what methods those distinguished folk were in the habit of employing.

"Yes, sir; they've gone to the governor's office," Juan answered.

"All right, let's go; follow me," Don Fernando ordered resolutely and marched off, followed by Juan.

Marcela was about to rush after them with Margarita, but Lucía took her by the hand to stop her and said, "Unhappy mother, don't you go, too; lift up your sorrow to the Lord of resignation. Your worries will be

11. *Wiracocha,* title of respect.

taken care of this very day; I promise you by the memory of my sainted mother. Sit down. How much do you owe the priest?"

"For burying my mother-in-law, forty pesos, niñay."

"And for forty pesos he attached your potato harvest?"

"No, niñay; it was for the interest."

"For the interest? And so you'd always still be in debt to him?" Don Fernando's wife asked with an eloquent expression.

"That's right, niñay; but death can cheat the father, too, because we've seen a lot of priests die and go to their graves without collecting their debts," Marcela replied, gradually regaining her composure.

The simple philosophy of the Indian, with its notion of requital, made Lucía smile; and she called a servant and gave him the written order she was holding, with instructions to bring the money at once. Then she offered Marcela a glass of gin to restore her strength and took a slice of bread from a wire basket and handed it to Margarita, saying, "Do you like sweets? This is a sweet bread made with cinnamon and sesame; it's delicious."

The girl accepted the gift with a melancholy and thankful air, and they all set to waiting for the return of one of the men.

The first to come was the servant with the money; and Lucía took forty *soles* and handed them to the Indian, saying, "Now, Marcela, take these forty *soles*, which are worth fifty pesos, and go pay off your debt to the priest. Don't say anything to him about what happened with the collection agent; and if he asks you where you got this money, tell him a Christian gave it to you in the name of God—that, and nothing else. Don't delay, and try to come back soon."

Poor Marcela was so moved that her trembling hands could scarcely count the money and constantly let it drop to the floor, one, three, or four coins at a time.

10

If we attack a people's depraved customs without first having laid the basis of an education grounded in belief in a Higher Being, we shall encounter an impenetrable wall of selfish resistance and find yesterday's peaceful lambs turned into raging wolves. If we tell the Canibus and the Huachipairis not to eat the flesh of their prisoners but do not previously impart to them the notions of humanity, brotherly love, and respect for the dignity and rights of others, then we, too, shall soon become food for those cannibals, whose tribes are scattered through the wild mountains of Ucayali and Madre de Dios.

We believe that what happens in Kíllac, as in every small town of the Peruvian hinterland, is only another form of that savagery. The lack of schools, the lack of good faith on the part of the clergy, and the obvious depravity of those few who exploit the ignorance and consequent docility of the many, drive these towns ever farther away from true civilization, which, were it ever solidly established, would enrich our country with large areas capable of making it great.

Don Fernando, followed by Juan, reached the town hall, where the governor, surrounded by visitors, was attending to matters that he called "most important." The visitors soon drifted away, until Don Fernando alone was left with Pancorbo.

Close by the entrance door squatted a little four-year-old girl, who, when she saw Juan, rushed at him as though pursued by a pack of hounds.

Don Fernando was serious and thoughtful as he entered. He was wearing a gray suit of Lucre cashmere, expertly made by the most famous tailor in Arequipa.

Don Fernando Marín was held in high esteem in the social circles of Lima; and his face showed him to be a just man, enormously learned, and as farseeing as he was prudent. He was rather tall than short, with regular features and fair skin; his luxuriant sideburns showed careful grooming with comb and aromatic oils. Eyes light green, nose straight, a high forehead, and black hair, slightly curly and carefully combed.

As he entered the governor's office, Don Fernando politely removed his black felt hat and, holding it in his left hand, stretched out his right to Pancorbo and said, "Pardon me, Don Sebastián, if I interrupt your work; but it's an obligation of common humanity that makes me come to ask you to let this man have back the daughter who was no doubt taken from him as a hostage for some debt, and to have the perpetrator of this crime punished."

"Sit down, my dear Don Fernando, and let's talk in peace and quiet. Frankly, these Indians shouldn't hear these things," Don Sebastián replied, getting up; and then, sitting down almost next to Don Fernando, he continued in a very low voice, "It's true they've brought his daughter—there she is—but, frankly, that's only a trick to make him pay the two quintales of alpaca that he's been owing for a year."

"Well, he's assured me, my dear governor, that that debt is the consequence of ten pesos that were *forcibly* placed in his hut last year, and that now he's being made to pay two quintales of wool, worth about one hundred twenty pesos," Don Fernando replied gravely.

"Don't you know that's the custom, and a lawful business practice? Frankly, I advise you not to be abetting these Indians," Pancorbo countered.

"But Don Sebastián . . ."

"And finally, just to clear everything up, frankly, my dear Don Fernando, that money belongs to Don Claudio Paz."

"Don Claudio is a friend of mine; I'll talk to him."

"That's something else again, so, frankly, I think we're done for now," Don Sebastián said, getting up.

"I don't think so, Señor Pancorbo, because I want you to have the girl returned to her father. If you accept my guarantee as to the money . . ."

"That's fine, my dear Don Fernando; Juan can take his little girl home, and you'll sign a guarantee," Don Sebastián replied, and going over to the table he took a sheet of paper, laid it down, and offered it to Don Fernando, adding, "It's not that I don't trust you, my friend; but frankly, this is the way it has to be done, because as the proverb says, a clear reckoning preserves a friendship."

Don Fernando drew up a chair, wrote a few lines, signed them, and handed the sheet to Don Sebastián, who patted his breast pocket and said, "My glasses . . . ?"

The glasses were lying by the tray. Don Sebastián saw them, put them on, and read the document; then he folded it, put it in his pocket, and turning to Don Fernando said, "Very well, frankly, now that's in order, Señor Marín. My respects to Señora Lucía."

"Thank you, and goodbye," Don Fernando replied amiably, offering a hand that the governor clasped; and he left, shaking the dust of that den of corruption from his feet. Juan, carrying little Rosalía, left with him.

No sooner had Don Fernando left the governor's office than the governor's wife entered it, seized him rather roughly by the arm, and proclaimed, "I can't take it any more, Sebastián! You'll make me as unhappy as the wife of Pontius Pilate, what with condemning so many innocent people and scratching your signature on so many papers you'd be better off not even reading."

A harsh "Come on now!" was Don Sebastián's only reply; but his wife went on, "I know exactly what you're all scheming against that poor Don Fernando and his family, and I'm asking you to stay out of it. For God's sake, Sebastián, stay out of it! Think of . . . our son; he'll be ashamed when he finds out."

"Go on, always the same song and dance! Frankly, women should stay out of men's business and stick to their sewing, their knitting, and their kitchens, do you understand?" Pancorbo answered angrily; but Doña Petronila continued to talk back to him, "Yes, that's what they all say, to still the voice of sense and conscience and send our sound warnings to the devil. Mark my words, Chapaco!"[12] she added emphatically, striking the table with the flat of her hand; and out she went with an expression of disdain on her face.

Don Sebastián uttered an "uff!" rather like a snort and calmly set to rolling a cigarette.

11

Doña Petronila Hinojosa, Don Sebastián Pancorbo's wife according to the law and sacrament of the Church, was approaching the age of forty and had come into possession of a robust and well-proportioned body, heavy without reaching the point of obesity. Her face clearly revealed a good heart that in the course of life and in a better place than the one in which she had been fated to be born might have distinguished itself for its nobility and high aspirations. Her dress is the finest you will find in Kíllac and the surrounding region. Her fingers are encrusted with inexpensive rings; enormous gold hoops with circles of choice diamonds frame her face; her beige wool skirt has five rows of delicately gathered flounces; and her cashmere shawl with its large scarlet and black checks is fastened on the right with a silver brooch in the form of an eagle.

12. *Chapaco,* diminutive for Sebastián, little used today.

Altogether, Doña Petronila is a typical upland provincial whose heart is as generous as it is virtuous, since her kindnesses are extended to all the living and her tears to all who die, whether or not she knows them—a type unknown along the Peruvian coast, where such women, whose heart of gold and angelic soul are hidden within a body of crudely fashioned clay, are inconceivable amid the elegance of dress and refinement of manners. The right kind of upbringing would have made of Doña Petronila an ornament to society, for she was a precious jewel lost among the rocks of Kíllac.

If woman is in general a diamond in the rough, to be polished by man and a proper upbringing, it is mainly left to nature to develop her noblest sentiments once she becomes a mother, as was Doña Petronila of a youth who showed extraordinary intelligence and who was to inherit her virtues, for by the grace of predestination or because his guardian angel had triumphed in the struggle against evil, he had escaped being contaminated by the deadening stream of depravation that runs through our minor towns, rightly called major hells.

12

M arcela, who headed for the rectory accompanied by her pretty Margarita and the forty silver *soles*, found Father Pascual sitting by the door of his small study, near a rustic old pine table covered with a cloth that hinted at having been blue in the days of its youth. In his left hand he held his breviary, with his index finger wedged between two pages half-way through the volume; and he was, albeit mechanically, reciting the prayer of the day.

Marcela stepped up to him timidly and greeted him with, "Hail Mary, *tata curay*";[13] and she bent down to kiss his hand, indicating to Margarita that she should do likewise.

13.   *Tata*, "father"; *curay*, from the Spanish *cura*, "priest."

The priest, without taking his eyes off the girl, replied, "Full of grace," and then added, "Now, you vixen, where did you get this good-looking strapping girl?"

"She's my daughter, tata curay," Marcela answered.

"And how come I've never met her?" Father Pascual asked, pinching the girl's left cheek with the first three fingers of his right hand.

"It's because I don't come here much, on account of what we owe you. That's why you don't recognize the child, tata curay."

"And how old is she?"

"I . . . I've counted about fourteen years since she was baptized, Father."

"Ah, then she wasn't baptized by me, because I only came barely six years ago. All right then, this year you'll put her in service to the church, won't you? She's ready to start washing dishes and socks."

"Curay!"

"And how about you? Still holding out on me? When are you going to do your *mita* here? Isn't it your turn?" the priest asked, fixing his eyes on Marcela and patting her on the back in a familiar way.

"Yes, curay," the woman replied shakily.

"Or did you come to stay on now?" Father Pascual pressed her.

"Not yet, sir; now I've come to pay you the forty pesos for burying my mother-in-law, so our potato harvest will be clear of debt."

"Oho! So we've got money, do we? Who slept in your house last night?"

"Nobody, tata curay."

"Nobody, is it? You've played some scurvy trick on your husband, and I'll teach you to fool around like that with a pack of bandits and set a bad example for this girl."

"Don't talk like that, tata curay," the woman pleaded, blushing and lowering her eyes, and at the same time placing the forty *soles* on the table. As soon as the priest saw the money, the focus of his attention changed; he put down the breviary, which he had absentmindedly held under his arm, and set to counting the coins and testing their authenticity. Once convinced as to the quantity and quality of the silver, he drew the bolt of an enormous wooden cupboard where he kept his money; and instantly turning once more to Marcela, he said, "All right, that's the forty *soles*. And now tell me, my dear, who gave you this money? Who went to your house last night?"

"Don't talk like that, tata curay; a rash judgment lies on the breast like a stone."

"And who's taught you all these tricks, you know-it-all redskin? Come clean!"

"Nobody taught me, tata curay. My soul is pure."

"And where did you get that money? You can't fool me, and I want to know."

"From a Christian, tata curay," Marcela replied, lowering her eyes and feigning a cough.

"A Christian! You see, there's some mystery here. Tell me . . . because I . . . want to give you back your money."

"Señora Lucía lent it to me, and now give me my change so I can leave," said Margarita's mother, abashed at having disobeyed her benefactress' first command with this revelation; and on hearing that name, Father Pascual, as though the viper of resentment had stung him, replied, "Change? What change? I'll give it to you some other day," and biting his lips with barely contained fury, he murmured, "Lucía! Lucía!"

The priest sat down again, lost in thought and taking no notice of Marcela's and Margarita's humble parting words. He saw them disappear as he kept on muttering broken sentences, perhaps continuing the prayers that Juan Yupanqui's wife had interrupted.

13

Don Fernando's return to his house was a joyous event. He came in triumph with Juan and Rosalía; he would now receive his wife's expressions of gratitude; he would savor the satisfaction of having done good, breathe the heavenly aroma that perfumes the hours after we have consoled a misfortune or dried a tear.

Lucía was weeping with pleasure. Her tears were the beneficent rain that brings peace and happiness to noble hearts.

Juan fell to his knees before her and ordered Rosalía to kiss her rescuers' hands.

Don Fernando gazed tenderly for a few seconds on the scene before him, then sat down on the sofa, leaning back into the corner and saying to his wife, "I'm not often mistaken, my dear, and I think Don Sebastián's pride has been deeply wounded by my intervention on behalf of this family."

"There's no doubt about that, Fernando; I'm sure of it. But then, what can he do to get back at us?" Lucía answered, coming up to her husband and running her hand over his hair.

"He can do plenty, my love, a great deal. I'm really sorry I invested in this mining company, thinking I'd be involved for at the most a year."

"Yes, Fernando dear; but remember that we're on the side of virtue," was Lucía's simple reply.

"I'll find a way to take care of everything," Don Fernando was saying, when Marcela and Margarita appeared, clearly showing their joy; and they both proceeded to give lively signs of their affection for both Juan and Rosalía, whom they had imagined already sold and carried off.

"Señor, señora, God bless you both!" Margarita said, turning to husband and wife.

"Juanuco, Rosaco! Ay, ay, where would they have taken you, child, but for the charity of this lady and this wiracocha?" the mother exclaimed in tender tones, picking up her daughter and covering her with kisses.

Lucía, eager to know the fruits of Marcela's errand, asked her, "How did it go? How happy you both are!"

Marcela set down Rosalía and assuming a respectful position answered, "Señoracha, tata cura has sold his soul to Rochino!"

"And who is this Rochino?" Lucía interrupted with curiosity; and a smiling Juan intervened to answer her, "Rochino, niñay, is the green wizard who they say lives in the Canyon of Sighs, smelling of sulfur and buying souls to sell them at a profit in Manchay-puito."

"Oh my, what a wizard! He really scares me!" Lucía said laughing and asked her husband, "Fernando, do you know what Manchay-puito is?"

"It's hell, the house of terror," replied Don Fernando, whose curiosity was also piqued by the start of Marcela's account, and who in turn asked, "Now then, why do you say the priest has sold his soul to Rochino?"

"Ay, wiracocha, when I told him I was going to pay him he started to ask me who had slept in my house last night and said it was a bandit with whom I cheated on Juan."

"The priest told you that?" Lucía interrupted, horrified.

"Yes, niñay, and he said other things to make me tell him everything."

"And so what happened?"

"I had to tell him."

"Tell him what?" Juan asked, with an intensity that made Fernando and Lucía laugh.

"The truth, of course."

"And what truth was that? Speak up!" Yupanqui insisted.

"That Señora Lucía has lent us the money."

"You told him?" Lucía asked angrily, picking up a handkerchief she had let drop to the floor.

"Yes, niñay. Forgive me for disobeying you, but otherwise tata cura wouldn't have let me leave his house," Marcela appealed in reply.

"That was bad, very bad," said Lucía, shaking her head in annoyance.

"This affair is simpler than our business with the governor, my dear, because if Don Pascual is willing to settle, what do you care if he knows the money is yours?" Don Fernando explained.

"That's right, sir, and he even said he'd give me the change another day; and he was pleased with how pretty Margarita is and said I should hurry and get her into the service of the Church," Marcela reported in her artless way.

"Margarita? Good Heavens!" Lucía said, not hiding her annoyance.

"Yes, niñay," Marcela replied, taking Margarita by the hand and presenting her to Don Fernando and his wife.

Don Fernando's searching gaze rested on the girl's face and demeanor, and he asked his wife, "Have you noticed the remarkable beauty of this child?"

"How could I help it, Fernando? Ever since I first saw her I've taken a special interest in her."

"This girl has to be brought up with every care," said Don Fernando, affectionately taking hold of Margarita's hand while she, like a flower, displayed her beauty and scattered the perfume of her charms in silence.

"She'll be our godchild, Fernando; Marcela already talked to me about it, isn't that right?" said Lucía, directing her question to Margarita's mother.

Juan and Marcela replied in unison, "Yes, niñay, yes."

"We'll talk about this tomorrow; for now, go get some rest," Don Fernando added, standing up and patting Margarita and Rosalía lightly on the cheek; and the whole Yupanqui family left, repeating the expression of their gratitude with the sublime words, "God bless you!"

"Goodbye; come back whenever you like," Lucía told them with a friendly gesture.

Don Fernando closed the door behind the Yupanquis and asked Lucía, "How old might Margarita be?"

"Her mother says she's fourteen, but her height, her beauty, the fire in her black eyes, everything about her bespeaks a woman in the first stages of puberty."

"There's nothing strange about that, my dear; this is an exuberant climate. But now we have to think about something else. Remember that we owe Doña Petronila several visits, and I want us to go see her tonight. That will counteract anything Don Sebastián may have told her."

"As you like, Fernando; I have the highest respect for Doña Petronila. As for the money, I beg you to settle with the governor by just paying him. Even a single peso that slips through their hands makes these people angry."

"You know them well, dear."

"Don't you see how quickly the priest was pacified? Here's the rest of the two hundred *soles* I asked you for."

"What an idea! Don't you worry about that, sweetheart; I'll take care of it, and there'll be no trouble for lack of payment."

"You're so good, Fernando! And I'll tell that to Doña Petronila, if the occasion arises. By the way, they say her son is about to come here."

"I'm sorry to hear it, because a young man will go to ruin in this place."

"I'm going to change," said Lucía, heading toward one of the inner rooms, "and I won't make you wait forever."

14

As soon as Marcela had left the rectory and he had finished his prayers, the priest called his *pongo* and said, "Run over to Don Sebastián's and tell him he has to come see me urgently, right away, and to bring along our friends."

"Yes, tata curay."

"And then go over to Don Estéfano's and tell him to come, and then set the tea kettle on the hearth and the chocolate pot on the embers and tell Manuela and Bernarda to stir up the fire."

"Yes, tata curay," the *pongo* replied, and dashed off like an express courier.

Don Sebastián just happened to be leaving his house, wrapped in his eternal cape, when the priest's envoy reached him; and after listening attentively to Father Pascual's message, he told the *pongo*, "You can go back from here; I'll inform our friends," and he headed for Estéfano's house.

The *pongo*, however, in order to follow his master's instructions to the letter, also went to Estéfano's; and with his light step he was back at the rectory in no time and went directly to the kitchen, there to carry out the second part of his orders.

When Pancorbo entered the house of Estéfano Benites, the latter was in a room that served him as both parlor and place of business, sitting at a small table covered with a vicuña poncho and playing cards in the company of the same individuals whom we met raising a glass at the governor's house. As soon as he heard the message from Father Pascual he threw down the cards and said, "Let's go, my friends; the Church is calling us."

"And I had a winning hand for sure," groused one of those present, called Escobedo, scratching his head with his left hand and caressing the cards fanned out in his right.

"Who had the two?" asked several others, getting up simultaneously and preparing to leave.

"The two was still in the pack," Estéfano answered as he straightened the hat that had slid toward the back of his head; and they all left together just as Don Sebastián came in and stopped them, saying, "Gentlemen, I was just looking for . . ."

"For us, right?" they all chorused, and Don Sebastián, laughing jovially, replied, "Aha, I'm glad to see you all together, because, frankly, our pastor needs us."

"All right, my friends, let's go; maybe he needs an acolyte for a *Dominus vobiscum*," Benites added roguishly, and laughing at the jest they continued on their way.

The influence that priests have in these places is so great that their word almost becomes a divine command; and the Indians are so docile that although in the intimacy of their huts there may be veiled criticism of certain acts of the clergy, the superstition that the priests maintain is powerful enough to crush all discussion and make their voice the law of their parishioners.

Estéfano Benites's house is only three blocks from the rectory, so the priest did not have to wait long; and as soon as he heard the group coming he stepped to his front door to receive his visitors.

"A very good afternoon to you, my fine gentlemen. You're men after my own heart, and attentive to your duty," he said, shaking hands all around.

"We're at your service, Father," they chorused in reply, taking off their hats.

"Please have a seat. My dear Don Sebastián over here . . . Don Estéfano . . . Please sit down, gentlemen," said Father Pascual, waving toward various seats and brimming over with cordiality.

"Thank you, we're fine."

"Frankly, Father, you're very kind."

"Well, gentlemen, things are getting out of hand, and I've had to bother you," the priest went on, walking about as though looking for something.

"No bother at all, Father," they all answered, speaking in chorus as provincials do.

"Fine, gentlemen. But let's not have any dry talk," Don Pascual said, drawing a bunch of keys from the right-hand pocket of his quasi-cassock, opening the cabinet where he had placed Marcela's forty *soles*, and bringing forth two bottles and some glasses. As he set them on the table he added, "This is a little liqueur made with viper root and anise; it's good against gas."

"You're very kind, Father, but, frankly, you're taking too much trouble; these young fellows can do the pouring," said Don Sebastián; and Estéfano stood up and, rushing over to relieve the priest of the bottle from which he was beginning to pour, said, "Allow me, Father; I'll do that."

"All right," the priest replied, handing him the bottle; and he went to sit in his leather armchair, next to Don Sebastián.

"To your health!"

"To yours, Father!"

With these toasts the first glass was downed.

Don Sebastián joined the others and then, spitting to clear his mouth, said, "What a comforting little drink! It's frankly first-rate!"

"It's the viper root that gives it the good flavor."

"All I notice is the anise."

"You must have a cold!"

These words were heard almost simultaneously; and Don Pascual, holding out his empty glass, said, "Well, my friends, I've been humiliated like some nobody by having the money that Indian Yupanqui owed me thrown in my face. You remember, that debt we were talking about the other afternoon."

"How's that?"

"What?"

"Frankly, Father, we can't put up with this; the same thing happened to me today," Don Sebastián replied; and Estéfano, never at a loss for words, said, "This is a direct attack against our pastor and our governor, but . . ."

"We won't put up with it!" they all replied in chorus.

"Frankly, we have to punish them," said Don Sebastián; and striking the floor with the heel of his boot, he added, "and while things are still fresh."

"Yes, my friends, otherwise we're just letting them poke their fingers in our eyes; and after all, we're still alive and kicking," the priest seconded.

"Let's decide right now; you tell us what we can do," Escobedo said, coming to pour another round without offering any explanation for this act of courtesy, but whispering to Estéfano, "Clumsy! You left the bottle uncorked."

"What the devil, I'll run the campaign!" Estéfano shouted enthusiastically.

"If you like, frankly, I'm ready, too," the governor volunteered.

"One step at a time," the priest put in, taking the glass Escobedo was offering him; and from then on each man drank at his own pace, so that the cabinet soon had to be opened once more to produce new bottles. Increasingly heated speeches began to sound as the liquor roused the spirits of the guests, and Father Pascual called over his *pongo* and whispered to him, "Is the water boiling?"

"Yes, tata curay; and the señora has come, too."

"All right, tell her to go in the bedroom and wait for me there; and you bring everything out here."

The *pongo*, thoroughly experienced in this line of work, quickly set the table with cups and a white china pot in which the tea was steeping, while the two Indian women who served in the rectory, Manuela and Bernarda, stood in the doorway.

"Let's have a cup of tea, gentlemen," said Father Pascual.

"You shouldn't have bothered," replied several of the guests.

"Let me do it; I'll take care of this," said Escobedo, seizing the handle of the teapot.

"Good and spiked, I hope; frankly, it's plenty cold tonight," Don Sebastián put in, rubbing his hands and simulating a bit of a cough.

"Now that we're going to talk in earnest, it was a very bad idea for us all to come over together," Estéfano pointed out.

"Quite right. We'll have to see that nobody notices us when we leave," observed Escobedo.

"We'll have to call the sexton and feed him some story," said the priest, taking two swallows of tea and setting his cup down on its saucer.

"The best thing is, frankly, to strike a conclusive and decisive blow."

"And no miscalculations, like when we attacked the Frenchman!"

"That was a case of bad planning."

"The thing to do is attack Don Fernando and Doña Lucía and cut off any escape route, and then . . ."

"Kill them!"

"Bravo!"

The sound of several cups set down on their saucers was the chorus that accompanied the last word of that criminal conversation that produced a death sentence against Don Fernando Marín and his wife.

The priest said, "First you've got to talk to the sexton, so that I'll be kept out of it, you understand?"

"Yes, Father; we'll tell him 'they say' some bandits are planning a raid on the church and that if it happens he should be ready to sound the alarm with the bell right away," said Benites; and Escobedo jumped up to add, "Good! I'll take care of the signal."

"What we have to do is spread the news all through town, in different ways. Frankly, we've got to take every precaution in case there's an investigation afterwards," Pancorbo said, and the others replied with:

"I'll say they're planning to rob the rectory."

"I'll say a battalion of troops is on its way."

"That's nothing! I'll say they're coming from Arequipa to carry off our miraculous Virgin."

"Splendid! But, frankly, people will head for the church," Pancorbo noted.

"No, sir; that's just to bring them together. Then we'll say the criminals have taken refuge at Don Fernando's, and, wham!" Estéfano Benites explained.

"Yes, that's the way; it's all downhill from there, because once the people have been aroused they don't think any more," was Father Pascual's opinion as he handed Estéfano and Escobedo each a glass.

"Let's not forget to get the justice of the peace in on it."

"Frankly, that's a must."

"You can always find him over at that woman's place, the one from Quiquijana. I'll drop by there now and start buttering him up," Benites volunteered.

"All right, let's go," they all said and began to shake hands with the priest, who sent them off with the words, "All right, careful, boys," and they went out one at a time, heading in different directions.

The priest was left in intimate conversation with the governor, not without frequent recourse to a nip of his pet liqueur, and said, "That boy Benites is worth his weight in gold! He's bold, and he's careful."

"He sure is, Father; frankly, we never thought of the justice of the peace."

"Yes, they're right when they say that young folks nowadays know plenty."

"And he's sure to find the rascal at that woman's place. Frankly, what a bouncy buxom one she is! And frankly, I think you used to be seen around there, too, my dear Father," Don Sebastián said in a jesting tone, to which the priest replied, laughing, "What are you saying, my dear governor?" and patted him on the shoulder.

"All right, then, Father, it's time to go home; and frankly, the night's so cold you'd think we were up on the *puna*."[14]

"Let's have a night-cap, since you're off to sleep and snore," said Father Pascual, pouring out two glasses and handing one to Pancorbo.

"Snore, nothing! Frankly, I'm not even going home. I'll wait over at Rufa's, so I can better see how the boys are doing."

"Fine, fine, my dear Don Sebastián; I'll be seeing you soon," the priest replied, shaking his friend's hand.

A quarter of an hour later, every little bar resounded with shouts, arguments, choruses of *marineras* accompanied with guitars, and the animated cries of the dancers, for the juice of the grape was flowing freely.

And the victims marked for sacrifice, their souls at peace and their loving hearts filled with happiness, were even then on their way to Don Sebastián's house to visit the wife of their covert executioner.

14. *Puna*, the Andean high plateau.

15

The sun of bliss was shedding its purest rays on Doña Petronila's house. Doña Petronila was a happy mother, because, after a long absence, her arms had held her beloved Manuel, the darling son who filled her dreams at night and was the joy of her gloomy days. He had left Killac a boy and had returned a fine upstanding man, not having wasted a single day of his schooling. Now he was sitting by his mother, holding her hands in his, gazing on her in rapture, and chatting about family matters.

Don Fernando and Lucía appeared in the doorway; and on seeing them, Doña Petronila and Manuel stood up and Doña Petronila introduced her son in that special language that good mothers have invented, saying, "Señora Lucía, Señor Marín, this is Manuelito, my boy, who was such a little fellow when he left."

"Doña Petronila, Señor Don Manuel," the Maríns said in turn.

"Señora, at your service. Señor Marín . . ." Manuel replied. And Doña Petronila went on in her simple way, "You haven't met him till now, because he's just come back after seven years and eight days. But please sit down," she said, pointing to the sofa.

"Your son's such a charming young man, Doña Petronila!" Lucía replied.

"Allow me, sir," said Manuel, taking the hat from the visitor's hand and setting it on the table. They all sat down in a close group, and a cordial, relaxed conversation began to flow.

Manuel was a youth of twenty, of a good height, that is, neither tall nor short, with a gentle expression on his face and a voice whose timbre won the hearts of all who heard it. A coal-black mustache grew above his fine red lips, and dark circles accented his large eyes. Easy speech and elegant manners were the final touches that made him an appealing young man.

"Have you decided on a career?" Don Fernando asked of Manuel.

"Yes, Señor Marín; I'm a second-year student of law, and I plan to become a lawyer, if my luck holds out," Doña Petronila's son answered modestly.

"Congratulations, my friend; the vast field of the law holds great charms for the mind," said Don Fernando, to which Manuel replied, "And so does any other profession, sir, when you dedicate your heart and will to it . . ."

Manuel was going to continue, when the report of a firearm was heard, making the ladies jump and startling the men.

As though struck by lightning, Lucía took her husband's arm and said, "Let's go, Fernando, let's go."

"Yes, ma'am, go right away, and make sure you shut up the entrances to your house," said a shaken Doña Petronila.

"And what might this be?" asked Manuel without giving the matter much importance.

"This sort of thing is unusual around here," Don Fernando replied, with Lucía adding, "Could it be robbers?"

"By all means, let's go," said Don Fernando, offering his arm to Lucía; but at that moment Manuel intervened, asking that he be allowed to accompany the lady; and once his arm had been accepted with an amiable smile, the three of them left.

Doña Petronila said to herself, "This mother's heart of mine can't rest as long as my Manuelito is out of the house," and with cautious steps she followed some distance behind the others.

Manuel, who from the first instant had felt a strong attraction toward the Maríns, said to Lucía, "When I came to Kíllac, señora, I thought I'd die of tedium in this wretched little place; but now I've found it embellished with your presence and that of your husband."

"Thank you, sir; you've been a diligent student of the gallant language of the city," Lucía answered with a pleasant smile.

"No, ma'am, my words are not just empty formulas of gallantry; without you and without my mother, what social relations could I have here?" replied Manuel, adding sorrowfully, "This afternoon I've come to know the inhabitants of the place, and I feel sorry for them."

"You're quite right, Don Manuel; but you have your parents, and you have friends in us."

"Yes, Don Manuel; this place is terribly depressing for a young man coming from the city; I'll agree with you there," put in Don Fernando, like a jealous husband giving notice that he hears his wife's conversation.

"I'm just sorry we may not stay here much longer, because I think Fernando's business will soon be taken care of," Lucía said.

"So much the worse for me if I have to extend my stay, which is only supposed to last four to six months," replied Manuel.

Don Fernando drew two paces ahead of the others to open the front door, since they had reached his house.

"I hope you'll come in to rest a moment, Manuel," Lucía said, releasing her companion's arm.

"Thank you, ma'am, but I can't. My mother would worry if I were out late, and I want to spare her that trouble," Manuel answered, taking off his hat to say good night.

"Remember that you're welcome here any time, my friend," Don Fernando urged.

"Thank you, I'll bear that in mind and visit you soon. Good night," Manuel repeated, shaking his friends' hands and disappearing down the dark streets crossed only by scattered drunkards.

Lucía and Don Fernando took some security measures, as Doña Petronila had urged; but seeing that all remained quiet, they went to bed.

The surface of a crystal lake that mirrors the image of the gulls is not as tranquil as the sleep with which Love, fluttering his shimmering wings above their foreheads, lulled Lucía and Don Fernando. Their hearts, linked by a single breath, beat in happy unison. But their rest was not like the eternal lethargy of mere matter. The spirit, which stirs and does not sleep, struggled against a powerful presentiment, that mysterious warning signal of virtuous souls; and as it agitated Lucía's body, it awoke her and caused her to feel uncertainty, fear, doubt, that whole complicated train of mixed sensations that come to us in sleepless nights. Lucía felt those nervous shudders, unable to understand or explain them as she faced an unknown danger; and her mind instantly recalled those midnight sounds that, like the rush of wings or the creaking of doors, first awaken our fears and then the thought of our loved ones, be they absent or joined to us in tender embrace.

That nervous energy that obeys the impulse of our spirit, which in spite of the work of Allan Kardec[15] is not yet understood, which frightens us with the sense of the unseen presence of a superior or dreaded being, and which scientific research is now exploring as it proceeds to change the face of the world with the astonishing lucidity of Charcot, Maira, and Benavente in their studies of hypnotism, had its full effect on the system of Don Fernando Marín's wife that night.

She lay awake.

The ancient and solitary town clock sounded the twelfth stroke that marks midnight, and at that same moment the ringing voice of the church bell vibrated through the night. Its brazen notes did not summon the soul to withdraw into itself for peaceful prayer; it called the townsfolk to battle and to the attack with the impressive signal agreed upon between Estéfano Benites and the sexton, who was posted in the

15. Pseudonym of Hyppolite Rivail, influential French spiritualist (1803–69).

tower. And like hail crashing down from black clouds amid flashes of lightning, a deluge of stones and bullets began to fall on the defenseless home of Don Fernando. Countless shadows flitted by in different directions; and the clamor began to rise like a gigantic wave that the storm raises in the depths of the sea, only to smash it against the shore with a powerful hoarse roar.

The commotion was terrifying. Shouted commands, savage and contradictory, now in Spanish, now in Quechua, resounded over the noise of the stones and gunshots. On all sides could be heard the cries of:

"Outsiders!"

"Thieves!"

"Súhua! Súhua!"[16]

"Meddlers!"

"Kill them, kill them!"

"Huañuchiy!"[17]

"Kill them!" countless voices repeated. And the rhythmic ringing of the bell sounding the alarm was the response to all this outcry.

Lucía and Don Fernando left the bed where they were resting, lightly dressed in their nightclothes and in whatever else they could lay hold of as they rushed either to escape or to fall into the hands of their implacable assailants, meeting an early and cruel death in the midst of this crowd drunk with alcohol and with rage.

16

J uan Yupanqui and Marcela, who had left Lucía's house after the events we witnessed earlier, had gone home with Margarita and Rosalía, those two stars that shed cheer on their hut and whose destinies were already sealed with the mark that God puts on those He chooses to play a part in the transformation of society.

16. *Súhua,* "Thief!"

17. *Huañuchiy,* "Kill them!"

There was no room now in Juan Yupanqui's brain for his criminal thoughts of the day before. No more would he stand at the gloomy threshold of a suicide that steeps the hearts of those who remain in mourning and kills the hopes of those who believe. God had sent Lucía to restore Juan's faith in Providence, torn from his heart by Father Pascual, the governor, and the collection agent or headman, that frightful trinity that embodied a single injustice. Juan once more believed in goodness, he felt renewed, and he would undertake life's labors with fresh zeal to show his eternal gratitude to his benefactors. No longer would Marcela be the widow of a suicide, of a deserter from life, whose corpse, buried on the bank of some river or by the side of some lonely path, would draw from his dear ones no sighs, no prayers, no peace.

Sitting in his hut, Juan said to his wife, "Let's pray to the Blessed Sacrament, and here and now I swear to you to devote my energies and my life to our protectors."

"Juanuco! Didn't I tell you? I'll serve them, too, as long as I live."

"And so will I, Mama," Margarita added; and all three set to explaining to Rosalía that it was thanks to the intercession of the Wiracocha Fernando and the Señora Lucía from the big house that "those men" had not taken her away. And making her kneel at the back of the room with her clasped hands raised to heaven, they made her repeat the sublime words of their prayer.

"Now stir up the fire," Juan said to Margarita.

"We'll roast some potatoes, and we have chili," Marcela added, taking out some packages of corn leaves tied with a piece of woollen thread.

"Tomorrow we'll kill a chicken, Marcela; I'm very happy, and I'm sure our new friends will lend us a couple of pesos," Juan said merrily.

"That's the way I like to see you, tata. Or should we ask for our change from the priest?" his wife replied, setting two plates of glazed earthenware by her husband.

"What change? What do we want all that for?" Yupanqui answered.

"Our Margarita will look so pretty once the señoracha is her godmother, won't she?" the woman said, changing the topic of conversation.

"You can be sure of that; *jay!*, she'll dress her in the kind of clothes they wear."

"But my heart aches when I remember that once our Margarita is a real young lady, she won't think of us the way she does now," Marcela said with a sigh as she came to lay wood on the hearth.

"What are you talking about? Señora Lucía will teach her to respect us," Juan replied.

"The blessings of Pachacamac[18] be on her!" Marcela added devoutly.

"Mama, when Señora Lucía is my godmother will I go live with her?" Margarita asked.

"Yes, child," the mother answered.

"And what about you and dear Juan and dear Rosalía?" Margarita asked again.

"We'll go see you every day," Marcela replied, continuing her preparations for supper; and Juan, holding Rosalía between his knees and caressing her, told his wife, "You seem pretty chatty tonight."

"I do indeed," Marcela replied, turning over the roasting potatoes; but Margarita kept up her questions: "And will you bring me blackberries and sparrows' nests?"

"Yes, we'll bring you all that if you learn to sew and do that pretty embroidery they say Señora Lucía knows how to do," Marcela replied, as she took the potatoes off the hearth and set them on the plates that stood by her husband.

It was a tasty and frugal supper; but Rosalía's prayer reached heaven and obtained a refreshing sleep for the family of Juan Yupanqui, resting on their humble bed of satisfactions free from the gnawing worm of doubt. A deep yawn coming from Juan showed Marcela that her husband was sound asleep and that her daughters had followed his example, leaving the hut plunged in absolute silence.

And while the spirits of peace dwell here, we shall see what is happening in the rectory.

17

A black shadow walked back and forth uneasily and impatiently from one side of the totally dark room to the other, afraid to light the linseed-oil lamp common in Killac or the tallow candle manufactured by the local candlemaker, who adds small amounts of myrtle and boiled rosemary to the grease to make it whiter and firmer.

---

18. *Pachacamac,* chief deity of the Incas, according to some chroniclers.

Crime is always most comfortable with the blackness of the night. Almost opposite a small window with wooden bars and shutters painted with yellow ochre stood an ancient bedstead of noble *zumbaillo* wood with a correspondingly ancient canopy of silk damask curtains over the comfortable wide bed. A handsome quilt composed of countless pieces of cashmere of different colors, ingeniously combined by the skill of some good housewife or by the hand of some pious city lady, had been partially pulled aside and lay somewhat rumpled. On an adjacent wooden bench, and leaning slightly toward the pillows, sat a woman who had entered the house secretly, and whose arrival the *pongo* had already announced early in the evening while the priest was holding his meeting.

Father Pascual was awaiting the outcome of his dreadful schemes, and he waited in darkness so as not to draw even the slightest suspicion on himself by being found awake and with his light on so late at night; and from time to time he put his ear to the cracks in the shutters.

"For Heaven's sake, what's the matter with you? I've never seen you this restless," the woman ventured to say.

"Didn't you hear that shot?" the priest stammered in reply, for the viper-root liqueur was having its effect and speech did not come forth freely.

"That shot! Why, hours have passed since then, and everything's peaceful," the woman countered.

"The church might be robbed; I heard some bad news from the neighbors this afternoon," the priest limited himself to saying, trying to throw the woman off the track, for he was obsessed by his need to appear innocent.

"Thieves in Killac? Thieves in our church? Ha, ha, ha!" the woman replied in a loud voice and burst into laughter.

"Hush, damn you!" the priest answered angrily, stamping his foot on the ground.

"But come on now, come lie down for a while . . ."

"Quiet, you devil!" Father Pascual interrupted.

"Don't get nasty with me now, after . . . all the other nasty things you've done," the woman replied as though spoiling for a fight; and the only way the priest could keep her quiet and stop her accusations was to go over and lie down next to her, taking a silken handkerchief from his pocket and tying it around his head.

And the sinister flutter of wings could be heard as an owl flew over the roof of the rectory, portending misfortune with that mournful screech that is the terror of simple folk.

• • • • •

Don Sebastián had not returned home.

Doña Petronila was ready to send two servants to find her husband and attend him; but Manuel, taking up his hat and a cane of fine *huarango* wood, said, "I'll go, Mother."

"I absolutely won't allow it. Ay, my boy, I don't know what it is I feel in my heart. That gunshot, your father's staying out so long, the comings and goings of Estéfano, everything worries me," Doña Petronila said sadly; but Manuel, inspired by the nobility of his feelings and perhaps by a twofold desire, replied, "That's just why it's up to me, Mother, to go find Don Sebastián and get him out of any dangerous or awkward situation."

"It wouldn't be any use, my boy; you don't know how stubborn he is. Ah! I beg you, Manuel," Doña Petronila added, affectionately putting her arms around her son, who stood for a few seconds in silent thought; and taking advantage of that silence, Doña Petronila continued her entreaties, "Your obligation is to take care of me, Manuel. I'm your mother; don't leave me alone! In God's name I beg you!"

"I won't go out, Mother," Manuel replied decisively, leaning his cane against the wall and taking off his hat.

"That's the way, Manuelito, that's right; now maybe I'll be able to sleep. Let's go to bed."

"Yes, Mother, go to bed. It's a very cold night, and very late."

"Go to your room, then, and I'll see you in the morning," said Doña Petronila, with a pleased look at her son.

18

At the first sound of bells and gunshots, Don Fernando's terrified staff had fled in search of safety, realizing they were in the line of fire. Don Fernando was getting ready to defend himself, and in his shirtsleeves he went for his hunting rifle with its good stock of ammunition; but Lucía stopped him, repeatedly begging him in her distress, "No, Fernando dearest, no! Save yourself, save me, let's save ourselves!"

"And how can we do that, my love? This is the only way, because if we don't defend ourselves we'll die," Don Fernando replied, trying to calm his wife's agitation.

"Let's get away from here, Fernando," said Lucía, spurred by her husband's concluding words.

"But how, Lucía dear? Every way in or out of the house is blocked," Don Fernando replied, taking a box of Remington cartridges and putting it in his trousers pocket.

Outside the shouts continued, ever more frightening and implacable: "Robbers!" "Newcomers!" "Outsiders!" "Yes, kill them, kill them!" Those were the words that could be made out amid the roar of the riotous mob.

Suddenly a new voice was heard—fresh, unclouded by alcohol— that with all the boldness and serenity of true valor said, "Get back, you wretches! You can't go murdering people this way!"

And another voice sounded in support of the first, saying, "We've been tricked! The scoundrels! There aren't any robbers!"

"All you decent people, over here!" another shouted bravely.

"Come over here!" ordered the first voice, and at that moment a woman arrived with a glass lantern equipped with a tallow candle that gave off a dim light.

The shots had stopped and the bell had fallen silent. Groups of people began to scatter in different directions, and the mood of the crowd was totally changed.

The entrance to Don Fernando's house was completely destroyed; and stones lay in large piles where they had fallen, next to the splinters that remained of the doors.

"Let's have that lantern over here!" a man shouted, making his way through the crowd; and as the lantern came near, by its dim light Manuel recognized Doña Petronila.

"Mother, you here!" he exclaimed in surprise.

"I'm by your side, son!" Doña Petronila replied, her terror showing on her face as she handed him the lantern; and together they began to look over the dead and wounded.

The first corpse they found was that of an Indian at whose feet lay a woman, likewise bathed in blood and tears, and calling out in desperation, "Ay! They've killed my husband! They've probably killed my protectors, too!"

As soon as the first shots had sounded, Juan and Marcela had come to defend Don Fernando's house. Juan fell when a bullet entered his right lung and exited breaking his second rib and grazing his liver. Marcela had a gunshot wound in her shoulder that was gushing blood, and next to her lay three corpses of unarmed Indians.

"Mother!" called Manuel to gain Doña Petronila's attention, "If she doesn't get help right away, this woman will be dead in no time."

"Let's get her away from here so the nurse can have a look at her," Doña Petronila replied.

"Some men over here!" Manuel commanded, and several men volunteered to carry Marcela. When he saw how eager all were to gather the dead and care for the wounded, the bold youth who had defied the wrath of a drunken mob, forced his way forward, and halted the tumult said to himself, "It's plain this riot stems from a misunderstanding that warrants pardon more than punishment."

Several men lifted a collapsed Marcela to take her away for medical treatment.

"Slowly, be careful!" said Doña Petronila.

"Ay, ay! Where are they taking me?" Marcela asked, clutching her wound with her hand and adding mournfully, "My daughters! Rosacha! Margarita!"

"What do you suppose happened to Don Fernando and Lucía?" inquired Manuel with growing concern, and at that moment a new day dawned to shine on the faces of the guilty.

19

There was someone whose interest in the fate of the Maríns was as strong as Manuel's. That was Father Pascual, who performed marvels of ingenuity to avoid discussing events with Doña Melitona, which was the name of the woman who had gone to keep him company on that sinister night. As soon as the bells were silent and the gunshots had stopped, he said to himself, "By now things are settled one way or the other." And turning to Melitona, he added artfully, "It seems all the uproar's over with, wouldn't you say?"

"Yes, curay, I think it's over. Lord, how scared I was!" Melitona answered, gesturing wildly, to which the priest replied, "And so was I, ever since I heard the first shot, thinking they were attacking the church, even though you kept insisting . . ."

"Fortunately we soon realized it was all somewhere else. And how could I have let you go out?"

"Lord bless me, Melitona, it's a good thing you stopped me, even though they say that women . . ."

"And what do you suppose it was, curay?" the woman asked in all innocence.

"It must have something to do with politics. Thank God I didn't go out, thank God," the priest kept repeating even as in his heart he grew increasingly anxious to know the outcome, though he managed to keep his emotions in check and appear quite at ease.

Sleep came to Melitona without further discussions, but not to the priest, who waited uneasily for the coming of dawn. No sooner had the first dim light of morning begun to appear and people could be heard walking along the streets than he coughed loudly, took off the handkerchief he had tied around his head, put it under the pillow, and said, "Run along now, Melitonita. Woman that you are, you must be feeling curious; find out what really happened last night in that neighborhood, which, as best we could figure, was . . . well, it seems to me, over toward Don Fernando's house. I'm going to get ready to say mass."

"Right away, curay," Doña Melitona replied, pleased with the commission. She crossed herself three times, got dressed, put on her black-fringed shawl of purple cashmere, and left.

The first persons she met gave her a fairly precise account of the assault on Don Fernando Marín's house; but since she wanted to return to the rectory with news confirmed by her own eyes, she proceeded right to the actual scene of events.

"Lord! What an outrage! What sort of heretics could have done this? Poor Señor Marín! Poor dear Señorita Lucía! Just look at that, everything's in pieces!" she said, walking among the ruins and gazing at the debris.

Lucía and Don Fernando were in the sitting room of their house, safe and sound and well accompanied; and Manuel, with all the indignation of his pure heart and all the fervor of his youth, was loudly saying, "It's hard to imagine wickedness like this, Señor Don Fernando. This town's full of savages, and it's a miracle you were saved. Tell us how you managed it."

"The miracle is Lucía's," Don Fernando answered dryly, tying the necktie that in his distraction he had left hanging loose, and taking great strides about the room.

"Señora Lucía!" was Manuel's only reply as he looked toward the sofa, where that lady half lay, deeply shaken and holding a small flask of

Bohemian crystal whose stopper she carefully raised just a crack now and then to sniff the salts contained within.

Don Fernando, as though continuing his line of thought, said, "What a fright! There must be many who know what it is to awaken to the noise of disorder, shooting, and killing, because in our country we tolerate and frequently witness those uprisings and that civil strife which, be it in the name of Pezet, Prado, or Piérola, are the bearers of shock and terror, whether in the storm of revolution or within the bastions of resistance. But there must be few who know what it is to awake from the sleep of happiness to the sound of murderous bullets and summons to slaughter shouted outside the walls of their own bedrooms."

"Stop, Don Fernando, that's enough!" several voices cried out in unison.

"How dreadful!" Manuel added, running his fingers through his hair; and Don Fernando, replying to Manuel's first question, which had gone unanswered in the natural tumult of his thoughts, said, "Don Manuel, I had decided to accept my fate and die defending myself with my weapon in my hand; but the tears of my good, my saintly, wife made me think of saving myself so as also to save her. We both fled along the left-hand wall and took refuge behind some stone fences that were right next to the scene of the attack; and from there we calmly observed the assault on our house and saw your heroism, Doña Petronila's motherly selflessness, the death of our unhappy Juan, and the wounding of poor Marcela."

"Poor Juan! Poor Marcela! Now that we're sisters in misfortune, all my efforts shall be on behalf of her and her daughters," Lucía said, sighing with deep sorrow and interrupting her husband.

"Ah yes! Margarita, Rosalía—from this day on those tender doves torn from the nest shall find their father's spirit in this house," Don Fernando declared.

"Let's have Marcela brought here so we can care for her properly," Lucía said, deeply touched; and especially addressing the young man, she added, "Manuel, I beg you in the name of friendship: take care of this," to which Manuel replied with youthful vehemence, "Right away, señora. You, the angel of the virtuous, will stanch a mother's wounds; and you and I, Don Fernando, will settle accounts with the guilty."

As he spoke these last words, a deathly pallor overspread his countenance, for the name of Don Sebastián passed through his mind—of Don Sebastián, his mother's husband, the man whom he called his father. Mechanically he took up his hat, bowed, and left quickly, passing by Doña Melitona, who was listening to everything from behind the door without missing a word.

Don Fernando sat down next to Lucía and took out a cigarette. Doña Melitona, thinking that she knew enough, retraced her steps to go inform the priest, who was impatiently awaiting the return of his "little woman" before going to say mass.

As she came in and took off her shawl, Melitona said, "Now I can fill you in on the latest, curay."

"All right, Melitonita; and what happened?" Father Pascual asked.

"They say there was some dispute about accounts between Don Fernando and some wool merchants, and that Don Sebastián took a hand in it, I don't know on whose side, and that's when the trouble started, and a row got under way, and other people thought it was thieves and rang the bells," Melitona recounted with gestures and movements of her head.

"So it was just a private quarrel? I'll give that sexton a good dressing-down so he won't be so free and easy with the bells," the priest replied cunningly.

"That's what they say, curay; but Don Sebastián's son, a young man who just got here, is over at Don Fernando's, just like one of the family, and saying he'll punish whoever's responsible," Melitona explained.

"He says that, does he?" the priest asked; and biting his lip, he added to himself, "Beardless puppy! And what'll you do when your father tells you, 'Hush, this is my business'? And even if he doesn't, we haven't lived all this time without learning a thing or two."

And soon after this the village bell was heard calling the faithful to mass.

20

The arrival of Marcela, carried on a rough wooden stretcher, wounded, widowed, and followed by the two orphans, at the same house she had left the day before cheerful and happy, had such a powerful effect on Lucía, who was alone at the time, that she could not restrain her tears as she went to receive her. She had the stretcher placed in a tidy room, put her arms around Rosalía, caressed Margarita, and spoke to both of them, calling them "my dears, poor little ones, my pretties." Then she sat down by Marcela and said to her, "Oh my dear, how much resignation you need now! I beg you to be calm, to have patience."

"Niñay, haven't you learned better than to protect us?" the Indian said in a weak voice and with a listless look; but Lucía, without answering her question, remarked, "How weak she is!" and turning to two servants who were near the door, she ordered them, "Get her a little chicken broth with a few slices of toast and a soft-boiled egg. I want you to take special care of her."

Marcela's countenance revealed her terrible suffering, but Lucía's words seemed to have given her some relief. Even though the local nurse had declared that the wound would very soon prove mortal, because the bullet had entered the left shoulder and remained lodged in the shoulderblade while Marcela's whole system was being attacked by fever, her virtuous protector had so powerful an influence on her that her spirits rose noticeably.

Two days passed like that, affording some hope of saving the patient.

Don Fernando had just come home, and Lucía asked him with a show of lively interest, "What about Juan's body, Fernando?"

"It's been taken to the cemetery with all the honors I could arrange for. I covered the expenses, and he's been buried in a temporary grave," Don Fernando answered, providing a detailed reply to the question asked by Lucía, who now inquired, "And why a temporary grave, my dear?"

"Because the judges will probably order a new autopsy, not trusting the one I had done," replied Don Fernando as he drew a piece of paper from his pocket.

"Good Heavens, what a lot of red tape! And what does that certificate say? Tell me!"

"What it says here," replied Don Fernando unfolding the document and reading, "is 'that Juan Yupanqui died instantly from the effects of a projectile fired from a certain height, which, fracturing the right scapula, followed an oblique path through both lungs, destroying the main arteries of the mediastinum.'"

"Will this report help in the search for the perpetrator?" Lucía asked eagerly.

"Ah, my dear, we can't have much hope of achieving anything there," replied Don Fernando as he refolded the paper and put it away.

"And what does Father Pascual have to say?"

"Bah, he was willing enough to say a prayer over Juan Yupanqui's grave, just as I was willing to set a simple wooden cross there," Don Fernando answered, twisting his mustache.

"Do you suppose he doesn't know the details of the attack on our house?"

"Not know them! That's nonsense, my dear. I think he's in on it."

"Really! It's enough to disgust you with all of these men. And what about the judges?" Lucía insisted indignantly.

"The judges and the authorities have taken some measures, such as seizing the stones piled up at the doors to our house as physical evidence," Don Fernando answered with a laugh followed by an expression of sadness that revealed the deep disillusionment and skepticism instilled in his noble upright heart by the recent events.

During this conversation husband and wife went down the corridor and reached Lucía's room, where they took seats facing each other, Lucía on the sofa and Don Fernando in an easy chair. Leaning back and crossing his legs, the husband said to his wife, "I'm going to trouble you for a moment, my dear. I think we have a little *chicha*[19] made of quinoa[20] and rice; let me have a glass."

"Right away, sweetheart," replied Lucía, getting up and leaving the room.

A minute later, she was back with a glass on a pottery saucer, holding a thick milky liquid sprinkled with ground cinnamon and appealing to both sight and smell; and this she offered to her husband. Don Fernando drank the chicha eagerly, set the glass on the table, wiped his mustache with a perfumed handkerchief, and resumed his former position, saying, "What a delightful drink, my dear! I don't know how some people can prefer that awful domestic beer."

"You're right, dear. I can't stand the beer they make at Silva y Picado's."

"And getting back to poor Juan, do you know, my dear, that I've taken an even greater interest in that Indian now that he's dead? They say the Indians are ingrates, but it was his gratitude that killed Juan Yupanqui."

"As far as I'm concerned, the upright and noble race that founded the empire conquered by Pizarro has not died out in Peru, even if our gentry here and others of their ilk have reduced the Indian to the level of a farm animal," Lucía answered.

"There's more to it than that, dear," said Don Fernando. "It's been proved that the diet of the Indians has enfeebled the functioning of their brains. As you've no doubt noticed, these impoverished people hardly

19. *Chicha*, a fermented beverage, usually derived from corn, of pre-Hispanic origin.
20. *Quinoa*, a highly nutritional grain, part of the Andean diet.

ever eat meat, and the discoveries of modern science prove to us that the activity of the brain is related to the nutrition it receives. The Indian has been condemned to the most absurd kind of vegetarian diet, living off turnip leaves, boiled beans, and quinoa leaves. Deprived of albuminoids and organic salts, his brain has no ready source of phosphates and lecithin. It only grows fat and thus plunges him into mental darkness, making him live on the same level as his mules and oxen."

"I share your views, dear Fernando; and I congratulate you on your fine dissertation, even though I don't understand it. I'm sure if you translated it into English any university in the world would award you a doctorate and consider you a great scholar."

"You scamp! But your laughter's been good for me this time," Don Fernando said, blushing slightly, for his wife's words made him realize that he had delivered himself of some possibly pedantic or inappropriate scientific pronouncements.

"No, dear. What do you think? If I've been laughing it's only because . . . of the solemnity with which we've been discussing these things over the grave of such an unusual Indian as Juan."

"No, Lucía, not unusual; and if the day of the Indian's true autonomy ever dawned, we'd witness the regeneration of that race that is today oppressed and humiliated," Don Fernando answered, once more letting his thoughts flow forth.

"I won't contradict you there, either, sweetheart; but here we are, arguing about the dead and forgetting the living. I'm going to see whether they've given Marcela something to eat," Lucía said, and hastened out of the room.

21

Manuel had not had a single hour's true rest since the beginning of the sad events that had shaken the people of Kíllac. As soon as he had arranged for and in part witnessed the removal of Marcela to Lucía's house, he devoted himself to making prudent inquiries, putting to use that good sense that is the product of a well-ordered and assiduous education. Prudence also caused him to avoid any immediate discussion with Don Sebastián, and he resolved that for the time being he would stay away from Señor Marín's home.

But matters have a way of moving on toward their resolution.

One morning, as he returned home, silent and pensive, absorbed by a single thought, he found his mother preparing some *suches*,[21] which, lying open in an earthenware pan with the appropriate accompaniment of pepper, chopped onion, salt, chili, and lard, were waiting to enter the oven to be cooked. When she saw her son Doña Petronila said, "Manuelito, how you used to enjoy baked suches! Do you remember, tatay? That's why I'm fixing them myself. Who else should be cooking for my son?"

"Thank you, Mother. Set that treat in the oven, and let me talk to you in your room," said Manuel, whose heart was soothed by that simple scene of domesticity; and as he walked toward Doña Petronila's room, he said to himself, "Bless all mothers! Anyone who hasn't been spoiled and caressed by his mother or kissed by the woman who bore him in her womb—ah, that man doesn't know what love is!"

Once in the room, he pulled a chair up to the table, sank down on it, and rested his elbows on the table and his head on his hands, with a meditative air. What conjectures were running through his mind! All the lines of investigation that he and his associates had followed led him to glimpse the true instigators of the assault on Don Fernando Marín's house, and foremost among them were Don Sebastián, Father Pascual, and Estéfano Benites.

At this point Doña Petronila came in, patted Manuel on the shoulder, and said, "Have you fallen asleep, Manuelito?"

Startled, Manuel let his arms drop, raised his eyes, and fixed them tenderly on his mother as he rose and answered, "Not at all, Mother; a troubled mind is condemned to wakefulness. Sit down, and let's talk"; and drawing up another chair next to his, he offered it to his mother.

"No, son, I'll just sit over here on this little bench; I'm more comfortable here," Doña Petronila replied, refusing the chair and rearranging the folds of her skirt as she sat down on her favorite seat, a low one covered with carpeting.

"As you like," said Manuel, sitting down in turn.

---

21. *Suches,* highly prized fish of the Andean rivers and lakes.

"I can tell what you want to talk to me about. Lord, the things that have been happening—terrible, aren't they? I'm still all in shock; I can just see the faces of the dead Indians, all covered with blood and dirt. Lord in heaven!"

"Ah, Mother dear! Why did I have to come here to see all this! But it's no use crying over things; let's make the best of it, do what we can, and see about getting Don Sebastián out of trouble," Manuel answered, as mother and son began to speak freely.

"Ay, my boy, what's the point of going into details? Ever since they made your father governor, he's a changed man, and . . . I can't cope with him any more."

"Yes, I know. Right from the start, I've understood it all, Mother dear."

"You talk to him, then; he'll listen to you."

"I'm afraid not. If I were really his son, the voice of a father's love would speak in him; but . . . you . . . you know . . ."

"And why are you bringing that up now?" Doña Petronila said angrily.

"I'm sorry, Mother; but let's get to the point. You have to help me, but affectionately, without any bitter words or accusations—none of that. We just have to get him to give up the governorship; I'll take care of everything after that. I've thought it all out. Now I've got to go face that scoundrel of a priest."

"Don't talk like that about a man of God! Good Heavens! You'll come to no good end if you don't respect what's sacred!"

"Mother, the man who abuses his ministry deserves contempt! But let's not talk about him; let's talk about Don Sebastián. Go see him in his room and talk to him, and try to get him in the right frame of mind for seeing me later on."

"Do you want me to go right now?" Doña Petronila asked, rising from her seat.

"Yes, Mother, there's no time to be lost," Manuel replied, buttoning his jacket; and Doña Petronila slowly left the room. When she reached the door of Don Sebastián's room she stopped for a moment and made the sign of the cross on her forehead before going in.

Manuel stayed behind, walking back and forth in his mother's room and busily making plans, because the interview with Don Sebastián was bound to be rather difficult. As he walked, his glance suddenly fell on a vessel displayed in a corner cabinet, which so powerfully attracted his attention that he stopped to examine it and remarked, "This must be a very important *huaco*.[22] What delicate clay! And such admirable decoration! How well it represents the needlework on the *lliclla*[23] of the *ccoya*[24] and the shadows on the loose cloak of the Indian, who must be some chief!"

"Manuelito, it seems Chapaco's in a good mood," said Doña Petronila cheerfully as she entered the room.

"What have you told him about this business?" Manuel asked eagerly as he returned the *huaco* to its place.

"I didn't want to push him, just as you said; but I told him it would be a good idea for him to leave the governorship because there's going to be trouble about arresting those responsible for the other night, and so on."

"You didn't tell him it's been said he took part in it?"

"Why would I tell him that? Good Lord, he would have turned hopping mad. I just don't dare . . ."

"But what did he finally answer you?"

"'I know what I'm doing,' is what he answered me, but in a good-natured way. Just you go see him," Doña Petronila said, taking hold of her son's hand.

Manuel kissed his mother's forehead and walked off to the room of Don Sebastián Pancorbo, governor of Kíllac.

22

Don Sebastián was slouched in an easy chair, wrapped in a shaggy poncho, a crimson silk handkerchief tied over his head with its corners knotted at the forehead. He was clearly uneasy.

"Good morning, sir," Manuel said as he entered.

"Good morning. Where've you been keeping yourself, Manuel? Frankly, I haven't seen you more than three times since you got here," Don Sebastián answered, concealing his anxiety.

22. *Huaco*, object found in a pre-Hispanic tomb.
23. *Lliclla*, brightly colored cloak or cape worn by Indian women.
24. *Ccoya*, Indian woman of high rank; a lady of the imperial court of the Incas.

"That's not my fault, sir; you haven't been home."

"Frankly, all these friends, and my official duties—my time's no longer my own; you're right, Manuelito," the governor said; and as though looking for a way to justify his behavior, he added, "As for the other night, frankly, son, I was in a lot of danger, but I couldn't stem the disorder. What can you do if you don't have any troops? But you behaved splendidly . . . and, frankly, that Don Fernando is also to blame for all this."

"I've come to talk to you seriously about what happened the other night. I can't just stand there with folded arms when I hear them accuse you."

"Me?" Pancorbo said, jumping up.

"You, sir."

"And who . . . ? Tell me now, who . . . ? Frankly, I'd like to know who that is."

"Don't get excited, sir; calm down, and let's talk as father and son, just the two of us," Manuel replied, biting his lips.

"Well, and what do *you* say? Let's hear it. Frankly, what an idea!"

"The result of all my investigations is . . . that it's practically certain that Father Pascual, you, and Estéfano Benites planned and directed this attack on Don Fernando, because of some repayment of money for advances and a burial."

Don Sebastián's color changed with each of Manuel's words; finally, pale, seized by a nervous trembling, unable to control himself, he said, "Is that what they say? Frankly, we've been betrayed!"

"It wasn't just you three; others were in on the plot, and a scheme hatched by many and while drinking doesn't bear the seal of silence," replied Manuel, calmly.

"It must have been young Escobedo; frankly, I never did trust that boy."

"*Somebody* told, Don Sebastián; what we have to do now is not speculate about that, but get you out of danger."

"And what's your plan, son?" Don Sebastián asked in a changed tone.

"It's for you to resign your governorship immediately," the young man replied.

"No, not that; frankly, not that! I should give up my position of authority in the town where I was born? No, no, don't even suggest that sort of thing, Manuel," Don Sebastián answered angrily.

"But you'll have to do it anyhow or face being dismissed, and I ask and advise you to do it. You've been swept along by the stream of events; it's the priest who's chiefly responsible. I'll deal with him, and you just sign your letter of resignation, Don Sebastián. Ever since I was a little boy I've called you my father, and everybody thinks I'm your son. You can't possibly question my concern or disregard my advice. I'm doing it all out of love for my mother and gratitude toward you," said Manuel, pulling out all the stops of his persuasive powers and wiping a forehead that dripped perspiration from a discussion in which he had again been forced to mention his origins, unknown to the public.

Don Sebastián was moved and embraced Manuel, saying, "Well, frankly, do what you think best . . . but don't leave out the priest."

"We'll see to it that everything turns out as well as possible for you, sir; and later on we'll go to Don Fernando's, because it's important for you two to be of one mind. Now I'm off to Father Pascual's. Goodbye for now," said Manuel, picking up his hat. And away he went toward the rectory, while Don Sebastián, shaking his head, kept muttering, "Young Escobedo or Benites . . . boys, nothing but boys!"

.   .   .   .

Meanwhile, Father Pascual was peacefully breakfasting in the company of two cats, one black and the other yellow and white, a shaggy dog stretched out across the doorsill and dozing with his head between his forepaws, and his *pongo*, who stood next to the dog with his arms crossed in a humble gesture, awaiting his master's orders. When he heard footsteps and saw Manuel, the priest raised a soup plate, turned it upside down, and used it to cover another plate that held a pigeon *a la criolla*, two split tomatoes resting on its wings and a sprig of parsley in its beak.

"Father," Manuel said as he came in, politely removing his hat.

"To what happy chance do I owe the pleasure of seeing you here, my young friend?" the priest replied.

"My reason for coming can hardly be a secret for you, Father," Manuel answered dryly and angrily, for he was not about to bandy courtesies with Father Pascual.

"You surprise me, my dear young sir," said the priest, changing his tone and absentmindedly picking up a fork.

Manuel, who was still standing, took the nearest seat and answered, "Let's get right to the point, Father: the assault that brought shame and mourning to this town the night before last was your doing."

"What's that, you insolent pip-squeak?" the priest said, shifting about in his seat and surprised at being addressed, for the first time, without the usual deference and in an accusing tone.

"Spare me the epithets, Father, and remember that it's not the priestly habit that brings a man respect, but the man who gives dignity to a habit that clothes both good priests and unworthy ones," replied Manuel.

"And what proof might you have for such an accusation?"

"All the proof that one man needs to accuse another man," was Manuel's straightforward reply.

"And what if instead of me you were to run into a person in whose presence you'd have to hang your head in shame?" said Father Pascual, throwing down the fork he still held in his hand and thinking he had dealt Manuel a decisive blow; but Manuel, unruffled and self-possessed, replied, "That person whom you're alluding to, Father, has been your unfortunate tool, just like the others."

"What's that you say, you schoolboy?" the priest said angrily, while through his mind flashed the question, "Could that rascal Pancorbo have told him all about it?"

"You heard me, Father, so let's not waste words," Manuel added.

"You'd better not waste time getting out of here," the priest answered angrily.

"That won't happen before I've done what I set out to do, Father."

"And what is it you're after?" the priest asked in a new tone, restraining his anger.

"That you and Don Sebastián repair the damage you've done before the law comes after the culprits."

"What's this I hear? Good Heavens! That pansy Don Sebastián has betrayed . . . !" the priest exclaimed, wholly vanquished by Manuel, who had just mentioned his father; but, as though finding a new line of defense, he went on to say, "Would you be so unnatural a son as to accuse your own father?"

"Of course not, since what I seek is a prudent and carefully thought-out remedy to mitigate the wrong; and there must be such a remedy, because our religion teaches us that unless we find pardon for our evil deeds, the gates of heaven will be closed to us."

"Aha! Is that what your teachers have taught you so you won't hesitate to accuse your own father?" the priest asked bitingly, still striving to undermine his opponent's position.

"They've taught me more than that, Father: that without righteous deeds there are no citizens, no family, no fatherland. Once again I tell you that I'm not accusing Don Sebastián; I'm looking for restitution that will attenuate his guilt . . ."

The young man was going to continue when one of Don Fernando's servants appeared, distraught and crying out from the doorway, "Help, Father, help, somebody's dying!"

"Go and comply with your priestly obligations, Father, and we'll talk later," said Manuel, seeing that they were not alone; and with a bow he left.

The priest went for his hat and, looking after the departing Manuel, contemptuously said, "Filthy Mason!" Then he uncovered the plate that he had protected from the air, sniffed it, and muttered, "My pigeon's grown cold . . . Well, I'll eat it when I get back."

23

T he Maríns spared neither expense nor diligent care to save their patient; but unfortunately her condition gradually worsened, and her life drew to its end. Just then Lucía was with Don Fernando, chatting with him in tender intimacy, and said, "What mysteries are these, Fernando? Marcela came to our quiet happy home seeking help, and for love of our neighbor we helped her and found delight in doing good; yet these virtuous, noble, and pious deeds have produced misfortune for all!"

"Remember, my love, that life is struggle, and that in the struggle between Good and Evil it's ignorance that digs the grave of Good. Victory consists of not letting ourselves be buried in it."

At this point Margarita came dashing to the door like a meteor, crying, "Godmother, Godmother, my mother's calling you!"

"I'm on my way," Lucía answered; and telling her husband, with a pat on the shoulder, "So long, sweetheart," she set off for Marcela's room.

Marcela was half raised in her bed, resting against several pillows covered in pink. When she saw Lucía her eyes brimmed over with tears, and in a weak and hesitating voice she exclaimed, "Niñay! . . . I'm going to die! . . . Ay! . . . My daughters! . . . Poor doves torn from the nest! . . . from their tree! . . . from their mother! . . . Ay!"

"Try to be calm, poor Marcela; you're very weak! I won't lecture you about God's mysterious ways; but you're good, you . . . are a Christian," Lucía said, rearranging the covers that were slipping off the bed.

"Yes, niñay!"

"If your time has come, Marcela, go in peace! Even if your daughters are torn from their nest, their new nest shall be here, and I shall be their mother!"

"God . . . bless you! . . . I . . . want to tell you . . . a secret . . . to be buried in your heart . . . until the right time comes," Marcela said, making an effort to speak without halting.

"What is it?" asked Lucía, drawing closer. And Marcela, her nearly icy lips close to the ear of Don Fernando's wife, murmured words that several times caused Lucía to turn her head and fix her astonished eyes on the dying woman, who, once she had finished, asked, "Do you promise . . . niñay?"

"Yes, I swear it to you by Christ crucified," Lucía answered, deeply moved.

And the poor martyr whose final hours were drawing close added, as she sighed deeply in what seemed to be her farewell to earthly concerns, "God bless you! . . . Now I . . . want to confess . . . and then . . . death is waiting for me!"

Father Pascual's arrival was announced, and Lucía returned his greeting coldly. Taking Rosalía and Margarita by the hand, she led them away to keep them occupied and prevent their witnessing their mother's leaving them forever.

The priest came up to the dying woman's bed and listened to the whispered confession of his victim.

Margarita could no longer avoid facing the truth. Her eyes were red from weeping, but still more tears would flow when she saw her mother carried out on the shoulders of strangers to be left forever in the damp earth of the cemetery. Poor Margarita! For all her suffering, she could not gauge the full extent of the disaster that had befallen her.

As she led the girls out and turned them over to a maid to be dressed in the new clothes being made for them on the Davis sewing machine, Lucía said to herself, "Ah, the wonderful innocence of childhood, which bathes all things in the golden warmth of a shining sun, while old age chills all things in the coldness of its skepticism! Are the old, who know mankind, right to be skeptical? Girls," she added aloud, "go with Manuela, who'll give you a piece of cake and some pretty dresses." And she went off to look for Don Fernando, who was working in his office. Almost at that moment Manuel and Don Sebastián arrived. When Lucía saw them, she wrung her hands and asked herself in astonishment, "Now what is going to happen in this house where in these few days such tragic events have occurred, events whose full significance we cannot yet assess? What new drama will be played out in my home, where an invisible hand is now gathering all the main characters, the persecutors and the persecuted, in the presence of a mother who stands at the edge of the grave dug for her by these *gentry*, who, with all their talk of alleged attacks against their customs, are only pursuing their personal interests, quite willing to stoop to the vilest means? Dear Lord!"

"Your servant, Señora Lucía," said Manuel, coming upon Señor Marín's wife almost at the door of the office, which they entered, followed by Don Sebastián.

"Gentlemen," Lucía replied, with clear distaste for Don Sebastián, who removed his hat and said, "Good morning to you, señora . . . señor."

"Hello, Don Manuel; how are you, Don Sebastián?" Don Fernando replied, mastering his displeasure at the presence of the second personage; but Manuel, expecting this reaction and trying to reduce tensions, initiated the conversation by saying, "Señor Don Fernando, we're here to reach an agreement with you as to how you might receive the fullest satisfaction from a town that has offended you as unwittingly as might a mad dog."

"Giving me satisfaction, Don Manuel, really isn't hard," Señor Marín replied, imparting to his words the severe tones of truth and reprimand. "I've more or less studied what this town is like, how it lives without the benefit of good examples and sound advice, and how at the price of its own dignity it tries to preserve what it calls 'venerable customs.' But how shall one repair the harm done to all those victims of violence?"

"And, frankly, how many dead was there?" Don Sebastián made bold to ask in a quavering voice.

"What! Don't you know, Don Sebastián? You, the chief local authority? That's strange, very strange indeed!" was Don Fernando's only reply as he took a step toward where his wife was sitting.

"You may well be surprised, Don Fernando," Manuel quickly said, "but you won't be once you realize that my father has not left his house since those events to which I was fortunate enough to put a stop, and that the lieutenant governor has taken charge as called for by the law."

"This preventive move, so carefully planned, does not make him blameless," Lucía observed with a woman's natural liveliness; but Manuel, ever prepared, replied, "Señora, I, who have arrived here at a time so tragic for Kíllac, for this town where I was born, could not remain unconcerned; I had to seek remedies, prevent new misfortunes; and I've persuaded my father to resign from the position . . . whose demands he's been unable to satisfy. I'm looking for a way to undo the harm that's been done."

"And are you going to struggle against bad habits fortified by their antiquity, against wrongs that flourish beneath the sheltering tree of 'customs' when nothing arouses the soul from the lethargy in which it has been plunged by abuses, by the desire for exorbitant gain, and by an ignorance maintained for the sake of profit? That won't be easy, Don Manuel," said Señor Marín.

Manuel was not ready to concede the argument and replied, "Yes, that, exactly that, is what those young Peruvians who live in these remote regions have to struggle against. Don Fernando, I live in the hope that the civilization we're working for under the banner of a pure Christianity will soon crystallize, bringing about the happiness of our families and, as a natural consequence, the happiness of society."

"And will you have the strength for that, my dear young man? Can you count on anyone to back you, apart from your mother and us, your friends?" asked Don Fernando, halting for the moment in his pacing around the room, and throwing toward the door a small piece of paper that all through this discussion he had been crushing into a ball.

Lucía crossed her arms as though she were tired, and Don Sebastián remained motionless beneath his historic cape like a post fixed in the ground.

"I count on this town's not being wholly vile. Its people are easily led, as we can see from the very events we so much deplore; and I think it'll be easy to lead them on the right path," Manuel replied heatedly.

"I don't deny any of that, Manuel, but . . ."

"Frankly, my dear sir, mistakes can also be rectified," ventured Don Sebastián.

"Of course they can, Don Sebastián, when their effects don't reach into eternity; but here we have seven wounded, four dead, and our unfortunate Marcela about to die, leaving behind her daughters—in a word, orphans, widows . . ."

"How do you propose to rectify those mistakes?" Lucía asked, placing her feet firmly on the ground as she came to the aid of her husband.

Don Sebastián covered his face with both hands like a child; Manuel turned pale, wiping the heavy perspiration from his forehead; and then they all heard the desperate cry of Margarita, "For God's sake, Godmother, Godfather, help!"

"Let's go!" said Lucía, rising instantly and conveying her order to the others with her glance. All rushed to the bedside of the martyred wife, whose existence ended with a sigh as down her cheek coursed the final pale tear with which we take leave of this vale of sorrows. Marcela had just taken flight to the regions of perpetual peace, leaving her mortal shell behind so that in its presence men might argue about the theory of organic decomposition that proclaims *nothingness,* and about the principles of a mechanical perfection set in motion by a *something* that, since its activity has both a beginning and an end, implies the existence of a guiding hand and reveals the Creator of the Universe.

There lay the corpse!

And there, before those remains, stood Don Sebastián and Father Pascual, the men solely responsible for the disasters that had occurred in Killac.

24

Rumors and comments went from mouth to mouth, some accurate, most distorted; and the Indians, ashamed of having so blindly obeyed the summons of the bells and allowed themselves to be tricked into attacking the peaceful home of Don Fernando Marín, were loitering at the edge of town, silent and afraid.

Estéfano Benites gathered his friends in the "study" of his house where we have seen them playing cards; and when he saw that his accomplices were wavering, he encouraged them by saying, "No use crying over spilled milk, old pals."

"I didn't think the shot would go wild," Escobedo replied, playing with his cane.

"If the magistrates come, you know what to do," Estéfano instructed them.

"And what if they question us under oath?" Escobedo asked.

"You won't know a thing, my friend, and . . . we'll decide on a firm plan, once things get started. It's not for nothing that I'm the secretary of the justice of the peace."

"Let's put the blame on the dead Indians," one of them suggested.

"We'll turn in the sexton. That Indian has some cows and can afford a lawsuit," said another.

"Listen, did you talk to him that night?" Escobedo asked the earlier speaker.

"Not me, that was Don Estéfano," was the reply.

"Yes, I talked to him," Benites confirmed.

"And what did you say? I plan to summon him because he's a good friend of mine and we've got a deal in the works about milling flour," Escobedo said with a show of concern.

"Well, what I told him was: 'Isidro, be on the lookout, because I've read that there are bandits around here who've come to rob churches; and since ours has a very valuable monstrance, we've got to protect it.'"

"That's fine. He's very fond of me; he's ready to follow me through hell and high water," Escobedo approved with a smile, tapping his cane against his feet.

"Very well, then, all of you make an effort to find out what's going on, all right? I'm off to Don Sebastián's to work on our story," said Benites, taking leave of his colleagues; and they went to occupy their usual stations in the town square, which they considered the proper place for gossip and idle chatter.

And so the riot had come to pass just as had been planned in the rectory, though without achieving the results sought by those fanatical defenders of corrupt customs. Once people had gathered in the streets, Don Fernando's house had been identified as the hiding place of the imaginary bandits; and since the mob, once aroused, is not given to sober thought, it believed and attacked. That was the tragedy. Afterward, the brave words of a young man almost unknown in town, backed by a woman as beloved and respected as Doña Petronila, produced a pause that preceded the restoration of calm; and then, with that lightning change of heart typical of the crowd, came repentance, abhorrence of what had been done, which the rosy light of dawn revealed as a criminal farce.

The magistrate visited the scene of the calamity, and two specially appointed experts issued a report in technical language that served only to confound any effort to find the truth.

．　　．　　．　　．

When Don Fernando, Lucía, Don Sebastián, and Manuel entered the room where Marcela had just died, her still-warm body lay on an uncurtained light iron cot, beneath a white blanket with blue and crimson stripes, a local product, and her arms lay on the covers with part of her shoulder bared. Father Pascual was kneeling by the death-bed, his hands over his face. Margarita, almost totally transformed, wearing a black percale dress, her hair hanging loose, and her eyes gleaming with the tears that welled up from her heart, was holding one of the dead woman's hands.

Lucía drew a white handkerchief from the pocket of her dress and covered the face of the deceased, with all the respect she felt for that martyr to a mother's love, to gratitude, and to faith. Her mind was astir with what Marcela had revealed to her in her dying moments. Don Fernando and Don Sebastián stood in the middle of the room; and Manuel, when he caught sight of Margarita, felt all the blood in his veins rushing to his heart.

Had he entered that room at one of those psychologically critical moments when the great passions of the human heart stir within us? Or was it that he first saw Margarita on so solemn an occasion, when so many warring impressions had prepared his soul for the violent onset of the most powerful of human passions? Was it his confused feelings or Margarita's remarkable beauty that conquered the heart of this second-year law student? We do not know; but Cupid with his arrows poured Margarita's soul into Manuel's heart, and at the side of a death-bed was born a love that would face an insurmountable barrier as it led that youth—born, it seemed, into a station higher than Margarita's—to the very threshold of happiness.

There can be no lively conversation in the presence of death. Low voices, cautious steps, whispered words, as though we were still caring for the sick—such is the scene in which we imitate the silence of the grave.

On this occasion, it was Father Pascual who, rising from his meditative pose, said in a clear voice but with wavering eyes, "Praise God, all of you, for even as He receives another saint into His heavenly glory, He is redeeming a sinner here on earth. My friends, forgive me! For I promise, here in this holy temple, before the relics of this martyr, that a new life will begin for this sinner, for me!" They all stood there amazed and looked at Father Pascual, thinking he had gone mad; but he noticed nothing and went on, "Don't think that the seed of virtue that the words of a Christian mother plant in the heart of every man has died in me. Pity the man cast into the wasteland of the priesthood without the support of a family! Forgive me! Forgive me!" And he fell once more to his knees, clasping his hands in a gesture of supplication.

"He's raving," said one.

"He's gone mad," others observed.

Don Fernando stepped forward, took Father Pascual by the arm, raised him, and led him to his office so that he might rest. To those who remained Lucía said, "Heavens! But . . . let us go and leave one who no longer belongs to this world in peace," and she pointed to Marcela's body.

Manuel, taking Margarita by the arm, answered in a sweet voice, "Señora, if Marcela has gone to heaven drawing forth our tears, this girl has come from there instilling hope!"

"You're right, Manuel. Margarita, though I couldn't make your mother's life a happy one, I shall make yours overflow with happiness. You shall be my daughter!" Lucía replied, turning to the orphan.

Those words fell like refreshing rain on the young man, who, as he gazed on Margarita, kept repeating to himself, "How pretty she is! She's an angel! Ah, I, too, shall do all I can for her."

"Let's go," Lucía said once more, taking the arm of Don Sebastián, who seemed to have been turned into a pillar of salt. "We must discharge our final duties toward what was once Marcela." And she led him out, leaving Manuel to escort the orphan, who, by a mysterious decree of fate, left the room where her mother had died accompanied by the man who would be the love of her life.

25

The man who, admitting that he is on the path of evil, stops to retrace his steps and ask for the help of the virtuous arouses a powerful sympathy in his fellow-creatures. No matter how heartless and egotistical our century may be, it is not true that repentance awakens no interest and merits no respect.

Father Pascual's words might have so moved the noble sentiments of Don Fernando Marín as to incline him unreservedly toward helping, or rather defending, the priest in any complications arising from the judicial process then under way; but Señor Marín was a man of the world who knew the human heart, and he saw more in Father Pascual's demeanor than would an ordinary person and said to himself, "This is an explosion of fear, the nervous shock produced by fear. I can't trust this man's words."

Meanwhile, Father Pascual, as though intuitively reading Señor Marín's thoughts, told him, "I don't want to waste any time, Don Fernando; once we hesitate, our resolutions fade. I've been more unfortunate than depraved. It's folly to spin a flimsy theory and then expect a priest to be virtuous removed from family and banished to the hinterland, when all our experience tells us, as plain as the hands on the clock, that you cannot change man or nature."

"You could have been a model priest, Father Pascual," Lucía's husband replied, almost confirming his interlocutor's concluding words.

"Yes, in the bosom of my family, Don Fernando; but now—I can talk to you!—alone, in this remote parish, I am the bad father of children who will never know me, I am only a memory for women who never loved me, I am a sad example for my parishioners. Ah! . . ."

The priest's voice was choking, great drops of perspiration ran down his forehead, and the look in his eyes produced fear rather than respect.

"Calm yourself, Father Pascual. Why all this agitation?" Don Fernando said compassionately, while surprise showed on his face, for this was not the Father Pascual whom he had seen and spoken to so often, this was a lion aroused from his torpor by the pain of a mortal wound, and tearing at his own entrails.

"Marcela . . . Marcela's secret," was the priest's only reply, as he hid his face behind his hands and then raised them to heaven as though seized by fear. Had those words of confession been so dreadful, had they perhaps had far-reaching and deep meaning? No doubt they had. Such as they were, they had fallen upon a spirit already battered by the terror born of the results of the riot, overheated by liquor and the pleasures found in Melitona's arms, and shaken by the words that Manuel had thrown forth like a frightful challenge. An explosion was inevitable.

In such a situation a man moves to one extreme of social life or the other: to virtue, or to crime. But the priest's poor system was totally drained, and his sudden turn toward virtue could not be taken as any guarantee that he would persevere on that path. He was in the grip of delirium tremens, which assaults the brain, conjuring up threatening ghostly voices. His lips were dry, his breath came forth scorching; but continuing the flow of words that an inner struggle had interrupted, he went on to say, "Women are like honey: take large portions and you'll destroy

your health . . . Don Fernando, I . . . am determined . . .!" Father Pascual
was delirious and fell unconscious to the floor. By the time he could be
raised, he was in the grip of a typhoid fever and had to be conveyed to his
house, where no assistance, no family's loving care awaited him.

None helped the unfortunate man other than his *pongo* and his unwilling *mitayas*;[25] none showed him affection but his dog.

26

The lofty peaks of the mountains that surround Kíllac were bathed
in that pale light that the lord of day sometimes pours forth as he
sinks into the west, and that locally is called "the pagan sun." It was a
peaceful afternoon, and the first chirping of the crickets announced the
approach of night.

Lucía and Manuel, accompanied by Don Sebastián, were busy making final arrangements for Marcela's burial, when Don Fernando came
into the room and was asked by his wife, "What do you say to all this,
Fernando? Is our poor priest still repentant?"

"My dear, Father Pascual is dying of fever, and in his delirium he says
things that make you tremble," Don Fernando replied, smoothing his
brow with his hand.

On hearing this, Don Sebastián jumped as though stung by a viper,
calling out, "God help me! All that's missing now is for the magistrates
to come. Frankly, this is horrible, just horrible!" he repeated, striking his
forehead with the palm of his hand.

"Calm down there, Don Sebastián; don't you get sick now," said Don
Fernando, laying his hand on the governor's shoulder.

At that moment the church bell began to sound, pealing for the
dead and asking, as it rang, for a prayer on behalf of Marcela, the wife
of Yupanqui.

---

25. *Mitayas,* women performing their obligatory service, or *mita.*

Lucía drew Margarita, who was by her side, to her breast, and pressing her against her heart, said, "Let's look for Rosalía; we haven't seen your little sister for hours"; and turning to her husband, she added, "Fernando, you take care of the funeral; I'm going to prepare a new home for the two little birds who've been *torn from their nest.*"

"Margarita, Margarita!" Manuel whispered into the girl's ear, "Lucía is your mother . . . and I . . . shall be your brother!" And a tear coursed down the young man's face, a precious pearl with which his heart repaid Lucía's affection for the orphan, to whom his soul had already raised an altar adorned with the chaste lilies of first love.

To love is to live!

PART II

1

The heart of man is like the cloud-covered sky: capable, it seems, of infinite variety, yet ever the same in the course followed by its violent upheavals. The stormy night gives way to a new day bright with sunshine. After the lamentable events that we reported in the first part of our tale, a period of calm settled on the people of Killac, not unlike the exhaustion that follows a time of excessive work, though the storm that had arisen in Manuel's heart, fanned by loneliness and idleness, kept gathering strength.

Several months passed in this way. A judicial inquiry was launched to discover those truly responsible for the attack; but the preliminary procedures, legalistic as they were, had neither found them out nor discovered any part of what we know, while the entire process was marked by that slowness that is the hope of the guilty and that in Peru serves to leave crime unpunished and innocence at times imperiled.

Nonetheless, the files were growing every day with the addition of sheets of testimony, for which stamp fees would eventually have to be paid and which contained lengthy declarations by witnesses who were unreliable even when stating their age, marital status, and religion. Don Fernando Marín was summoned to make a declaration as an injured party; and although he had intended not to become entangled in the inquiry, he obeyed the summons and appeared before the justice of the peace who had been charged by the court with the investigation.

The justice of the peace, Don Hilarión Verdejo, an elderly man, thrice widowed, tall, pockmarked, owner of the villa Manzanares, which he had bought from the estate of Bishop Don Pedro Miranda y Claro, was in his office, solemnly seated at a pine table on a wood and leather chair, one of those that used to be made in Cochabamba, Bolivia, forty years ago and are now museum pieces in the cities of Peru. Verdejo was accompanied by two men who knew how to write their initials and who were to serve as witnesses to the proceedings. Don Fernando soon arrived, and the judge received him by shaking his hand and saying, "Excuse me for making you come down here, Señor Don Fernando; I would have gone to your place, but the court . . ."

"Please, no apologies, your honor; this is only proper," Marín answered; and Don Hilarión began to read aloud some documents that once more convinced Don Fernando that it would be absurd for him to persist in a case that should have been handled by serious people.

"Shall we get under way, your honor?" Don Fernando asked.

"Let's wait a little longer, my dear sir; my clerk will be here any minute to write it all down," Verdejo replied, somewhat flustered, as he hung his hat on a corner of the table and looked anxiously toward the door, where eventually Estéfano Benites appeared with a pen over his right ear.

The new arrival uttered a rapid greeting, drew up a chair, and said, "I'm very late, sir; please excuse me"; and at the same time he took hold of his pen, dipped it in the inkwell, and positioned himself to transfer onto the paper before him the words of Don Hilarión, who said, "Get your heading on there, Don Estéfano, and in a real nice handwriting, because this has got to do with our friend Señor Marín."

After writing several lines, Benites answered, "Ready, sir."

Then Don Hilarión coughed to get his voice in tune; and in a magisterial tone, or rather, like a schoolboy who recites his memorized lesson, he began thus, "Upon being asked does he know for a fact there was some disturbances and with firearms in this here town on the night of the fifth of this month, he replied . . ."

"That he does know it for a fact because his house was attacked," Don Fernando hastily answered, wishing to spare the judge some of the labor of composition.

"This here declaration will crush your enemies, my dear Don Fernando," Verdejo said, interrupting his dictation. Don Fernando preferred to say nothing, and the judge went on, "Upon being asked does he know who attacked his house or who was planning the attack . . ."

"That he does know," Don Fernando said firmly.

On hearing this reply, Estéfano looked up, understandably surprised by this unexpected blow, and scrutinized Marín's face; and though he could see nothing there to make him suspect that Don Fernando was aware of his role in the matter, his writing changed slightly at that point, which proves that his hand was not quite steady.

The witnesses exchanged an expressive glance, and the judge allowed himself to comment, "In that case somebody's heading for jail"; and believing himself to have worked long enough, he added, "That's enough for today, Don Fernando. God willing we'll go on tomorrow, because right now they're waiting on me to decide about some property lines. Lord, a judge is real busy, and still there's no . . .", and as he spoke he scratched the palm of his left hand with the fingers of the right.

"As you wish, your honor; I'm in no hurry," replied Don Fernando Marín, picking up his hat and taking his leave. He was about to step out when Estéfano came up to him with a mysterious air and in a low voice said, "Excuse me, Señor Marín: who's going to pay my . . . secretary's fees?"

"My friend, I haven't the slightest idea," Don Fernando answered, shaking his head and leaving the temple of the law.

As soon as they were alone, Verdejo turned to his clerk and remarked, "He says he knows 'em, did you get that?"

"I did, Don Hilarión; but words are cheap and proof is golden, as old Cachabotas would have said," Benites replied, wiping his pen on a piece of paper.

"That's what I been thinking, Don Estéfano; all them years as judge has taught me a thing or two."

"And now that I think of it, sir: just to have everything in order, we first have to attach the sexton's cattle, because as of now he's the only one our record shows to be involved in all this," was Benites's advice, in keeping with his plan.

"Right, it clear slipped my mind. Draw up a real tough order."

With the judge's approval, Benites proceeded to draw up a sort of writ of attachment of the cows, sheep, and alpacas of Isidro Champí, the sexton of Kíllac, for whom these animals represented a lifetime of indescribable sacrifices on his part and that of his family. After writing, Estéfano consulted the judge as follows, "The law requires a receiver, and that could be our friend Escobedo, who is honorable, trustworthy, and on our side, your honor."

"Escobedo . . . ?" Don Hilarión repeated, scratching his ear; and after a short pause he added, "All right, good enough; put down Escobedo."

And with that, Verdejo collected the papers scattered all over the table and took his hat in preparation for departure.

2

Manuel was in an extremely difficult position. During the long hours—all day and most of the night—that he spent shut up in his room, he would frequently say to himself, "Even though Don Sebastián's name does not yet appear in the court records, it's on everyone's lips as a guilty party. For now I can't give a satisfactory explanation of my conduct to strangers who might see me visit Don Fernando Marín's house, and what they're likely to say won't be to my credit. And so I'll have to be strong; I'll accept the sacrifice so as some day to be worthy of her . . . I won't go there any more. But good God, what a time to be banishing myself! Just when my heart belongs to Margarita, when I yearn to take part in the plans Señora Lucía is making for her upbringing! Oh heartbreak, your name is Fate, and I am your child!"

As he spoke these last words Manuel dropped onto the sofa in his small room; and with his elbows resting on his knees and his head between his hands, he sat like one plunged into the boundless seas of speculation and doubt.

Manuel certainly had a plan, formed by his brain but perhaps inspired by his heart; and feeling compelled to carry it out, he had begun to prepare the terrain for doing so. One day, after much struggle and hesitation, his feelings triumphed over his will, and he told himself, "Whatever people may say, I'm going there tonight." And for the first time since his arrival he took pains with his hair and his clothes. From the depths of his trunk he took out some gloves that he had bought for his examinations at the university; he prepared his patent-leather boots; and he went out into the garden of his home to wait for the right time.

Thoughts of Margarita glowed brightly among the flowers; and given over heart and soul to his hopes and dreams, he picked a number of the pretty violets that grew in such profusion beneath the myrtle and combined them in a fragrant bouquet, which he placed in the inside breast pocket of his overcoat, saying, "The violet is the flower that symbolizes modesty; and modesty is a virtue that shines more brightly in a beautiful woman, because an ugly one has no choice but to be modest. Violets, then, for my Margarita! When you pick them at my age, guided by the rays of that light that shines on a heart in love, you can't help attaching a piece of your soul to each flower so that all of it may fly away to be joined with the soul of your beloved. They say the age of twenty is the poetry of life, and flowers are its rhymes, and love is life itself. Oh, it's love that's made me feel and know that I'm alive!"

The yearned-for time was finally at hand; and putting on his gloves and sprinkling some perfume on his clothes, Manuel plunged into the dark streets of Kíllac, dashing over their uneven pavement with gigantic strides until he reached Don Fernando's house, his heart throbbing with emotions that for him were pure ambrosia.

As he entered the parlor he found Lucía finishing a watchcase of light blue satin on which she had embroidered a forget-me-not in colored silk, with her husband's initials at one end. Margarita was nearby, prettier than ever, her flowing hair tied over her forehead with a silk ribbon, busily filling a cardboard box with the pieces from a spelling game, all of whose letters she had already learned. Rosalía and another little girl her age were laughing as merrily as could be at a rag doll whose face they had just washed with some left-over tea from a cup.

For some moments Manuel stood speechless in contemplation of that lovely scene of domesticity in which his heart saw Margarita as the angel of Happiness.

Lucía turned her head, expecting to see Don Fernando; but on seeing Manuel, she set down her needlework and said in surprise, "Ah, it's you, Manuel."

"Good evening, Señora Lucía. How surprised you are to see me! If I were superstitious, I'd see a bad omen in that and fear for my life," Manuel cheerily replied, removing his hat and shaking Lucía's hand.

"Don't say that. If I'm surprised, it's because you've been hiding yourself all these days," Don Fernando's wife answered pleasantly, returning Manuel's greeting and motioning him to a seat.

"All the more reason for all of you to be ever present in my memory and my heart," the young man replied, fixing his eyes on Margarita, whom he then greeted by saying, "And how is the lucky godchild?" And as he took her little hand and held it in his own, both young people could feel the contact between two souls.

"I'm fine, Manuel, and I already know all my letters," the girl answered with a smile of satisfaction.

"Bravo!"

"It's hard to believe, but every day I'm more delighted with my godchild, isn't that right?" said Lucía, looking at the orphan.

"Well, let's see; I'm going to test you," declared Manuel. He took the box, poured out the pieces, and began to choose letters and show them to Margarita.

"A, X, D, M," the girl said with touching enthusiasm.

"You pass," Lucía said, laughing.

"Now you've got to combine them, and I'll be your teacher," Manuel suggested, picking up six letters, and then nine; and setting them down in order, he said, "Look!" and he made her spell out, "Margarita, Manuel."

Lucía understood Manuel's meaning and in a pleasant tone said to him, smiling, "My fine teacher, you're looking out for your own interests. You want to imprint your name in your pupils' memories."

"I'm bolder than that, señora; I'd like to imprint it in their hearts," Manuel answered as though in jest.

Margarita's eyes did not leave the game board, and we could safely wager that she already knew how to combine those two names. Manuel was stirred by the turn things were taking, and as though to cover his emotion he asked, "Is Don Fernando not at home, señora?"

"Yes, he is; that's why when you came in I thought it was he. He'll be here any minute. But tell me now, why haven't you come to see us?" Lucía asked.

"Señora, I don't want to trouble you with painful explanations; it just seemed prudent to me, as long as these judicial matters are still going on."

"You're very discreet, Manuel; but we, who know all about it and know you saved us . . ."

"I wasn't worried about what you might think but about others," Manuel quickly said, fully aware of the interest with which Margarita followed her godmother's words.

At this point Don Fernando came in, set his hat on a chair, and stretched out his hand to Manuel, who stood up to receive him.

3

Father Pascual miraculously survived the bout of typhoid fever that confined him to a sickbed for a week. Compassionate care put him back on his feet; but his convalescence promised to be lengthy, in spite of the mild climate and an abundance of milk and nutritious food. His brain needed a change of place, of concerns, and of habits to rid itself of the images that accompanied the constant gnawing of remorse; and he decided to go to the city in search of consolation and medical help, leaving his parish in the temporary charge of a Franciscan friar whose monastery had been shut down and who arrived in Kíllac almost at the same time as the new subprefect appointed by the national government to rule the province.

The person chosen for this post was Colonel Bruno de Paredes, a man well known all over Peru, both for the connections he had made in gastronomic tournaments, alias banquets, and for his frequent corruptions of justice. Furthermore, Paredes was an old comrade of Don Sebastián's and had even taken part with him in an uprising on behalf of some military chieftain—either Don Ramón Castilla or Don Manuel Ignacio Vivanco.

Don Bruno must have been at least fifty-eight years old, yet he preserved an appearance of youth with the aid of a little Barry dye for his hair and the services of Dr. Christian Dam for his teeth, novelties that he brought from Lima the first time he returned from the capital as the alternate deputy for Sacramento. He was tall and heavy, with coarse features and a swarthy complexion; and when he laughed his great laugh he showed Dr. Dam's teeth behind lips guarded by a mustache trimmed into the shape of a brush. He wore black trousers, a blue vest buttoned to the neck with yellow uniform buttons, a larger version of which appeared on his coffee-colored coat, also adorned with a colonel's enormous epaulettes. On his broad-brimmed black wool hat, a miniature horseshoe held in place the broad striped ribbon of twilled silk. True, he had never received any instruction in matters military; but circumstances put him into an officer's uniform one fine day, and he was not so simple-minded as to refuse it. His education had been minimal, and his speech was far from refined.

On arriving in Kíllac he immediately sought out his old comrade Don Sebastián, went to his house, learned what had occurred in the town, and spoke to him as follows, with all the open frankness of old times, "What the devil! And you, my dear Don Sebastián, a full-grown man, let your life be run by a schoolboy like Manuelito? Well, that's the limit!"

"Frankly, my dear Colonel, I tell you there's no way out. That boy's put things to me with the clarity and eloquence of a book, and Petruca's driven the point home with her crying."

"That's just wonderful! Let women's tears be your guide, and we'll see what our country comes to. No, sir; you just dig in your heels, and I'll support you. Yes, indeed."

"But, frankly, Colonel, my resignation's already been submitted to the prefecture."

"Good Lord, you'd think you were a babe in the woods, Don Sebastián. Don't you know what connections are for? Where's that old spirit? Yes, sir!"

"But what's the solution? Because, frankly, this is serious business," Don Sebastián replied with surprising cheerfulness.

"The solution is child's play. Yes, sir: either you take back your resignation, or you don't and I reappoint you as governor," said the colonel, putting both hands in the pockets of his trousers, which he then held up as though with a belt as he calmly walked back and forth.

"Frankly . . . ," said Don Sebastián, running his fingers through his hair as though in search of ideas, and then adding, "It's almost Easter, and we could donate a bull for the prefect's bullfight; but . . . frankly, what about Manuel, Colonel?"

"Forget about Manuel! You don't have to tell him a thing. And now, man to man, just like old times, I'll tell you something straight, my dear Don Sebastián: I need your support; I've come here counting on you. This subprefecture has to get me out of a bit of a bind. Yes, sir: you know a man has certain expenses, and you know I've been trying to get this job for five years, and I've made my plans."

"Well, frankly, if that's the way it is, that puts another face on things," Don Sebastián replied, drawing closer to his interlocutor.

"Come now, do you take me for a fool, Don Sebastián? I know that if you rent a cow you milk it thoroughly before handing it back. Do you suppose I haven't had to sweat blood to get this job?"

"True enough, Colonel, and there's more than one that's come here all skin and bones and left here good and fat. But still, frankly, what about the inquiry into that riot?"

"The inquiry? Ha, ha, ha! It's plain to see you're new at all this, a real country boy! Afraid of an inquiry! My dear sir, leave it to your great-grandchildren to fret about the inquiry, and meanwhile let's forget about it."

"Frankly, Colonel, you've just cheered me up!"

"And what's become of Father Pascual?"

"Our priest's gone to the city to recover, Colonel. Frankly, he almost died on us."

"I'm sorry to hear it, because the good father would have been a big help in our plans. We've got to collect plenty of *soles* this year," Don Bruno said, taking his hands out of his pockets.

"Of course, Colonel. Frankly, we could have used Father Pascual, good fellow that he is, and so cooperative."

"And is he still such a ladies' man?"

"As for that, Colonel, you know: the leopard doesn't change his spots. And frankly, after all, a man's a man . . ."

"Yes, sir, a man's a man. And what about Estéfano Benites, and our other friends here?" Don Bruno asked eagerly.

"All of them fine, Colonel; and frankly, I'm very fond of Benites."

"Well, get them over here, Don Sebastián. I want to make sure we're agreed on a plan for running things before going on my way, because I mustn't delay taking my oath of office."

"Right away, Colonel, though, frankly, they'll come soon enough to congratulate you, because everybody must already know that you've come to town," Don Sebastián replied, his spirits newly raised. At the sound of Colonel Paredes' voice all the scruples that Manuel's words had awakened in his mind had vanished as quickly as a golden summer cloud changes its shape or a good idea succumbs before the superior skill of its enemies.

4

M anuel's visit to Don Fernando's house was decisive for one important aspect of his life, as we shall see later.

Don Fernando Marín informed Manuel in detail of what had happened in court and concluded, "And doesn't all of this show you our authorities in the worst possible light, Don Manuel?"

"Don Fernando, I'm wounded to the quick by it all; and every time I hear something like this I feel the wound anew. Ah, if only I could tear my mother away from here!" the young man said with feeling, setting down a piece from Margarita's game that he had been handling absent-mindedly.

"That's why we've decided to have the girls brought up somewhere else," said Lucía, entering into the conversation.

"And where have you decided to do that?" Manuel asked eagerly.

"In Lima, of course," Don Fernando answered.

"Oh, yes, Lima!" Lucía said. "There they form the heart and train the mind, and then in a couple of years I expect Margarita to find a good husband. With that face and those eyes, she won't be single long!" and she chuckled contentedly; but Manuel grew pale as he continued his questions, "Have you already decided when the girls will leave?"

"We haven't picked the day, but it will be before the year is out," Don Fernando answered, getting up from his chair and walking about the room.

"Going to Lima is like reaching the gate of heaven and glimpsing the throne of Glory and of Fortune. They say our beautiful capital is a fairy city," Manuel answered, hiding his emotion; and from that moment on he was determined to follow Margarita to Lima.

Lucía had a few private words with her husband, who had come to stand by her side; and Manuel took advantage of this small distraction to hand his bouquet of violets to Margarita, rapidly whispering, "These flowers remind me of you, Margarita; I hope you'll always be modest like them. Take them and keep them."

Margarita quickly grasped the bouquet and nimbly hid it in her bosom, like a child hiding a toy from the greedy eyes of a playmate.

Why is love born with this instinct for secrecy? Why does the flower of affection bloom among the weeds of egotism, deceit, and lies? Who could have told Margarita it is forbidden to accept flowers bedewed by a young man's love? Ah, mysteries of the human soul! What told her was the fire that leapt from Manuel's glowing eyes to set her heart aflame, the virginal heart that was beginning to feel those light tremors, unnoticed at first, that finally leave a tear of love quivering in the eye. A tear of happiness! A tear that awakens the heart to its feelings, that drops like rain on the flower of hope! A woman's heart is the heart of a child from the moment of her birth until she dies, unless it has been chilled by the dreadful storms that alone can affect it, loss of faith and loss of virtue.

Lucía, changing the topic of conversation, said to her husband, "Do you know that Manuel has great reservations about coming to see us?"

"He needn't have any as far as we're concerned, my dear; but he's right with regard to other people. Still," he said to the young man, "you can come evenings."

"Thank you, Señor Marín."

"And they tell me our new subprefect has arrived today. Do you know where he'll be staying, Manuel?" Don Fernando asked, to which Manuel replied, "Yes, sir; he stopped at our house today, but then he continued on his way. I saw him and greeted him in passing. I don't think we hit it off. He knew me when I was a child . . ."

"I'm sorry your meeting wasn't more cordial. One young man like you is worth twenty old fellows of his stripe. I don't say it to flatter you, but I think the subprefect would be the one to gain the most if he made friends with you."

"You're too kind, Don Fernando; but those who knew us when we were in diapers are usually reluctant to see us any other way," Manuel answered, smiling and picking up his hat to leave. "Good night, señora, Señor Marín, Margarita," he said.

"Good night," the others replied, and Margarita added, in a pleading little voice, "You'll come again, won't you, Manuel?"

Soon Manuel found himself alone with his thoughts in the midst of the gloomy streets of Kíllac, whose stillness would have struck fear into the heart of anyone who remembered the tragic events of the fifth of August and the scene of Juan Yupanqui's death. But Manuel was so intensely concerned with what his heart was saying to his head that he could fix his mind on nothing but his love. Thinking aloud, he told himself, "Yes, I'll go to Lima! In three years I'll be a lawyer and Margarita, a beautiful woman of sixteen or seventeen, in the lovely blooming springtime of her youth . . . How pretty Margarita will become in that pure and gentle climate of Lima, where flowers blossom rich in color and aroma! . . . And then . . . and will she be capable of returning my love, ah . . . or will she see me as the son of her parents' murderer? . . . Oh, thank you, Lord, thank you! For the first time in my life I'm glad of who my real father is. But . . . why can't I bear his name, that name respected and venerated by all? . . . No, it is not God's command, it's human folly, it's a cruel law, a dreadful law! . . . Margarita, my Margarita . . . I'm . . . ready to tell Don Fernando the truth, and then you'll be my wife! Love spurs my aspirations; I want to become a lawyer as soon as possible! . . . I'll follow her to Lima; I'll study day and night at its famous University of

San Marcos. Yes, man's will can achieve anything! . . . But she . . . she has to love me! . . . Ah, perhaps I'm only dreaming . . . She does love me, because she accepted my violets with all the enthusiasm of love; and as I was leaving she asked me to come again! . . . Am I imagining it all? . . . If she were a woman I could tell her all I think; but Margarita is still a girl, and that girl has stolen my heart. Yes, I shall be worthy of Lucía's godchild, the godchild of that angel!"

Manuel was speaking so heatedly that he seemed quite mad, when the barking of a dog that threatened to chew on his legs awoke him from his reveries, showing him that he had reached the front door of his house, which stood open because a mother's ever-watchful love, that supreme love undaunted by sacrifice or sleepless nights, was awaiting his return.

The house was far from still; no sooner had Manuel set foot in its entrance hall than a tremendous uproar struck his ear.

5

The news of the subprefect's arrival in Kíllac spread as quickly as Don Sebastián had anticipated, and with the same speed the citizens of the town gathered in the governor's house. As they arrived, they addressed the subprefect, who solemnly awaited them in Don Sebastián's parlor, in these terms:

"We were delighted to hear your excellency was coming, Colonel," said one.

"Yes, your excellency. Now things will be run properly," added another.

"All the gentry of the town congratulate your excellency," yet another explained.

And they all made their comments on events, repeating the "excellency," which they seemed to consider an appropriate title, and speaking, as usual, in chorus.

The colonel answered them as he stroked his broad-brimmed hat, "I come here with the soundest intentions, firmly committed to support the townspeople in everything."

"That's what we want!" shouted several of his audience.

At that moment Estéfano Benites arrived.

The subprefect added, "In turn, I expect you gentlemen to support me . . . Hello there, Benites, my friend!" Don Bruno concluded, catching sight of the new arrival.

"Count on us, your excellency; and a very good evening to you," Estéfano answered in high good spirits.

"Yes, excellency, we're with you," said others.

"I'm going to leave my instructions with the governor, and I hope my friends will aid and support him," said the colonel, pointing to Don Sebastián.

"Is Don Sebastián still our governor, excellency?" they asked in chorus.

"Yes, gentlemen, and I expect you won't complain about that," the subprefect replied.

"That's the way! That's just what I told everybody we needed," Estéfano replied, looking round him.

"All right now, this is the season for our advance payments, and let's be moderate about it, do you understand? Because I don't like abuses when it comes to matters of law," said the colonel, hiding his true meaning and looking at the portraits that served as wallpaper.

"Yes, frankly, that's fair, and that's how every subprefect does it, Colonel," Don Sebastián said in support of Paredes.

"Yes, nothing unusual about that; it's the custom, and by buying right here we benefit the Indians," commented Escobedo, who was also present.

"And does your excellency know about the to-do with Don Fernando Marín?" asked Estéfano Benites, taking a sounding to see how he should proceed.

"I do indeed, but you've had bad . . . advice in this business. That's not the way we do things. In future you have to . . . be prudent," said the subprefect, modifying his original thought as he realized he was about to say something he shouldn't.

"That's just what I told them, excellency; but the only one to blame here is that scoundrel of a sexton who started off ringing the bells and getting everyone in an uproar," was Estéfano's reply, which won him the admiration of his colleagues, who said, "That's the truth, as you can see in the inquiry."

"Is there documentary proof of that?" the subprefect asked eagerly.

"Yes, your excellency; and up to now no measures have been taken against this Indian, and only the reputations of respectable people have been besmirched," Estéfano replied, and Don Sebastián slyly added, "Frankly, Colonel, if the sexton hadn't had this harebrained idea, nothing would have happened, because, frankly, Don Fernando is really a decent enough fellow."

"And who is this sexton?" Don Bruno said.

"Isidro Champi, your excellency, an insolent Indian who thinks he's somebody because he's got a lot of cattle," Escobedo replied.

"All right, Governor, send a message to the judge right away urging him to be diligent, order the arrest of Isidro Champi, have him jailed and held at the disposition of the court, and . . . when I come back we'll settle all this," said the colonel.

"That's the way, we have to act vigorously and fairly," commented Estéfano.

"Marvelous, my dear Colonel; frankly, that Indian, Champi, really ought to pay for what he's done," Don Sebastián seconded.

"All right! And now, with your leave, gentlemen . . . Where's my horse?" said the colonel, stepping to the door.

While these decisions were being reached, Don Sebastián's agents and deputies had gathered a large train to accompany the new subprefect in his departure; and many horses were waiting ready-saddled in the courtyard, along with a band composed of drums, bugles, trumpets, and a clarinet. The mayor—in dress uniform of vicuña hat, silver sun on his chest, black cloak, and tall staff with silver ornaments, his hair in a braid interspersed with threads of vicuña—led out a spirited sorrel, which Colonel Don Bruno de Paredes proceeded to mount. Outside, a troupe of *wífalas* was waiting, Indians dressed in petticoats with a colored kerchief draped over one shoulder and another kerchief tied to a reed, which they waved in the air to the sound of the drum, dancing in honor of the subprefect and following after the horses.

"Long live our subprefect Colonel Paredes!" "Long may he live!" came the shouts of many voices.

With this resplendent escort, and pleased to hear himself acclaimed by all those unfortunates, the subprefect started down the left bank of the river, puffed up like the frog in the fable and satisfied with himself like every man who rises to a position he does not deserve.

Don Sebastián signaled Estéfano to stay behind, and together they set about planning how to carry out the subprefect's orders.

"Well, frankly, my dear Don Estéfano, you're a jewel," said Don Sebastián, shaking Benites's hand.

"I'm delighted if what I came up with hit the mark," Estéfano replied with satisfaction.

"Now we're in the clear! Frankly, once that Indian Champi is in the pen, nobody's going to let out a peep."

"Right you are, so let's draw up the warrant."

"Warrant? What warrant? Frankly, Don Estéfano, you go right now with two constables and arrest him, because all of us here have heard the subprefect's order," the governor replied, and Estéfano happily hurried off in search of the constables.

Don Sebastián was left alone, but his contentment quickly faded at the prospect of a new battle on the home front. His wife and son would soon be brandishing their dialectical weapons and might succeed in puncturing the new bubble of his ambitions, which lulled him into the most pleasant dreams as his heart swelled in response to Colonel Paredes's encouraging promises and the cleverness of Estéfano Benites. Would he once more taste defeat, a humiliating defeat? He would have to arm himself, entrench himself, fortify himself, strengthen his determination. For this purpose Don Sebastián had recourse to the coward's supreme source of strength: pounding on the table, he declared in a haughty tone, "What the devil! Frankly, I won't take it lying down any more!"; and "*Pongo!*" he shouted with all the verve of a man with a few pesos in his pocket. His shout was answered by the usual Indian, who appeared in the doorway and whom Don Sebastián ordered, "Go on, on the double, and tell Doña Rufa to send me . . . frankly, a bottle, and to put it on my tab."

The Indian was off and back again in no time with a green bottle and a glass. Don Sebastián poured himself a healthy serving and, mumbling the ritual words of the devotees of Bacchus, "Sweet little drops, come close to my heart," he raised the glass, finished off its contents, grimaced, wiped his lips on a corner of the tablecloth, and went on, "All right, frankly, I'm ready for them; let's have it out!"

What Don Sebastián had drunk was not even a grape liquor, but alcohol distilled from sugar cane and slightly diluted with water, which gave it a whitish sheen. It was designed to have an instant effect; and so its vapors quickly spread through his system, storming the redoubts of reason in the brain, subduing all that is human and leaving intact all that is brutish.

Doña Petronila had been carefully watching developments in her house since the arrival of the new subprefect, whom she had not gone to greet; and when she saw the *pongo* enter her husband's room with his supply of alcohol, she was close to rushing in, seizing the bottle, and smashing it against the floor. But a flash of her good sense made her see matters more clearly and checked her first impulse; and saying to herself, "No, tatay, it's better to wait for Manuelito; he knows how to deal with it," she set to walking about inside the house, never suspecting that out in the garden her son, under the aegis of the winged gods and with his heart steeped in love's supreme ambrosia, was picking every violet she had grown.

These, then, are life's illusions. While Doña Petronila was hatching the most prosaic plans to keep Don Sebastián from drinking, Manuel was dreaming golden dreams. Oh happy time of our youth, when we can love! Fortunate first budding of manhood, when tender, fragrant bonds of love bring happiness! Blessed season of life in which our joy flows from the fleeting touch of a dress, from the treasured flower stolen from the hair, from the sweetness of a glance that one soul sends forth in search of another!

Had Manuel's mother been able to discern the nature of her son's dreams, she would have watched over them not daring to awaken him, stifling in her breast a tender sigh that murmurs, scarcely audible, "A mother's love is a woman's sacrifice."

It was already late at night. Suddenly a hoarse voice could be heard exclaiming, "What the devil! Frankly, nobody orders me around!" And at the same time there was a thud as though of a chair violently knocked over. Doña Petronila rushed into the room and looked for a few seconds at Don Sebastián, who kept on shouting like a madman, "No sir! That's the limit! Frankly, nobody . . . but nobody orders me around!" His tongue had trouble speaking clearly, as did his feet holding him up. As soon as he saw Doña Petronila he shouted, "Here's the beast! Frankly, fire!" And he seized a chair and hurled it toward his wife.

Doña Petronila calmly answered, "Good Heavens, it seems you don't recognize me. I'm going to put you to bed. It's late." And she took hold of his arm and tried to lead him away; but Don Sebastián, seeing this as an act of despotism, brusquely shook himself loose and seizing the now empty bottle and everything else within reach, threw it all at Doña Petronila, shouting and raising an infernal ruckus.

"Damn you, woman, not now! Frankly, nobody's going to put a halter on me!"

"Good Lord, what's happened here?"

"I'm the governor, frankly, whether you like it or not, damn it!"

"What's going on here? What's got into this town? For Heaven's sake, Sebastián, calm down!" Doña Petronila kept on begging; but

Pancorbo, with the stubbornness of the drunkard, replied, "Nobody orders me around, do you understand?" And another chair fell near Doña Petronila, who scurried from one side of the room to the other in search of safety, wiping her tears with her shawl.

The noise brought in some of the neighbors; and Manuel, who, as we have seen, was just coming home, rushed in, caught Don Sebastián around the waist, raised him to his full height, and led him off to his bedroom.

6

It took Estéfano Benites little time and less effort to find the constables currently on duty; and as soon as he had done so he went with them to the hut of Isidro Champi, who was taking leave of his family to go to the belltower and toll the Angelus, which is done at nightfall with the great bell.

Isidro Champi, known by the nickname Tapara, was a tall and powerful agile man of forty, married and the father of seven children, five boys and two girls. That afternoon he was wearing his only suit of clothes, consisting of black trousers with red stripes, scarlet shirt and vest, and a light green jacket. His thick long hair fell on his back in a braid tied with vicuña ribbons, and his head was covered with the jaunty Andalusian cap that the Conquistadors brought to Peru and that the Indians, with their love of picturesque and brightly colored dress, continue to wear.

The arrival of Estéfano and his crew greatly alarmed Isidro's whole family, since experience had taught them that such visits were the immediate precursors of disaster. Estéfano was the first to speak and said, "Well, Isidro, you've got to go to jail, by order of the new subprefect."

A bolt of lightning striking their hut would have had less effect than Benites's words on the Indians, who had been anxious and fearful from the moment they first saw him. The women knelt down before Estéfano raising their clasped hands in supplication and weeping copiously, the children rushed to their father, and amid all this confusion Isidro could barely utter, "Niñoy wiracocha, why . . ."

"It's no use carrying on like this; just go and don't be afraid," Estéfano interrupted him; and turning to the wife, he said, "And you there, yelling your head off, there's nothing to it; we're going to look into why those bells were ringing, that's all."

When he heard this, Isidro's clear conscience restored his confidence, and he told his wife, "Just calm down, and bring me my ponchos after a while"; and he resolutely set off in the company of the constables.

His wife's heart could not calm down, because it was the heart of a woman, a devoted mother and wife, and thus ever fearful for her loved ones; and calling over her eldest son, she asked him, "Miguel, when the pot boiled over and the milk curdled, didn't I tell you there'd be trouble?"

"And I've seen the hawk fly over the barn about five times, Mama," the boy replied.

"Have you really?" his mother asked, her face pale with terror.

"I really have, Mama. And what shall we do now?"

"Well, I'll go see our friend Escobedo; he can speak for us," the woman answered, putting on her brightly decorated *llicllas*; and she left the house, followed by two shaggy dogs that Miguel called back by whistling in a special way and shouting their names, "Zambito! Desertor! Pst, pst!" In obedience to this command, Zambito returned, briskly wagging his tail; but Desertor, less docile or perhaps more loyal, followed his mistress's footsteps, panting and occasionally showing his tongue.

7

Don Fernando's concern about the future that awaited him in Kíllac grew with each passing day. He was paying for confidential investigations that kept him informed about what was going on in the town and convinced him that the prevailing calm was merely apparent and not to be trusted, although Lucía's delicate condition led him to keep his information from her. Providence was going to bless their home with offspring; and this caused the father-to-be to think often about his need to reach a clear decision and put an end to the vacillation that had continued for three months, ever since the visit during which Manuel had conceived such far-reaching plans.

One day Don Fernando's ideas began to take a more definitive turn, and he said to himself, "The progress Margarita is making, the pliant temperament of Rosalía, who promises to be a good little girl, my Lucía's condition—all of this augurs a delightful future for my family. My duty is not to waste this opportunity and to seize all the happiness that could be mine with a wife like Lucía. Yes, I must reach a decision!"

During those days the new subprefect, after taking the prescribed oath of office, was traveling from one town in his jurisdiction to another, while his subordinates offered him sumptuous banquets by requisitioning food from the Indians.

Important issues, nothing less than the election of a president and of the people's representatives, were being debated in the country.

When Don Fernando learned that the sexton of Kíllac was languishing in jail, he trembled, more with indignation than with alarm. "That man is weak and defenseless, and the sword of justice meant for the guilty will fall on him," he was saying to himself when a somber voice resounded throughout the land telling of the bloody murder of the Gutiérrez brothers,[26] which spread a cloud of human ashes over the face of civilization. This news made Don Fernando tremble, for he had good reason to fear a new attack like that of the fifth of August, not being unaware of the brief but encouraging words that Colonel Paredes had pronounced in his meeting with Don Sebastián. The deeply melancholy demeanor of Manuel, who kept up a studied reserve, only confirmed his opinion, because he could tell that a relentless struggle was going on between the young law student and Don Sebastián; and at the same time he began to suspect that so decent and thoroughly honorable a young man could not be the son of the unscrupulous governor of Kíllac.

"I'm going to cut this Gordian knot with a sword of unshakable will," said Don Fernando, striking his forehead with the palm of his hand; and he went to find Lucía and tell her of the decision he had just reached.

---

26. The Gutiérrez brothers, military officers of middle rank, overthrew President José Balta in 1872. Faced with the angry reaction of other officers and of the population of Lima, they murdered the president. Shortly thereafter they were themselves lynched by an enraged mob.

When Don Fernando entered his wife's bedroom he found her standing before a full-length mirror that shone from the door of a perfectly varnished black mahogany wardrobe, its bright surface reflecting her slender figure dressed in a loose piqué robe, her blond hair falling over her shoulders in elegant silken waves. She had just stepped from her bath. As Don Fernando reached the threshold of the room his reflection also appeared in the mirror; and when Lucía saw it she smiled and turned around to receive the original, who was advancing toward her with open arms.

"I've come to give you some good news, my love," Marín said, embracing her.

"Good news in these disastrous times? Where did you find good news, Fernando dear?" she asked, embracing him in turn.

"In the strength of my own will," he replied, withdrawing to the middle of the room.

"That's fine, but tell me what you mean."

"We can't be happy in this place, my dear Lucía; you're going to be a mother, and I don't want the first link in the chain of our joyous union to start life here."

"And so . . . ?"

"Within three weeks, come what may, we'll leave here for good."

"So soon! And where are we going, Fernando?"

"No arguments, my dear. I've thought it all over, and I've just come to tell you to prepare the few items that should make up your baggage."

"And where are we going, Fernando?" the wife asked again, more and more surprised at so sudden a decision.

"I'll take you to a land of flowers, to Peru's fair capital, where you'll taste happiness tending our child's cradle," Don Fernando answered, drawing near to Lucía and taking a lock of his wife's loose hair, twisting it around his fingers as he spoke, and then releasing it.

"To Lima!" Lucía cried enthusiastically.

"Yes, to Lima! And once the child we're expecting is strong enough for a long journey, we'll go to Europe. I want you to know Madrid."

"And what about Margarita and Rosalía? What will become of our orphans without us? Simple gratitude obliges us to look after them, dear Fernando."

"They're our adopted daughters. They'll go to Lima with us; and there, just as we've planned, we'll place them in the school that will best prepare them to be wives and mothers, without the false piety of constant rote prayers," was Marín's straightforward reply.

"Thank you, Fernando dear; you're so good!" said Lucía, once more embracing her husband.

At that moment there were two gentle measured taps on the door.

"Come in," said Don Fernando, drawing away a little from his wife; and Margarita's charming figure appeared, made even more strikingly beautiful by the care and affection lavished on her.

"Godmother," the girl said, "Manuel is in the parlor and says he wants to talk to my godfather."

"Has he been waiting long?"

"Yes, Godmother."

"I'm off to see him," said Don Fernando and stepped through the door, leaving behind his wife and her godchild. Lucía spent a few moments in rapturous contemplation of Margarita, saying to herself, "Someone has said that woman responds more than any other creature to gentle and kind treatment. Ah, my Margarita is the living proof of that theory!"

And Lucía was right. A woman who is cherished and pampered gains a hundred percent in beauty and moral qualities. If anyone doubt this, let him think of those wretched women victimized in the privacy of their homes by groundless jealousy, worn out by their husbands' inordinate appetites, forced to breathe stale air and take sparse nourishment; and instantly he will see before him an unfortunate woman, ill-tempered, pale, hollow-eyed, her mind ever prey to gloomy thoughts, her capacity for action engulfed in dreamy lethargy.

8

To understand how events in our story are linked to each other, we must now go back to the characters we have left behind.

Father Pascual's lofty sentiments of Christian repentance, his confession by Marcela's death-bed, and the serious condition in which he was taken back to his empty house all produced their natural effect in Lucía's generous heart, arousing an intense concern for the fate of that forlorn creature. The nurse of Kíllac, skilled in the battle against typhus, which was endemic in that town, cared for the priest and saved him; and once on the road to recovery, Father Pascual decided to head for the city, leaving a substitute in his place.

The demands of moral purity can rarely be met for long by an organism corrupted by vice. The man who has sullied his youth in the mire of excesses far removed from the moderate pleasures of chaste love, who has spent his nervous energy in those physical passions that weaken the mechanism of his body until it has neither the strength nor the coordination to fulfill the functions that an all-wise nature has assigned to it, who has not husbanded his physical vigor by subjecting it to the moral law that governs human nature and has, instead, perversely followed only his animal instinct and squandered his life in debauchery, that man is seriously ill, and cannot simply recover his health whenever it suits him. Nonetheless, the rehabilitation of a man banished from the ranks of the virtuous is within the realm of the possible as long as those delicate fibers of his heart that vibrate in sweet response to the mention of God, fatherland, and family are not paralyzed.

For several days Father Pascual forswore alcohol and the company of women; and this abstinence greatly irritated his nervous system, stimulating his imagination, which, as he traveled over hills and meadows, was all the more active in evoking pictures that flashed before his eyes like magic visions. Voluptuous apparitions, some ridiculous to see, others terrifying and bearing the marks of orgies; white-winged angels bearing green triumphal palm-fronds with which to touch the pure forehead of a mother or a wife, by the side of a child born of holy wedlock or before the altar of God . . . Oh, how much there was to agitate that brain on the verge of becoming unhinged in the struggle against its own ghosts!

Had Father Pascual lived in a weak and enervating climate, his path would have ended in the madhouse; but the frigid air of the Andes had invigorated his brain and thus protected it from the violent and irreparable upheaval of insanity. Would this man triumph in his struggle, martyred or purified?

Aghast at all the events he had witnessed and, indeed, brought about; ever mindful of Marcela's mysterious revelation; weighing and assessing his own actions, Father Pascual was in despair and immediately sought to flee the scene of his lamentable deeds; and while his mental state was such as we have described, he would have liked to flee from himself.

Conscience, placed in the engine we call our heart as the great argument against those unfortunates whose answer to the problem of life is the void of death, conscience may at times sleep soundly; but when it awakes it hammers unceasingly within the soul of man.

Father Pascual was able to run from the scene of his crime, and he could have traveled the world over; but his inexorable judge spoke to him without letup in the fearful language of remorse, to which reform is the only answer. And in this dismal state of mind the priest traveled mile after mile at the steady pace of his mule, until he reached the slopes of El Tigre and saw the post-station with its fair owner at the door. He put the spur to the animal's flanks; and ten minutes later he was dismounting and asking for a bottle of "refreshments," which he emptied thirstily, not without inviting his landlady to join him.

Farewell, airy dreams of reform! The merry words of other days sprang to his lips and struck the ears of the landlady. Alcohol reclaimed its old abode, and meditation yielded to the drunkard's ravings. The landlady's husband, who had charge of the post-horses, came at this point and said, "This gentleman's a bit befuddled; let's get him up in the saddle."

"Let's do that, Leoncito, because in this case the mount knows more than the man and will take him straight home," the landlady replied.

No sooner said than done.

When Father Pascual found himself in the saddle, he sat up straight and applied spurs and lash to his mount, which compliantly went on its accustomed way. That had been the last post-station; and two hours later the traveler was entering the city, his destination, whose high towers and steeples seemed to him so many ghosts ready to pounce on him. As his reason tottered in the twilight between reality and illusion, his mule suddenly swerved and began to curvet wildly, bucking, jumping, and kicking. The first thing to fly off was Father Pascual's hat, which increased the skittishness of the animal, already startled by the little flags that identified some establishments selling stew and *chicha*. The rider swayed for a few minutes, finally losing his balance and falling unconscious to the ground.

All this happened near the Franciscan monastery. A curious crowd soon gathered, and compassionate hands bore the stranger to the monastery gate, where the charitable friars received him.

The guardian of the monastery was a venerable monk whose heart held untold mysteries of virtue and who had met Father Pascual on various journeys through Killac. He took the sick man in his care and, when he had come to, said to him, "The mercy of the Lord is great, brother," and assigned him lodging in one of the cells.

In the monastic silence Father Pascual found himself once again morally naked and alone, absolutely alone in the world. Yet no: his ghosts were still with him, and he fell anew into a fevered delirium, saying, among sobs and disjointed mutterings, "Yes, Lord. Thou hast made man to live in society; Thou hast implanted the bonds of love, brotherhood, and family in his heart. The man who rejects and flees them, flees from the order of Thy creation, abhors Thy law of nature, and . . . falls, falls alone, like me in that remote parish! Who, who has succeeded in such a flight? How many are there? Even here . . . in this solitude, in these halls of stone: one? a thousand? Have they adorned their brows with the crown of virginity, whether in health or in sickness? . . . No! No!" And he clapped his hands.

Father Pascual's words had become incoherent. His eyes were bloodshot; his lips, dry; his breath burned like the steam that rises from a live coal plunged into water. The veins of his temples bulged noticeably, and the thirst that was consuming his breast drove him to drain a glass of water that he saw by his night-table.

"This drink will give me new life," he said, taking hold of the glass with his trembling hands and lifting it to his lips. Though hardly able to drink while his teeth chattered convulsively against its rim, he drained it to the last drop and then, before he could return it to its place, fell to the floor with a scream. His body, stretched out at full length, shook and gasped; and with a low final "Ay!" his face sank into the rigidity of death.

A lay brother passing by heard the feeble voice of the sick man and entered the cell; and seeing the new guest stretched out on the floor, he rang a bell hanging by the main gate with such urgency that several friars, among them the guardian, soon appeared.

"He's fainted!" said one.

"Good heavens, he's ice-cold! Let's give him absolution," said another, and uttered the words prescribed by sacred ritual.

"Call the community together; perhaps we can still give him the last rites," the guardian commanded while the others raised the body and set it on the bed. "Is he already dead? Oh merciful God!" he exclaimed, folding his hands and raising his eyes heavenward.

"Requiescat in pace," the friar who had pronounced absolution said solemnly. In the meantime the whole community had gathered, and it now proceeded to chant the usual prayers for the dead and to sprinkle holy water.

The guardian called a lay brother and said, "Brother Pedro, get a shroud ready and go with Brother Cirilo to prepare a grave." And he left the cell in the company of another friar, to whom he remarked, "In spite of Büchner's claims for materialism in his *Force and Matter*, the truth, Father, is that the way a man dies and the respect accorded his remains are the epilogue to his life and way of being."

"According to that," replied the other friar, pulling up his hood, "Father Pascual must have been a good Christian, since he died in peace and has found kind hands to bury him; and yet there's all kinds of talk, Father Guardian."

"God save us from a sudden death; but if we judge with Christian charity, we know that sincere repentance is the gateway to salvation. That priest may have expired on the wings of contrition," the guardian answered, crossing his arms and plunging his hands into the sleeves of his long robe.

"Sudden death may suit the man who doesn't believe in the next world, or the just man ever ready to depart; but for those of us who are not prepared, yet do not doubt that within man there is an immortal animating spirit, the truth, plain and dreadful, is also this: we die as we have lived," the friar remarked as they reached the door of the guardian's cell, where they parted.

These philosophers knew nothing of the cruel moments that Father Pascual lived before yielding his soul to God. The torture of his spirit as he realized that he could have been a virtuous and useful man but for the folly of human laws that contradict the law of nature; his anguish, with no friendly hand to sweeten so much bitterness, no word to console him in his tribulations—could these have equaled the sufferings of a lingering death?

For us the sudden demise of Father Pascual is a great misfortune, since we hoped to put the course of his life to good use. Yet such is the reality of man's existence. Death falls upon us unexpectedly and strikes us just when our life is most necessary, when its threads have become part of the social fabric that makes up the ever-varied human tapestry. The only words we can pronounce before the solitary grave of that unfortunate priest, deprived of a lawful family and robbed of the bonds of affection by the laws of man, are the laconic, "May he rest in peace!"

Let us return to Killac.

9

In view of Don Sebastián's weakness of character it was to be expected that his situation would grow more difficult after his meeting with the subprefect and after what passed between him and Doña Petronila.

Manuel felt that the scene that had taken place in Don Sebastián's bedroom, when he had dragged him away by force to save his mother from abuse by a drunkard, was humiliating; yet Manuel also knew that there are domestic scenes that entail no humiliation if they take place within the family home, and so he met the insults of his mother's husband with manly composure, until sleep closed Don Sebastián's eyes and restored peace between father and son.

Once Pancorbo was sound asleep, Manuel went to look for his mother and found her weeping. He kissed her on the forehead, wiped away her tears, and said, "Courage, Mother; save your tears for when I am no longer by your side."

"Oh Manuel, I'm so unhappy!" Doña Petronila answered, sobbing.

"You unhappy, Mother? That's blasphemy against the Lord! Hasn't He given you a son, don't you have my heart and the blood in my veins, which I'm ready to shed for you?" the young man replied heatedly and with a certain tone of resentment.

"Yes, it's blasphemy; but God will forgive me just as you forgive me for having forgotten you. Yes, Manuelito, my dear son, I am a mother!" Doña Petronila exclaimed, taking her son's hands and making him sit by her side.

"Poor Mother!" Manuel uttered with a sigh, contradicting what he had just said.

"'Poor women' is what you ought to say, Manuelito. No matter how happy we may seem, there's always a worm to gnaw at our hearts," replied Doña Petronila, a little calmer now and stroking the tassels of her shawl.

"Mother dear, let's stop complaining and talk calmly. Let's discuss something concrete."

"What is it you want? Tell me."

"I want us to see what our income is. In this world, Mother, you can't take a step without coming up against that gate they call *receipts and assets.*"

"What's this? Do you mean you want to go back to your studies and leave me here in this madhouse?" Doña Petronila asked in surprise.

"Don't jump to conclusions, Mother. As you say, I'm a child; but remember that contact with books and with men matures us: it gives us experience and teaches us to think. I consider myself a man!" Manuel said with a spirited air.

"And so you are!" Doña Petronila affirmed, looking proudly into her son's face.

"Yes, Mother. What I mean is that I've done some serious thinking and hope to carry out my plans for your future and mine. Apart from that . . ." He was about to say something harsh; but Margarita's name flashed through his mind like a gentle moonbeam reflected on the surface of a tranquil lake, causing him to pause and sigh deeply.

"What a pleasure it is for me to hear you talk like that, my boy. Yes, Don Fernando and Doña Lucía are right when they keep congratulating me on having such a son."

Manuel hesitated for a moment and then replied with renewed vigor, "Mother, I want to know what our income is, but . . . not counting Don Sebastián's."

"Our income?" Doña Petronila repeated, again catching at the tassels of her shawl and playing with them distractedly. "How should I calculate our income? We have some good land that produces corn, wheat, barley, oca,²⁷ beans, potatoes, and quinoa. We have several hundred sheep, cows, alpacas, and the wild mares we use for threshing the harvest. I work the fields and turn the wool and grain into cash, and part of that goes to you for your studies. Is that account enough for you?"

Manuel listened to his mother attentively and with satisfaction; and when she concluded he went silently and thoughtfully to kiss her forehead, offering in his heart the prayer of thanksgiving and admiration called for by a mother's sacred selflessness and love. The account had, however, yielded no numbers for his calculations; and so he timidly asked once more, "And haven't you saved anything?"

"What do you mean? Do you think I'm a spendthrift? Don't I know I have a son? Don't I have your future to be concerned about? Don't I think about how some day you'll want to marry? Come now! I've saved half of everything and I've got five bags well hidden away, each one with two thousand shiny *soles*. You won't have to scrape like some who marry with only the shirt on their back."

---

27. *Oca,* a sweetish tuber.

"Bless you and all mothers like you: you find your happiness in the welfare of your children! All right, I'll use the ten thousand *soles* as the basis for my calculations. I'm going to propose a plan to you, and . . . then, not one more second," Manuel said resolutely.

"There, it's just as I said, you're going to leave me."

"Remember, Mother, that if I lose a year from my studies I may lose the chance to enter my chosen profession; but I won't leave unaccompanied, and I won't go to a provincial university like San Bernardo."

"All right, whatever you wish; but above all remember that I am Sebastián's wife, bound to him by . . . gratitude, and that you must respect him like . . . a real father," Doña Petronila answered, twice lowering her eyes.

"I won't forget it, Mother dear; and now let's get some rest after such a strenuous day," Manuel replied, bidding his mother good-night by kissing her hand.

10

Once the sexton Isidro Champí had been locked up in jail, the doors to his freedom remained shut.

Let us see what happened to his wife that afternoon when she went to the house of her friend Escobedo in search of aid and counsel.

"So my good friend's in jail?" Escobedo said after the reciprocal greetings and once the Indian had told him the news.

"Yes, wiracocha. So what should we do? You help us!" the woman replied, downcast, upon which Escobedo gently patted her on the shoulder, saying, "Aha, but that's no way to come asking for a favor, with empty hands, when you've got all that cattle, eh, my friend?"

"You're right, friend wiracocha; but I dashed from my house as though the witches were after me, and later on, tomorrow . . . I won't be ungrateful, like a dried-out field."

"Fine, fine, that's another story; but if we're going to talk to the judge and the governor, you have to tell me what we're going to take them."

"Should I take them a chicken?"

"Foolish woman, what are you talking about? Do you think they're going to do all that paperwork for a chicken? They've already written up my good friend as being involved in that ruckus when Yupanqui and the others died," Escobedo said slyly.

"Good Heavens, what are you saying?" she asked, wringing her hands.

"I'm telling you the facts; but with the right connections, we'll get him out. Tell me, how many cows do you have? I think with four . . ."

"Will my Isidro go free for four cows?" asked the woman in alarm.

"Of course he will. We'll give one to the governor, one to the judge, one to the subprefect, and, well, the fourth would be for your good friend here"; and as he made this distribution, Escobedo paced back and forth across the room, while the Indian, plunged into dark doubts and despair, went over her cattle in her mind, identifying each animal by its color, age, and special markings, and sometimes confusing her children's names with those of her beloved heifers. "Good Lord, there you are, thinking it all over! Anybody would say you're tight-fisted and don't really love your husband," Escobedo broke in.

"God forbid I shouldn't love my Isidro whom I've known all my life and with whom I've been through so much together, ay, but . . ."

"Well, let's forget it. I'm very busy," Escobedo said, forcing the issue.

"Excuse my foolishness, friend wiracocha, and . . . I say, yes, we'll give four cows, but . . . young ones, all right? I'll go set aside the two brown ones, a black one, and a piebald one; but will you get my Isidro out, now that . . ."

"Of course I will now. In a little while I'll get to work on it; and tomorrow, or the day after, or by the third day, it'll all be settled. Remember that first I've got to talk to that Don Fernando Marín, who is the one that lodged the complaint."

When the sexton's wife heard the name of Marín, a ray of light shone through the gloom within her mind, and she said to herself, "Why didn't I go to him in the first place? Maybe I'll still be in time if I go the first thing in the morning"; and she left, saying to Escobedo, "Friend wiracocha, get busy on it; I've got to take some clothes to Isidro and I'll tell him that you're going to save us. Goodbye."

"You're in the trap, little mouse," Escobedo said to himself with a laugh and then prepared to go looking for Estéfano Benites to tell him of the deal he had made, in which they would share equally, exempting the four heifers from the attachment, since they would be listed as belonging to Escobedo or Benites.

11

Political events in the nation's capital were to have a strong and direct influence on the outcome of the plans for advance payment that the new provincial and local authorities had undertaken with such enthusiasm.

Subprefect Paredes was inspecting one of the small towns under his jurisdiction; and there he met with a pair of eyes set in a remarkable female face, eyes that penetrated to the very "marrow" of his heart. Since the colonel, when it came to battles fought on the green fields of Cupid, was a veteran who bore not only decorations but even wounds of which he would boast at merry all-male gatherings, and since there are always persons eager to do the bidding of those in power, his excellency was confident that breaching this rampart would be an easy matter.

It should be noted that in Kíllac as well as in the neighboring villages where a straightforward and unsophisticated morality prevails, that blight on society that undermines the foundations of the family by diverting young men from marriage and that appears in the unfortunate guise of the "fallen woman" is absolutely unknown.

A clever seduction is always linked to misfortune and almost always involves some potentate whose power and unscrupulousness overcome the victim while leaving the victimizer secure. This time, the colonel's candidate for inclusion in the already long list of martyrs to his spirit of adventure was an attractive young woman in whose home the new subprefect had been made heartily welcome.

Teodora had turned twenty; she was short, with bright yet serene eyes. She wore an elegant dress of pink muslin with coffee-colored trimmings; a crimson silk scarf hung around her neck like a short cape, pinned together on her breast with a brass brooch displaying an imitation topaz. Her long and carefully groomed hair fell in braids whose tips were bound in black silk ribbons. Teodora's heart was not free. She was engaged to be married as soon as her fiancé could come from the estate he was administering, where he saved part of his salary to pay for a "proper wedding" with distinguished attendants, three days of feasting, and a band of wind instruments. Teodora had been born with a firm and impetuous character, passionate once she had left her childhood. She loved her fiancé; and his absence may have intensified the warmth of her maidenly dreams, making her sigh for his daily visits and those tender words whispered at deliciously romantic moments that are the gateway to the castle of matrimony.

Five days of constant carousal had gone by in Teodora's house, instigated by the subprefect, who devoted himself wholly to the rustic beauty, whose resistance was soon plain to him but only intensified his desire. Barrels of wine, cases of beer—there was plenty of everything. The town's two blind violinists gave no rest to their bows, drawing *moza-malas* and *huainus* from their violins' tuneful strings.

The colonel called the lieutenant governor aside and whispered something in his ear. The lieutenant governor smiled slyly and replied in a low voice, "We'll catch that mouse soon enough. Be patient, sir; persistence pays off, and I'll see to this right away, your excellency," and he rushed out.

Teodora, who had already had to hear the colonel's repeated urgings and suggestions, called her father to the door and, more distressed than fearful, said, "Father, my heart's going through Purgatory!"

"How come, Teoco? You ought to be happy, what with all these visitors."

"That's just the trouble. The subprefect has dishonorable intentions toward me, and if Mariano finds out . . ."

"What's that you're saying? How about that! So this is his excellency's idea of how to behave!" Don Gaspar replied, passing his hand over his moist lips.

"Yes, Father; he's told me that with or without my consent, he's going to carry me off," the girl said, turning red and lowering her eyes.

"Hm!" the old man snorted furiously, biting his lips; and turning around as though to survey the field, he added, "This is one tidbit he'll never swallow. Not while I'm still around!"

"Father . . . !"

"Just go in there and act as though nothing's happened and let him spend some of the money he's been stealing from all these towns, and . . . keep your heart true to Mariano, all right? I know what to do next," said Teodora's father, pushing her toward the center of the party.

One of the guests, seeing this, muttered, "What a foxy old fellow! Just look how he hands over his daughter!"

Soon after this, dinner was announced and everyone sat down at the table, where, on cloths neither quite white nor entirely black, a well-prepared meal was served, featuring roast stuffed guinea pigs, chicken almondine, potatoes cooked with green beans, and a stew, *locro colorado*, with cottage cheese. The subprefect sat down next to Teodora and, drawing the edge of the tablecloth over his lap, said in rather a triumphant tone, "Gentlemen, I always make myself at home next to a good-looking woman."

"Naturally, and that's the right place for your excellency," several of those present replied knowingly.

"And what's become of Don Gaspar, Señorita Teodora?" one of the guests asked slyly.

"My father? He'll be here in a minute," the girl answered as she looked about her.

Two of the younger guests exchanged roguish whispers, and another murmured, "That old fellow's a sharp one . . . and he doesn't want to stand in the way."

At that moment Don Gaspar appeared, rubbing his hands; and picking up a bottle to serve his guests, he said merrily, "A little aperitif, gentlemen!"

"All right! Our Don Gaspar has perfect timing!" the subprefect replied. And dinner got under way with lively cheer, while Teodora's complaisant manner led the colonel to believe that the fortress had been taken.

12

After bidding his mother good-night, Manuel went to his room, where, sleepless and plunged in thought, he awaited the arrival of the new day. At a suitable time he took his hat and went to Don Fernando's house. He entered the parlor, where he found Margarita alone, reading the tales of *Thumbkin* in an illustrated booklet. Happy to see her, he told himself, "What a good chance to probe her heart and declare my feelings!" and coming up to the girl and embracing her, he said, "All by yourself, and so beautiful!"

"How are you, Manuel?" the girl answered, setting the booklet on the table.

"My pretty Margarita! This is going to be the first time I talk to you alone. We may only have a few minutes, because I've come to see Don Fernando, and so I ask you to listen to me, my Margarita," Manuel said, taking hold of one of the girl's hands and caressing it between his own, his heart's fond dreams reflected in his eyes, which sent forth rays of tenderness and love with each glance.

"Good Heavens, Manuel, you're acting so strange today!" said Margarita, fixing her lovely eyes on his and then artlessly lowering them.

"Don't say I'm strange, Margarita; you are the soul of my soul; from the moment I met you I've given you my heart, and . . . I want to be worthy of you!" Manuel replied, stressing the final words, because what he most feared was that Margarita would reject the son of Marcela's murderer, a thought that could not occur to the child she was but very well could to the woman she would become.

The orphan kept silent, blushing like a poppy; and Manuel continued to caress her tiny hand, lost between his. There are times when silence is more eloquent than speech. Manuel was drunk with love as he feasted his eyes on the girl's beauty, and once more he addressed her, "Speak, answer me, my Margarita! Yes, you're still a child, but you already know I love you! Remember that by the bedside of your sainted mother I asked to be your brother; today . . ."

"Yes, Manuel, ever since that day I, too, see you in my joys and in my sorrows; and so you shall be my brother," the girl replied; but Manuel heatedly corrected her, "No, my angel, brother is so little, and I love you so much. I want to be your husband!"

"My husband?" asked a startled Margarita, in whose soul the veil of childish fantasies had just been rent, stirring her whole being and piercing her heart with that hypnotic dart that wounds us when we are young and that, plunging her into the sublime languor of hearts in love, would make her dream of the poetic world of fears and secrets, laughter and tears, light and shade, that enfolds the chaste soul of a virgin. From that moment on, Margarita knew she was a woman, knew she was in love.

For Manuel, one impression followed another with lightning speed, though his emotions differed from Margarita's, since his soul had already lost that virginity that consists of not knowing the true mysteries of life. Manuel loved deliberately and with full knowledge; Margarita, with her feelings alone. Manuel's first impulse was to seal the word "husband" with his lips as it emerged from those of the woman he loved; but mind restrained matter as the bridle restrains the galloping steed, and he limited himself to saying, "Yes, your husband!" and to kissing Margarita on the forehead.

It was not the kiss of the glowing ember on the fresh leaf of the lily, but it left an indelible mark. Margarita felt an unknown current course through her veins; her cheeks were tinged with scarlet, and she ran from the parlor, saying, "I'll call my godfather." As she headed for Lucía's rooms, instinctively she paused in the hallway to regain her composure.

Manuel remained in that ecstasy of the soul that has nothing in common with the sleep of the body, and only the calm words of Don Fernando jarred him out of it.

Manuel was the slave of a woman. A woman, who, after all, is only,

for the physician, the means of reproduction;

for the botanist, a delicate plant;

for the fat man, a good cook;

for Vice, sensual pleasure;

for Virtue, a mother;

and for a noble loving heart, soul of its very soul!

We expect no argument as to the accuracy of these definitions, which, to be sure, are not original with us; but the truth is that the last one legitimately applied to Manuel, which is why, as he saw Margarita leave, he sent her on her way with the sigh that says, "Soul of my soul!"

13

Once she knew of her husband's decision and found herself alone with Margarita, Lucía gave vent to her pleasure at the idea of the journey and said to her godchild, "Margarita, you're going to be very happy with the news I have for you."

"Godmother . . . ?" the girl interrupted, looking Lucía in the face.

"You and Rosalía won't travel to Lima alone."

"Who else is coming? Are you?" the orphan asked eagerly, while the myriad butterflies of anxiety, enthusiasm, and curiosity fluttered in her mind.

"I am, and so is your godfather—the whole family," Lucía answered, nodding her head as she registered the tally on her fingers.

"You, and my godfather, and Rosalía! Oh, how wonderful! And will Manuel come, too?" Margarita asked excitedly.

Lucía scrutinized her godchild's face to assess the impression her answer would make and said, "Manuel won't come; his parents live here."

A brief silence ensued.

Margarita's eyes filled with tears, which she tried in vain to dissemble as she asked, "Lima's a beautiful city, isn't it?"

"The most beautiful in Peru. But . . . why are you crying, child?" Lucía asked, taking both of Margarita's hands, making her sit by her side, and saying, "Look, my child, I've noticed you're very fond of Manuel; and now I see that young man's made an impression on your heart, a child's heart today, and I begin to fear that tomorrow the woman's heart will belong to him."

"But Godmother, Manuel is very good, I've never seen him do anything bad," Margarita replied timidly.

"That's just it, child: his goodness has made you fall into a snare that has to be cut so you may regain your freedom. You cannot love the son of the man who murdered your parents! Ah, I shudder at the thought! . . . Poor Manuel!"

Lucía was deeply moved as she spoke these words; fear and doubt assailed her heart and noticeably affected the timbre of her voice. One after another, tormenting thoughts flashed through her mind; and she silently asked herself, "Was it indiscreet of me to talk to my godchild of love? Have I marked Manuel's forehead forever, so that from now on Margarita will see him as the son of her parents' killer? And then, what of Manuel? . . . Ah, the deep caverns of the human heart, its tangled mysteries!"

And how full of meaning this momentary silence was for Margarita! She sat there, speechless and trembling, like a lily on whose stalk the nightingale has tried to alight, never folding her wings because the plant's weakness has forced her to fly on in search of better shelter. Coming immediately after her conversation with Manuel, her godmother's declaration gave her cruel pain; it devastated her soul, it cut down the flowers of hope newly born in two hearts linked by the ties that make for human happiness, two hearts in love.

Don Fernando's wife finally managed to regain her composure; and putting an end to the previous conversation, she told Margarita, "So make sure your trunk is ready by Thursday, and don't forget your little sister's things, all right? You're the elder, and you have to help her."

"Yes, Godmother," Margarita replied, distractedly picking up a skein of blue silk she saw on the floor. She set it on the table and left. Once alone, Lucía again said, "Poor Manuel! Such fine qualities, such noble aspirations! There's no doubt he loves Margarita, but a chasm lies between them! But then . . . doesn't experience show us that our wayward hearts see the most poetic part of love precisely in the unfathomable? Can there be any fire comparable to the fire of an impossible love? Can there be a yearning like the yearning to forge ahead toward possession of the beloved object, overcoming obstacles, conquering mountain after mountain of thorns that have drawn blood from the feet, climbing steep ranges where the snows of the impossible, melted by the sun of love, have produced torrents of tears? Heroes of sorrow, poor exiles from the paradise of Happiness, the world understands you not! Sacrificial victims on the altars of misfortune, whom generous souls may envelop in the incense of their sympathy, in sorrow will your love endure!"

At the conclusion of this soliloquy Lucía dropped onto the sofa, lifting her right hand to a forehead bathed in abundant perspiration that ran down over her cheeks, burning with the color of the poppies of May. Then, interweaving her fingers and pressing them against each other until the knuckles cracked, she asked herself, "And so what shall I do? My situation is difficult and dramatic, as are Manuel's and Margarita's. If theirs is a first love, it will grow ever more exalted with each sigh that bears the aroma of a virginal passion and springs from a breast yearning for its beloved. What if I took some firm action? . . . Ah, but my Fernando will resolve my doubts. We'll share our ideas, and I'll see the light, because I can never forget that as Marcela was dying she bequeathed to me these two pieces of her heart."

Lucía was right; she would share her doubts, her fears, and her hopes with Don Fernando and drive away the shadows that now hung over her. Manuel would be able to share the sorrows that afflicted his heart with the noblest of all hearts, his mother's, take refuge at her knee, and shed a man's tears now with her who yesterday had dried the tears of his childhood. But what of Margarita? A poor orphan, torn from the nest, she would be forced to seek the shelter of an alien tree, there to sing, beneath its foliage, the song of a soul bound to another; she would be forced to conceal her thoughts, with laughter on her lips and tears within her heart. For Margarita, Lucía was the best of women. But she was not her mother!

14

Now we shall go for a moment in search of Colonel Paredes, whom we left as he was sitting down at table in Teodora's house.

Dinner was abundant and animated; and as soon as it was concluded, when night had already fallen, all headed for the parlor to continue their revels with the *zapateo* and the handkerchief dance.

Don Gaspar called his daughter aside and told her peremptorily, "Follow me, Teoco." And the two of them went to a nearby fence where an Indian waited with three horses, one of them bearing a sidesaddle and everything else needed for a woman to ride.

"Where are we going, Father?" Teodora asked.

"To Kíllac, to my friend Doña Petronila's house. As you know, she's a woman of character, and you'll be as safe with her as the monstrance is on the altar," Don Gaspar replied while still walking with long firm strides in spite of the darkness.

"Fine, and all the better now that Don Sebastián is no longer governor, so nobody will bother us before Mariano comes," Teodora answered, her little steps following her father's hurried ones.

At that moment a tall shape wrapped in a poncho stepped from the shadows.

"Anselmo!" Don Gaspar called out.

"Yes, sir," was the succinct reply, and the three of them went on until they reached the horses. The two men lifted Teodora, who with a countrywoman's nimbleness seated herself on her horse, Chocllopoccochi, doubtless so called because he was black with white fetlocks. Don Gaspar and Anselmo, who was a trusted servant, then mounted; and Teodora's father commanded the Indian, "Go home, see to the lights, and make sure there's plenty of tea, well laced. If they miss us, you know what to do, right?"

"Yes, tatay," the Indian answered as he headed for the house.

Three simultaneous cracks of a whip on the croup of a horse sounded as the three mounts dashed into the darkness of the night, bearing the weight of their riders, snorting through flared nostrils, and furiously champing at their bits.

The old man was lost in thought, for our brain is always fashioning its ideas, and this process will not cease just because the body is at rest.

"Father, let's slow down," said Teodora, pulling up her horse; but Don Gaspar either did not hear his daughter or paid no attention, so that she again said, more loudly, "Father!"

"What? Are you tired already?" the old man answered, also slowing down.

"Nonsense! I'm not tired! But I've thought of something."

"What's that?" Don Gaspar replied, managing the reins so as to draw closer to Teodora.

"It would be better if you turned back right here. In half an hour you'd be home, and by being there you'd avoid all suspicion and they'd go on for a while and never miss me . . . and then . . . you'd present my excuses."

"And you . . . you'd go on alone?" Don Gaspar asked, coughing repeatedly.

"I'm perfectly safe with Anselmo, Chocllopoccochi is gentle and knows the way very well, it's not far any more, the moon will soon be out—and above all, if they've got it into their heads to ask about us and they happen to find out we've left, you can be sure they'll come after us, catch up with us, stop us, and then, good and drunk . . ."

"Right! That's the Gospel truth, Teodora!" the old man interrupted her, stopping his horse; and with a sly smile he added, "There's no denying it: for planning one of these escapades there's nobody like a woman." And again he coughed violently.

"That's it, then. You've already caught cold. Just go back; and if anybody's following us, your return will throw him off the track."

"Right you are! And before I tell them where to find you, they can skin me alive," Don Gaspar answered, then calling to the servant, who was some way off, "Anselmo, Anselmo!"

The servant brought his horse up to the others, and this dialogue took place between father and daughter:

"Goodbye, then; I'll come for you within four days."

"Goodbye, Father. Put something over your mouth to protect it; you've got a bad cough."

"Knock discreetly, and tell my friend Doña Petronila the whole story. I know what to expect from her."

"Yes, yes, I'll tell her everything."

"Anselmo, take care of my girl. I'll see you soon." As he finished his sentence Don Gaspar turned his gray horse around, dug his spurless heels firmly into his flanks, and applied a couple of smart blows with the whip to his croup, all of which filled the beast with new energy, as did the prospect of returning home.

Teodora and Anselmo dismounted at Doña Petronila Hinojosa's front door at about eleven that evening. They made vigorous use of the small bronze monkey that serves as a doorknocker; and four or five dogs answered their knocks with frantic barking, while a sleepy and annoyed voice asked, "Who is it?"

"It's me, and I've come from Don Gaspar Sierra to deliver something to Doña Petronila."

The doorman, the usual *pongo*, needed no further explanations; he unbarred the front door, and its leaves turned on their hinges to admit the fugitive Teodora, who was received by Doña Petronila with her customary warmth.

Don Gaspar had not advanced two miles from the spot where he had left Teodora when he heard shouts and saw a swarm of horsemen. Within moments he was convinced these were the followers of the subprefect.

"Teoco was so right! What the devil, women are witches, all of them! And the funny part of it is that we men all let ourselves be bewitched! That's plain to see, whether we realize it or not," Don Gaspar said to himself and rode on at the steady pace of his gray horse.

15

Teodora's flight was soon noticed by the revelers. The lieutenant governor was the first to remark on it, saying, "This is the rotten old man's doing, Colonel, because she was obviously ready to oblige your excellency."

"Are they trying to make a fool of me? I won't put up with it, no sir! By my honor I won't!" said Paredes, striding back and forth across the room.

"Let's go look for her, my friends," the lieutenant governor proposed, seizing a burning candle and ready to leave.

"Yes, sir, I'll retrieve my little houri from the very bowels of the earth, yes, sir!" the subprefect repeated furiously while those eager to please him went off to search the house and drag the servants before their in-quisition, receiving the same reply from *pongos* and officials.

"They've gone out," they all said.

One questioner, stumbling onto the trail, asked, "On foot?"

"No, sir, on horseback," one of the officials replied.

"All right, your excellency, we'll go after them," they said as one, "be-cause there's just one road, and an easy one at that."

"Very well, my friends, go to it; and whoever brings me the girl . . ."

"I'll be the lucky one, I guarantee it," the lieutenant governor interrupted. A committee was appointed, and its members went for their horses.

The subprefect's rage was near the bursting point, and he said to himself, "Miserable old scoundrel! Yes, sir, if he showed up here now, I'd shoot him without bothering with a court-martial. I'm not subprefect for nothing. But . . . these boys are clever, and . . . I'd better have a little rest," and as he said this he stretched out at full length on the couch in the corner and began to doze.

Soon thereafter a troop of horses could be heard, and Don Bruno Paredes, opening his eyes, muttered, "That's them . . . they're off! Yes, sir, I'll soon have what I want, thanks to the zeal of my . . . subordinates. Why, these boys are worth all the silver in Cerro de Pasco!" And with a grunt he closed his eyes again.

At the same time that the posse was leaving in pursuit of Teodora, a constable serving as a *chasqui* or messenger was arriving from the provincial capital after having, with astonishing speed, followed the winding path through the mountains on foot. This *chasqui* bore an enve-lope sealed with red wax bearing the arms of the Republic and addressed to "Colonel Don Bruno de Paredes. Official and urgent." Once the mes-senger had handed the document to the subprefect, the latter, without getting up, began to read it; but no sooner had he taken in the first lines than he jumped up as though impelled by an electric shock, his face at first pale and then flushed with all his blood as he stood motionless for some seconds holding the open sheet of paper. Suddenly he threw it on the bed, stamped on the floor, and said, "Damn! This doesn't look good! I'd better get out of harm's way, yes, sir . . . Hello! Is anybody there?" and several Indians and the guardsmen of his escort came in response to his shouts. "My horse, quick, quick!" Don Bruno cried; and as though by magic, he was instantly obeyed. He mounted and, followed by three others, galloped off toward the city on his dappled horse, muttering to himself, "Best to lie low! I won't have any trouble finding a hiding place in the city till this storm blows over."

The men who had gone out to search for Teodora and had come upon Don Gaspar surrounded the good old man, and the lieutenant governor accosted him with, "Well now, old pal, what a way to abandon your guests! Where's young Teodora?"

"What?" Don Gaspar replied, feigning concern. "You're looking for my daughter? But didn't I leave her at home with you? Good Lord! Fortunately she's a good girl, and . . . she must be there, let's go," and he applied the whip to his horse, making him leap impetuously.

"Hold on there, *taita*,"[28] some said, turning around their mounts; and the lieutenant governor threatened, "All right, let's go; but if you don't deliver the goods, Gaspar, your goose is cooked."

"Yes, let's go back," others said; and as they whispered to each other someone opined, "Her ladyship must still be at home, because the old fellow hasn't had time to take her to any nearby town and come back."

"And if you didn't go out with Teodora, Don Gaspar, what are you doing here?" the lieutenant governor asked.

"My, my, tatay, you must be a stranger in these parts; maybe you've come from Lima with your cane and your stiff collar. I'm out here checking on my pastures," Don Gaspar answered solemnly.

"He's out here for the round-up," said one.

"Let's have a drink!" shouted two, and the group came to a halt.

The lieutenant governor drew a bottle of *pisco*[29] from his saddlebag; and they took turns drinking from it, downing as much as they could before the next would-be drinker whistled for them to stop; and this procedure was repeated very often in the course of their return to Don Gaspar's house, where they arrived between midnight and cock-crow.

The full moon shone all its silvery light onto the plain of Saucedo, where stood the cheerful huts of Peruvian Indians, through whose doors, at the first glimmer of dawn, pass the gray deer and the succulent partridge.

Don Gaspar's house was bare and abandoned, as though its owner had fallen on hard times. Only the *pongos* were snoring away huddled in the entry; they had to be shaken awake before they could answer questions.

"What's become of the subprefect?"

"Is he asleep?"

28. *Taita*, "dad."

29. *Pisco*, a liquor originally manufactured in the Peruvian town of the same name.

"And what about Teodora?"

"Come on, light a match!"

And so it went, until one of the *pongos* resolved their doubts by telling them, "His excellency's gone off on his horse."

"I'll be damned!" the lieutenant governor exclaimed.

"We must have been taking too long, and so he went after us."

"That's it! Waiting's no fun, and when you're in love . . . but hush!"

So saying they came into the parlor, which stood open. Don Gaspar lit the candle that was by the couch, and the first thing they saw by its light was the letter whose contents had made Colonel Bruno de Paredes take to his heels. They gathered around to read it; and when they had finished, Teodora's father said, "And so our subprefect's run away."

"Well, the great colonel of the National Guard was a fool!" declared the lieutenant governor.

"A colonel of toy soldiers!"

"A coward!" added one.

"What do you mean? A merchant, an embezzler, I know it for a fact," said another.

"A coward! A deserter!" was yet another opinion.

"An ex-subprefect!" Don Gaspar explained with the laugh of a man who has lived much and seen much; and picking up a guitar that stood in a corner of the room, he began to strum it and sing in a voice made hoarse by his cold,

> "Little bird that flutters
> With the sea beside you,
> Of course you're very frightened,
> With no map to guide you . . ."

And since to the tune of this strange song the would-be abductors and the injured party were reconciled, we shall return to Kíllac, where our friends are waiting for us.

16

Don Fernando found Manuel still immersed in the impressions left by Margarita's sudden departure. "Hello there, Don Manuel," he said as he entered the room and held out his hand to the young man.

"Excuse me for coming at this inopportune time, Don Fernando, but in cases like this the urgency of our business has to serve as an *open sesame*, "Manuel answered, shaking his friend's hand.

"Please, no formalities, Don Manuel. You know I'm your friend, and that should be enough," said Don Fernando, pulling up a chair and inviting the young man to sit down.

"I do know that, and without that friendship I'd have gone crazy: the awkward situation in which I stood with you after that attack; all the delicate and contradictory matters that have developed since I came to this town, where the leading citizens respect neither law nor religion; and everything I've been thinking and meditating—it's enough to drive anyone mad."

"It's true, my dear Manuel, that the present condition of our little society here is appalling; but I worry more about the news I've just received from the city than I do about you."

"I suppose it must concern you privately."

"No, it concerns everyone. It's about the sad end of Father Pascual, that unfortunate man whom we heard lamenting bitterly that future priests are deprived of the salutary influence of the family."

"So he died?"

"Yes, my friend, and in an awful way."

"How was that, and what did he die of?" Manuel asked, with growing interest, and intent on the reply.

"He died in the Franciscan monastery. He was dragged by his horse, taken in by some compassionate people, and cared for by the friars. They say the end came as he was drinking a glass of water," Señor Marín replied.

"Drinking a glass of water in the monastery?"

"Yes; the doctors believe he had a cerebral hemorrhage."

"Poor man! May he rest in peace."

"There's even more serious news that has given me pause."

"I wonder whether it's what we heard at home, too: the outbreak of a political storm in the capital that's been brought under control only after frightful excesses."

"Precisely, friend Manuel. But . . . come to think of it, that sort of thing is threatening at the outset because abnormal situations demand violent measures; but once that's over, it's different. I have faith in the administration of Don Manuel Pardo,"[30] said Don Fernando, rising from his chair.

"So do I, Don Fernando, because he's an outstanding man; but what weighs on my mind right now is . . . I'll tell you, my friend, even though it's a sudden change . . ."

"Of opinion?"

"No, sir, of topic: it's the storm at home that weighs on my mind. I see that it's not possible to live in this town oppressed by the tyrants who call themselves gentry."

"Friend Manuel, tell me something I don't already know! I've learned the sexton is in jail, accused of being responsible for the attack on my house."

"What did I tell you? It's enough to drive you crazy! And since, apart from that, I must finish my studies and be admitted to the bar, I have to get out of here; but I can't make up my mind to leave my mother in the midst of this wolf-pack."

"Well, friend Manuel, it so happens that I've just decided on the same solution for this problem with respect to my family. We're leaving in a few days."

"You, Don Fernando?" Manuel interrupted, as surprise, tinged with sorrow or doubt, appeared on his face.

"Yes, my friend; I've arranged for the sale of my mining stock and my personal property to some Jews who are paying me twenty percent of their value, and even so I'm glad to be leaving."

"And where will you go?"

"To the capital. I assume that in Lima a man's home will be safe and the authorities will understand their obligations. I'd just like to do something to get the sexton set free before I leave."

"Don Fernando, count on me! Together we'll do what it takes for that unfortunate Indian. Now fate seems to be smiling on me. I've come to talk to you about something related to my plans."

"I'll be delighted to listen."

"As I was saying, I want to get my mother out of here. I've made the necessary arrangements to take her to Lima, supposedly for a visit; and once we're there, there'll be no ship to bring us back."

30. President of Peru from 1872 to 1876, seen by some intellectuals as the best hope for putting an end to domination by the military.

"I understand, but what about Don Sebastián?" Don Fernando asked, his curiosity aroused.

"You know that in every home the mother is the sun whose warmth our heart seeks; once I've taken away my mother . . . I'd take Don Sebastián, too, because his future here is also very dark . . . Ah, Don Fernando, you have no idea what acts of oppression I put up with, for my mother's sake."

"How is that? Don Manuel, your way of talking about your father has been attracting my attention for some time," said Don Fernando, his tone of voice leading the young man to feel he could trust him.

"I thought it would, Señor Marín. My birth is shrouded in a veil of mystery; and if I ever lift it, it will be for you, who are a gentleman and my best friend," the young man said, flustered.

Don Fernando had just learned all he needed to know, because he had not failed to notice the impression that Manuel and Margarita had made on each other. Manuel was not, could not be, Don Sebastián's son.

"Who might his father be?" Don Fernando thought. "I could ask him more questions, demand that he confide in me as a friend, find out his secret, and be master of the situation; but I have to respect this young man's prudent reserve. The right time will come eventually." And addressing Manuel, he said, "Thank you, Don Manuel. I believe your trust in me is justified, but . . . let's get back to what you wanted to ask me. You were saying . . ."

"That I'd like you to help me transfer some funds to Lima and place them in a guaranteed account."

"I'd be delighted, Don Manuel. We'll get drafts on some bank: La Providencia, the Bank of London, Mexico, and South America—in a word, whichever one you like."

"The Bank of London."

"Fine, and how much do you want to send?"

"For now, about ten thousand *soles*. And another ten thousand later on, because I plan to liquidate all our properties here," the young man replied.

"Consider it done, my dear Don Manuel. You can leave the money in my name with Salas this afternoon, and tomorrow you'll have all your drafts. Now let me congratulate you on your decision. That's good thinking. You'll be useful to our country like so many others who have gone from the provinces to the capital; and you'll be an honor to your family, I can assure you," Don Fernando said, stressing the last sentences.

Manuel bowed his head to acknowledge the compliment and held back some inopportune words that were already on his lips, for he was about to reveal to Don Fernando that the motive behind all his aspirations was Margarita. A second thought checked this impulse.

"Has your mother had to suffer a great deal?" Don Fernando asked, breaking the brief silence and drawing forth a cigarette.

"Terribly! She has an angel's soul and a woman's heart. Poor Mother!" Manuel answered with a sigh. And as his thoughts took a new turn, he added, "I don't think you've heard the other big news from last night, which is right in keeping with this situation."

"What news is that?" Don Fernando asked, his curiosity aroused.

"A young woman from the next town, from Saucedo, has come to our house to take refuge from Subprefect Paredes."

"I suppose that girl must owe some taxes, maybe a property tax . . ."

"Nothing of the sort, Don Fernando; the colonel took a liking to her youthful good looks and without further ado, just because he felt like it, decided to make her his," Manuel said, laughing heartily.

"And . . . ?"

"She ran away from home."

"So around here those who escape the frying pan of the priest fall into the fire of the authorities?"

"That's it, exactly," Manuel answered, visibly disturbed by Don Fernando's words.

"That's frightful! And if we look at the Indians, the heart despairs at the oppression they suffer from the priest and the local headman."

"Ah, Don Fernando, these things upset any honorable man who comes from the outside and has eyes to see and a heart to feel. When I write my thesis I plan to use all this information to prove that our priests must marry."

"You'll be dealing with a vitally important point, one that has to be settled in the course of social progress before we ring down the curtain on this nineteenth century."

"I'm convinced of that, Don Fernando," said Manuel.

"And what do you say to the officials that come to govern these remote towns of our rich and vast country?"

"Ah, my friend! They're looking for a job, a salary, and an easy life, without ever having learned from the words of Epaminondas that 'it is the man who lends dignity to the office,' which is what they teach us in school."

"It's just that our country is run by favoritism," Don Fernando said, taking a box of matches from his pocket and lighting the cigarette he had been holding, ready to be smoked, for some time.

"Could you tell me how the investigation into the assault on your house is progressing, Don Fernando?" Manuel asked, taking advantage of a brief pause in the conversation to change the subject; and as he asked that question, his cheeks turned bright red.

"The investigation . . . I don't know what to say, my friend. Just yesterday I asked about it when I heard they'd arrested the sexton, whom I consider to be completely innocent. Are you interested in that?" Don Fernando answered, blowing out smoke.

"Very much so, Don Fernando. We've already agreed to save the sexton, whatever his name is; and besides that . . . if some day Margarita finds out the details of all this, I'd like her to see them in a different light."

"Ah! The girl's parents met such a tragic end!"

"What wouldn't I give to have your worthy godchild know all the facts about that tragic end! Margarita! And Margarita . . ."

Manuel was about to reveal his innermost secret when Doña Petronila appeared in the doorway accompanied by Teodora, whom she introduced with evident affection.

17

After sacrificing four heifers to her friend Escobedo's greed, Martina, the wife of Isidro Champi, ran home, frightened by the news that her husband's imprisonment was due to his having rung the bells at the time of the riot; and once home, she collected Isidro's ponchos and went to the jail. The jailer let her come in, and when she saw her husband she burst into uncontrollable tears.

"Isidro, Isidrocha, what have they done to you? Ay! Your hands and mine are clean, we haven't stolen anything or killed anyone. Ay!" the poor woman said.

"Patience, Martica; save your tears and pray to Our Blessed Mother," Isidro answered, trying to calm his wife, who dried her eyes with the edge of one of the ponchos and replied, "You know, Isidro, I've gone to see our friend Escobedo and he says he'll have you out in no time."

"He said that?"

"Yes, and I've paid him, too."

"What have you paid him? I suppose he asked you for money."

"No, what he said was that they brought you here because you rang the bell that night there was all that ruckus at Don Fernando's house. Lord, all those people killed! And that wiracocha has money, he said, and he'll prosecute us," Martina said, crossing herself as she spoke of those killed.

"That's what Don Estéfano said, too," Isidro answered; and coming back to his earlier question, for he knew the town's gentry all too well, he said, "And what did you pay him? Come out with it!"

"Isidrocha, you're getting angry, you're turning as bitter as the bark of the terebinth," his wife replied timidly.

"Now then, Martina! You've come here to torment me like the worm that gnaws on a sheep's heart. Speak up, or if you won't do that, go away and leave me alone. I don't know why you don't want to tell me . . . How much did you pay him?"

"All right, then, Isidro; I gave our friend what he asked, because it's you that's here in jail, because I'm your faithful turtledove and it's my duty to save you even if it costs me my life. Don't be angry, tata; I've given him the two little brown ones, the black one, and the piebald one," Martina itemized, drawing closer to her husband.

"Our four heifers!" the Indian said, raising his clasped hands to heaven, and with a sigh so deep that we do not know whether it took a terrible load off his heart or merely replaced one load with another.

"Look, he wanted me to give him cows; and all I could do, and it was like pulling grass up by the roots, was to get him to take the heifers, because one is for the governor, one for the subprefect, one for the judge, and the piebald one is for our friend."

When Isidro heard this account he lowered his head in gloomy silence, not daring to say any more to Martina, who, after a few moments, went in search of her children, wiping away renewed tears and with her heart split between the jail and her hut.

Meanwhile Escobedo found Estéfano and said, "All set, old pal."

"Set and settled?" Benites asked in reply.

"And just as we thought. Our Indian Isidro's already coughed up four good heifers."

"How's that?"

"You heard me: his wife came by, sniveling; and I told her this is no joke, because he was jailed for ringing the bell."

"And then . . ."

"She offered me chickens. Can you imagine, pinching pennies like that!"

"But then she coughed up heifers?"

"Well, she did. Now then, how do we split them?"

"We'll give one to the subprefect—why not eliminate the middleman?—and the three others are for us," was Benites's decision.

"Fine. And what about the Indian: does he go free or doesn't he?"

"Right now it's best if he doesn't. We'll keep him tangled up here a couple of months, and then we'll see what the decision is. One step at a time, old chum," Benites proposed.

"True enough, easy does it. And what about the attachment?"

"The attachment has to be duly processed, and that way we'll get at least another . . ."

"Four heifers, of course. Really, Estefito, you know more than a judge, and I can see why you're everybody's secretary," Escobedo added, rubbing his hands.

"Well, why did I study with old Rebenque if not to give orders and make a living and become a respected public figure," Benites said emphatically, taking out his plain handkerchief and wiping his lips.

"And when do we attach his goods?" Escobedo asked.

"We can do it in a couple of days; and now that I think of it, what the . . . You stay away from the hearing, and that way we'll make the Indian think that because you're his friend you've insisted on taking charge of his cattle because any other receiver would just grab them for himself."

"Very cagey! A great idea!" replied Escobedo, laughing and then asking, "What will Don Hilarión say?"

"The old fellow doesn't even read what I write; he just says 'Amen' to everything. It comes from having a priest for an 'uncle,' if you know what I mean."

"Watch what you say!" Escobedo warned, and then asked, "And what about Don Sebastián?"

"Don Sebastián will say, '*Frankly*, that's fine with me,' and from then on you and I will have new clothes and horses for the Kíllac fiesta," was the laughing reply of Estéfano Benites, whose brain had already forged a complete plan for taking advantage of Isidro Champi's innocence with the help of his friend Escobar, who was godfather to the sexton's second child.

"All right, old buddy; and now that we've made our plan it's time for a drop of something," Escobedo suggested.

"Absolutely, old pal; we'll stop by for a couple of drinks at the Quiquijana place or at Rufa's," Estéfano answered, accepting his partner's proposal and smoothing the brim of his hat.

18

W hen we were speaking of events in her town, we already had occasion to describe Teodora in the flower of her youth. Her hair was so long and abundant that had she not worn it braided it would have covered her back like a broad mantle of undulating vapor. With that sweet expression that conquered every heart, her appearance was so pleasing and attractive that in his mind Don Fernando could find something like an excuse for the subprefect. He asked the newcomers to sit down and called through the doorway, "Lucía, Lucía!", at the same time throwing out the stub of the cigarette he had been smoking.

Meanwhile Doña Petronila said to her son, in a low voice and smiling slyly, "I've caught you, you rascal; I see where you've been spending your time."

"Mama!" Manuel brought out like a child making excuses.

Don Fernando asked Teodora, "Have you just arrived?"

"Yes, sir, I'm from Saucedo, and I've only been here a few hours," the young woman answered with an easy air.

Lucía was not long in coming, and as she entered the room she said, "To what do we owe this honor, Doña Petronila? And who is this young lady?" and she embraced them both.

Doña Petronila, taking the shawl from her shoulders, exclaimed in her straightforward fashion, "What do you say to this blessed Colonel Paredes, who first sows the seeds of discord in my house and then goes to my friend Don Gaspar's to try to rob him of this jewel?" and she pointed to Teodora.

"Mother!" timidly put in Manuel.

"Bah! Why shouldn't I come right out with it?" Doña Petronila went on. "After all, Don Fernando knows them very well and so does Señora

Lucía," and she gave a detailed account of all that had happened in Saucedo. By the time she had finished, with the Maríns listening and looking first at one newcomer and then at the other, Teodora's cheeks were two cherries and she was staring at the floor, not daring to raise her eyes. She was experiencing one of the most difficult moments of her life, repeatedly joining her feet under her chair and wringing her hands beneath her cashmere shawl. Manuel smiled from time to time. Lucía was hemming the border of her delicate handkerchief, alternately twisting and releasing it.

"And so this young lady is a heroine of love, all for the sake of her betrothed?" said Don Fernando.

"Well done! Good for her! Every woman in love should be faithful like her!" Lucía exclaimed.

"What a blessing to find such affection! I envy Mariano," added Manuel.

"Well, I'm delighted by the trick they played on the subprefect. Well done, Señorita Teodora!" said Don Fernando, rising from his seat and shaking Teodora's hand. "It seems to me life in these towns is getting to be more difficult day by day," he went on. "Here everybody's corrupt and nobody chastises wrongdoing or encourages virtue, though, amazingly, there's no comparison between the conduct of the men and that of the women."

"If the women were wicked, too, good Heavens, this place would be unbearable!" Lucía interrupted, putting her handkerchief into her pocket.

"Doña Petronila, you must save your husband and your son, who is a perfect gentleman," said Don Fernando, addressing Manuel's mother, whose eyes gleamed with the light of maternal joy. Manuel smiled and bowed his head, understanding that his friend was aiming to smooth the way for him to convince Doña Petronila.

Lucía came to her husband's support, saying, "Yes indeed, dear friend. This is no place for us any more; we have to fly away to more tranquil climes. We're leaving soon."

"Leaving? You're leaving?" Doña Petronila asked with a start.

"Yes, ma'am, that's what we've decided," Don Fernando answered, seconding Lucía.

"Good Heavens, and I came over here for sad news like that!" said Doña Petronila, to whom Manuel suggested, "Now what we need is for you to make up your mind, Mother, and then we can all feel better."

"We'll see about that."

"What do you mean, 'we'll see'? Ah, we'll soon find out which one of us is going to have his way," replied Manuel, marking his concluding words by tapping his heels against the floor.

"Margarita, Margarita, come here!" Lucía called when she saw the orphan passing near the door. She wanted to see what impression the girl would make on Doña Petronila's heart, for ever since her conversation with her godchild, whose heart felt an inclination toward Manuel stronger than she could gauge, she worried about the orphan's future.

"I'd like to introduce my godchild Margarita," said Lucía, holding the girl's hand and addressing Manuel's mother.

"What a pretty young lady!"

"Charming!"

So said Doña Petronila and Teodora, simultaneously.

"Margarita—that's the name of a flower. Don't you agree that it suits her?" added Manuel, as his mother embraced the orphan, showering on her words of praise that sounded like heavenly music to Manuel's heart, which, drunk with happiness, threatened to burst from his breast.

This scene of joyful tranquillity was interrupted by the arrival of a frightened, tearful, and distraught woman who, as she reached the door, called out sobbing, "Señor Fernando, wiracocha, take pity on us, for Our Blessed Mother's sake!"

"Who is this poor woman?" Marín asked with surprise.

"This is Martina, Tapara's wife," replied Doña Petronila, while Lucía covered her eyes with both hands, murmuring, "Marcela, Marcela! She could be her sister!"

Don Fernando said, "Tell us who you are and what you want."

"I'm the wife of Isidro Champi, the sexton . . ."

These words cleared up the mystery. Don Fernando and Manuel were visibly affected, and the former said, "Ah, I know: your husband's in jail, isn't he?"

"Yes wiracochay, and now they've also taken away all our cattle."

"Who?" "Who did that?" Manuel and Don Fernando asked at the same time.

"The law, sir," was Martina's laconic reply.

"The law! But what law is that?" Manuel asked.

"Heavens! The things that happen!" Doña Petronila exclaimed, while Lucía, moved beyond words, could barely open her lips to tell Margarita, "Go to Rosalía, dear, and ask for a glass of water."

Manuel, who under other circumstances would have regretted Margarita's departure, cast at Señora Marín a glance that betrayed all his gratitude, and continued to look at her for several seconds without opening his lips.

"The justice of the peace and the governor, wiracochay. Have pity on us!" said Martina, falling to her knees before Don Fernando, who, as he reached down to her, repeatedly urged her, "Come, get up . . . and be calm!"

"I swear to you, we'll save you; everything will be all right, just calm down!" said Manuel, drawing closer to Martina.

"And so you won't prosecute us?" Martina asked Don Fernando.

"No, my dear, not at all."

"And you'll save us and get Isidro out of jail and our cattle out of where they penned them up after they took them away?"

"Yes. I'll defend you."

"You will?"

"What cruelty!" "Heartless people!" sounded again and again; and as Martina left, the promises of Don Fernando and Manuel sufficed to fill her with a hope that her loving wifely heart wanted to convey at once to that of her imprisoned husband.

19

The change in the governing authorities of the province took place peacefully. The new subprefect sent the usual circulars to the local officials, invoking Law, Justice, and Equity.

Once the festivities at Teodora's house had ended, Don Gaspar came to Kíllac to give his virtuous daughter a personal account of all that had happened in Saucedo after her flight, to thank his friend Doña Petronila for her hospitality, and to return with Teodora to their peaceful country life until the time should come for her to marry honest Mariano.

No one could account for the whereabouts of Colonel Don Bruno de Paredes, because after a few miles' ride he had dismissed his escort and gone off by himself to look for a safe hiding place. In subsequent days it did transpire that the property tax fund was notably depleted and that the Indian population held a sizable number of receipts for payment of a mandatory individual tax specially invented by his excellency and titled Public Education Fee.

Don Sebastián, dispirited and distressed, was beating his breast, saying over and over again, "Frankly, my wife and Manuel knew what they were talking about; frankly, I'm very sorry I didn't follow their advice."

Such a confession strengthened Manuel's hand as he sought to carry out his plans for the family, which would eventually respect and abide by his views. Manuel did not sleep that night but spent it writing and erasing numbers with a pencil on a sheet of paper and walking rapidly around his room, stopping occasionally to jot something down or rest briefly on the sofa.

"And why am I so anxious to get away from my home town," he said to himself, "when by nature every man loves to see his birthplace flourish? Why not aspire to live here, where Margarita was born and where knowing her made the flower of my love bloom in all its vigor and beauty? Ah, my aversion to this place is all too understandable when I think about my experiences here. A place where neither property nor family is secure will lose its population: whoever can afford to emigrate to a civilized community will do it; and when one finds oneself, as I do, in a lonely struggle against two others, or against five thousand . . . the only recourse is to flee and seek the peace of my family and the eternal springtime of my heart elsewhere . . . Margarita, my Margarita! You would grow numb in the winter of disillusionment on this *puna* where every virtuous sentiment is frozen by the cold of wrongdoing and bad examples. Your beauty shall flourish in a place where your soul is understood and your loveliness admired. You shall be the sun that gives me warmth and life beneath an alien tree!"

Countless glistening strands fluttered and floated through the mind of Doña Petronila's son, bearing a swarm of fond dreams that two powerful forces, the nobility of his sentiments and the purity of his passion, kept alive in his heart. Deep in thought, he took a few absentminded turns around the room, then drew a cigarette from a small rubber case. Manuel rarely smoked. Tobacco was for him not a vice but a form of recreation. He prepared the cigarette and, after lighting it from the tallow candle, taking three puffs on it, and blowing out the smoke through his mouth and nostrils, said, "Yes! They're leaving soon. I'll join them, even if it's in the farthest corner of the earth! And once we're far away from Kíllac, far from the scene of the tragedy of the fifth of August, I'll reveal my heart to Don Fernando, I'll ask for Margarita's hand; and once I've been accepted and we've agreed on a time, I'll work with faith and enthusiasm to complete my chosen course of study. Yes, my decision is made! I'll reveal the secret of my birth to Don Fernando, to Lucía, to my

Margarita, because that revelation will guarantee my happiness; but . . . first I'll talk to my generous mother, on whose head I can never bring . . . even the shadow of dishonor. Mother, dearest Mother! Fate placed me in your womb, and ever after . . . ay! . . . my existence has been the torment of your life and drawn the aversion of a stepfather. And now that I'm a man, why is the warmth of my affection not for you alone? . . . Margarita! . . ."

Through cracks in the door and window, the serene first light of a new day crept into Manuel's bedroom, where he had spent a sleepless night from dusk to dawn, the first sleepless night he owed to love and duty.

20

Doña Petronila had visited the Maríns not only to introduce Teodora and bring the news from Saucedo, but also to ask Don Fernando to intercede with the new subprefect; and therefore, as soon as Martina, the sexton's wife, had left, she said, "My dear Don Fernando, I've come to trouble you with a request."

"No trouble at all, my dear Doña Petronila."

"I've heard you're a friend of the new subprefect's."

"I do know him, but very slightly; still . . . what did you have in mind?"

"Too bad! I wanted a letter to certify that my friends Teodora and Don Gaspar are worthy citizens entitled to be treated with respect. After all that's happened, you can imagine how those poor folks are trembling when they think they may get other boorish visitors like that colonel," said Doña Petronila, fastening her shawl.

"I'm sorry to say I can't help you directly, but I'll try to use the influence of a friend," Marín answered.

"Salas is related to the new subprefect," Lucía pointed out.

"Yes, but I don't plan to appeal to him but to Guzmán, because he'll help me to work on behalf of Isidro Champi."

"And meanwhile you, Doña Petronila, could see how Don Sebastián might take care of this matter of the sexton," Lucía recommended.

"Leave it to me, and . . . I'll see you soon," said Doña Petronila, preparing to leave with Teodora and Manuel, to whom Don Fernando said, "We'll get together soon to decide about Champi."

Margarita, who had left the room in search of Rosalía, was breathing easier away from her godmother, whose glances she had come to distrust after the revelation she had made to her and the way she had spoken of Manuel. When, plunged in sorrow, a heart struggles for breath, it draws from solitude an air redolent of melancholy and warmed by the balsam of consolation.

Love is like a plant. In rich, fertile soil, it grows with surprising rapidity. Margarita's vigorous temperament and robust constitution favored the powerful swell of her inclination toward Manuel, as did the circumstances in which fate had placed her and which revealed to the fourteen-year old girl all the impulses of a mature mind and all the joys of a twenty-year old heart.

When Don Fernando and his wife found themselves alone in the parlor, Lucía said, "Don't call it a case of woman's intuition, Fernando dear, but I think I can tell that Margarita and Manuel love each other, and . . ."

"I'd be happy if that were the case."

"But Fernando! What about propriety and conscience? Margarita is the daughter of Marcela, a heroic mother and the victim of Don Sebastián; and Manuel is the son of her murderer!"

"There I'm one step ahead of you, sweetheart," said Don Fernando, smiling and taking Lucía's hand. "Manuel has hinted to me that there's some mystery about his birth. I expect to know that story in due time, but I assure you I've never believed that such a worthy young man could be the son of Don Sebastián. I've never thought so, even before Manuel let a few words slip in an unreserved moment."

"Good Heavens! That ugly old fellow! Maybe you are a step ahead of me, Fernando. What you're telling me may help to solve a problem that's very painful for me, because I've planted the seed of antipathy in our Margarita's young heart."

"How did you do that?" Don Fernando asked in surprise, releasing Lucía's hand and looking at her intently.

"By pointing out to her that Manuel is the son of the man who killed her mother."

"That was most unwise!" Marín exclaimed bitterly; but then, as though he had found a remedy, he added, "If she loves him, no hatred will have sprung up, and the day she finds out that Manuel is no son of the corrupt governor of Killac will be a doubly happy one."

"From today on, Fernando dear, I'll do what I can to wipe away the shadow that my rash words have cast on my godchild's heart. I do realize that Manuel would be a truly desirable match for our Margarita."

"None better, my dear Lucía. I love studious and serious young people who are spurred to work by their own impulses. That's why I love Manuel; and I can foresee that he'll be a distinguished attorney, an ornament of our legal system. Apart from that, Lucía, you should know that his financial situation is more than adequate for the comfortable support of a family."

"I can't tell you how delighted I am by what you're saying, Fernando. They must find happiness!"

"We're duty bound to strive for Margarita's happiness, darling."

"Yes, dearest Fernando. That's what I swore to Marcela when on the threshold of death she gave into my keeping the secret that Margarita is the daughter of that man, with all the details I told you. Then Margarita will be as happy as I am, if she loves Manuel the way I love you, Fernando."

"Flatterer!" said Don Fernando affectionately, embracing Lucía.

Why had Lucía revealed Marcela's secret to Don Fernando? Is it true that a woman can never keep a secret? No! Lucía loved her husband too much to keep anything from him; and we must understand that marriage entails an intimacy that embodies the charming vision of two souls blended into one, allowing the happy husband to read, as in an open book, in the heart of his wife, who when she gave him her hand gave also the tenderness of a loving soul as an offering of everlasting love sworn before the altar of God.

Marriage ought not to be, as people generally think, merely the means for the propagation and conservation of the species. Such may perhaps be the propensity of the senses; but something higher exists in the aspirations of the soul that seeks the responsive throb of another soul, the two forming a single spiritual being united by the power of memory, will, and understanding, and linked by the holy bonds of love.

When Lucía, born and raised in a Christian home, put on a bride's white robe, she left the business and tumult of life to her husband and chose for herself the new home and the joys of the love of her new family, fondly recalling those great words of the Spanish author that in her childhood she had more than once read by her mother's side: "Poor women," she had written, "forget your dreams of emancipation and liberty. Those are but theories of diseased minds that can never be put into practice, because woman is born to poeticize the home."[31] Lucía's calling was to teach through motherhood, and Margarita was the first pupil to whom she would transmit the domestic virtues.

"Very well, Fernando; it's resolved that I completely change my mind about the love between Manuel and Margarita, for whom I'll think of an explanation within the limits of prudence," Lucía answered.

"Fine, but I have to do something about the sexton and his poor family."

"Fernando, dear Fernando! My heart trembles with fear. Ah, when Martina came I thought I was seeing the image of Marcela, and you have no idea what gloomy forebodings came to my mind. I didn't say anything, I kept quiet, because you come first, and I'm afraid . . ."

"Don't be afraid, sweetheart. I won't charge into anything head-on, but I can't just let them calmly murder yet another man."

"I wish we were already far away from here so I wouldn't have to see these things! . . . And what will Manuel do?"

"Be patient, darling; you won't be in this hateful place much longer. Manuel will take care of everything, together with Guzmán; and I'm going to write to Guzmán this very minute," said Don Fernando, going to his study. Lucía also left the parlor.

Seated at his desk, Don Fernando wrote as follows:

Kíllac, December 13, 187–

Señor Don Federico Guzmán
Aguas-Claras

My dear friend:

I am about to move to Lima, a decision I have reached for reasons well known to you.

I need your friendship and influence with the new subprefect in order to free Isidro Champi, our town sexton, from the jail where the real culprits of the attack of August 5 have confined him. I am wholly convinced that this Indian is innocent; but nothing can be done here against the concerted machinations of the local gentry who make up the three powers of our society: the executive, the judicial, and the ecclesiastical. I can almost guarantee that the real culprits are Estéfano Benites, Pedro Escobedo, and Governor Pancorbo, now that Father Pascual Vargas has passed away.

---

31. The source of this quotation is a book of essays by María del Pilar Sinués, *El ángel del hogar* (1859), vol. II, chapter 13. We thank our colleagues Susan Kirkpatrick and Cristina Enríquez de Salamanca for leading us to it.

Perhaps it surprises you that I should ask the executive authorities to intervene in a matter that is before the courts; but if you think for a moment about who administers justice here, you will recognize our need for an upright and well-meaning authority to enforce the laws.

I am not interested in continuing prosecution in this matter. All I want is to save the sexton, whose fate I lament; and that is all I recommend to you. If you can accomplish that, I shall be deeply grateful to you.

I also need a letter of recommendation from you to the subprefect on behalf of Don Gaspar Sierra and his family. Such letters are still accorded great importance around here, my friend; and I see this as a good sign that people still believe in friendship and disinterested favors and have not caught wind of the fact that elsewhere the only possible recommendation is a gold piece.

Call on me for whatever service I can render you, my dear friend. My Lucía sends you her regards, and I remain

Ever faithfully yours,

Fernando Marín

After folding it and enclosing it in a blue envelope, Don Fernando placed his letter in the inner pocket of his coat and left the house, hoping to meet Manuel.

21

Martina rushed panting into her husband's cell; but as she came from the bright light of day, her eyes were temporarily blinded by the darkness reigning in the place. Gradually such scanty light as seeped through the cracks between the adobes obstructing a wide skylight fell on her retina and at last allowed her to make out the walls, the floor, the bench that served as a bed, and, seated on it, her husband, who looked at his visitor not daring to ask her anything, for fear of hearing news of additional misfortunes.

As soon as she could see him, Martina said, enthusiastically, "Isidro, Isidro! Cast sorrow from your heart! The wiracocha Fernando is not prosecuting us. I've seen him, and that's a lie."

"You've seen him?" Isidro asked without any show of interest.

"Yes, I've seen him, I've talked to him, and he's told me he's going to save you, to save us!"

"Is that what he said? And you believe him, don't you?"

"Why shouldn't I believe him? He's not from here, Isidro; and it's only here, in our town, that the devil shook out his poncho and scattered so much trouble and lies."

"And what sort of payment did he ask you for?"

"None at all! He didn't even ask me whether we have any sheep."

"Really?" Isidro asked, opening his eyes wider.

"Really and truly, Isidro; and he says he's not pressing any charges. Ay, ay! I think he'll save us, just as he's taken in Yupanqui's daughters. Believe me, Isidro, otherwise the Machula we pray to, Our Blessed Mother, will be angry . . . The clouds cover the sun, the afternoon grows dark; but the same One who brings on those clouds takes them away again, and the sun comes out and shines and warms us once more."

"Maybe, Martinacha, maybe," said Isidro, sighing and stretching out his legs.

"For Our Blessed Mother's sake, Isidro! Our suffering will also come to an end. No doubt you didn't commend yourself properly to Our Lady when you were ringing the bells at dawn, and that's why all these disasters have fallen on us, like the frost that turns the leaves of corn yellow, and ruins the ears," said Martina, sitting down by her husband.

"That's possible, Martina, but . . . it's never too late to repent! The earth that yields nothing for a year, or two, or three, or even four, suddenly awakens and . . . fills our barn with its harvest."

"That's right, so pray to the Blessed Sacrament and . . . I'll see you tomorrow. Now I'm going for our children."

"What are our children saying? Why don't you at least bring me the little one?"

"When they ask me about you, I say you've gone on a trip. Miguel looks down and is quiet, because he's old enough to understand and I can't fool him. You say I should bring them? Good Heavens, what for? Ay, it's enough that you and I know what a jail is. I'll see you tomorrow," she said, and kissed Isidro with the calm and chaste kiss of the dove.

While this scene took place between Isidro and his wife, several of the townspeople were gathered at Estéfano Benites's house, talking over recent events between one glass and another, when Escobedo arrived and said from the doorway, "All right, what are you drinking? Where there are this many flies, there must be honey."

"Come in, old pal," answered Estéfano, preparing to pour out a glass for the newcomer.

"You'd think he'd been summoned with a constable," said one.

"He just followed his nose; he's smelled the booze," another explained laughingly.

"Sit over here," the first speaker added, offering Escobedo a seat.

"No thanks, old buddies. I'll just have one standing up, because I'm in a rush," Escobedo answered, taking the glass from Estéfano, to whom he whispered, "I need you; there's big trouble brewing!"

"Your health, everybody!" Estéfano toasted, whispering to his friend, "I'll be with you in a minute." And after drinking, they withdrew toward the door, where the following conversation took place sotto voce:

"Do you know that our friend Don Fernando's coming to the rescue of the sexton?"

"Oho! But isn't he supposed to be leaving?"

"Yes, he really is leaving; but that doesn't keep him from wanting to defend that Indian, and if he gets involved we'll lose the whole kit and caboodle."

"That can't happen, we can't just let him take away our four—no, at least eight—cows. Impossible!"

"Don Sebastián's son is also scurrying around . . ."

"What? I can't imagine what that little pedant is after. You're right, there's big trouble brewing."

"So what's your plan?"

Estéfano was still for a few seconds, his eyes on the floor, and then suddenly said, "I'll just disappear, along with the records."

"Fine."

"The important thing now is to know when that rascal Marín is leaving. As for that busybody Manuelito, I'm not afraid of him. After all, Don Sebastián's involved in this; and if worse comes to worst, we'll give him a beating."

"Good! I'll find out right away when Marín's leaving, and what it is they're doing, and . . ."

"And I'll disappear right away into the bowels of the earth. Let 'em try to catch me! Pss!" said Estéfano, letting out a whistle and wiggling his lower lip with his right index finger.

"Marvelous! No sooner said than done, and we'll skin that meddler Marín alive."

"Let's have another drink, and then it's get to work," said Estéfano, holding out his hand to his comrade.

"All right, pal," replied Escobedo, shaking his hand; and they stepped up to the table, filled all the glasses, and Escobedo, inviting his friends to drink, said, "Gentlemen, your health! This one's for the road." He emptied his glass, wiped his mouth on the edge of the tablecloth, and went off to carry out his mission.

22

As day followed day, the clouds were swept from the sky and the financial arrangements made in Manuel's home turned out to be more promising than he had expected. Manuel would go to Lima to enroll in the School of Law. His spirits were buoyed by the hope of living near Margarita, whose enrollment in one of the best schools in the capital had also been decided on.

Meanwhile, all the efforts of Don Fernando and Manuel to free Isidro from jail were fruitless, for the justice of the peace barricaded himself behind a mountain of legalisms, requested a report from the prosecutor's office, and would go no further than to assure the parties of a rapid resolution of the matter.

Don Fernando could no longer delay his departure, and he said to his wife, "My love, I've thought of a way to bring about a general reconciliation between us and these people in Kíllac, but for the sole purpose of getting Isidro released."

"And what's that, Fernando? May God give you an inspiration, because we'd certainly hate to leave with that poor man still in jail."

"We'll give a farewell banquet on the morning of our departure, and there we'll get everyone to pledge support to Isidro. I think these people have put him in jail just to be able to produce a culprit and pass themselves off as innocent. Once we're gone, there's no more reason to go on with the case, and Isidro's sure to be released."

"I approve your plan, Fernando dear; and I'll go right now and give the order to prepare everything, although it's going to cost us quite a bit, because I've noticed that in Kíllac they take advantage of you when you first get here and again when you're leaving."

"That makes no difference, dear. So much money is wasted on useless things! And anyhow, let's call it a whim of ours to want to set that Indian free. A hundred *soles* ought to be more than enough, don't you think?"

"Much more than enough, dear. Don't you know that a chicken costs twenty centavos, a pair of pigeons, ten centavos, and a whole sheep, sixty centavos?"

"Good Lord, that little! And still there are people who want to steal from the Indians!"

"Yes, you may well wonder at that! Poor Indians! Poor race of people! If only we could free all of them as we're going to save Isidro!"

So Lucía was saying when there was a knock at the door. It was Manuel, who was coming with a roll of papers in his hand. He greeted the Maríns, set his hat on a chair, and said to Don Fernando, "I'm very frustrated, Señor Marín. After so much running around and after submitting these two petitions that have already been ruled on, it turns out that Estéfano Benites has the records and that he's not to be found in Killac. His wife has assured me he's gone to Saucedo and will be back in three or four days."

"How annoying, friend Manuel!" Don Fernando replied.

"Maybe he's gone into hiding. That young fellow has every mark of a Pontius Pilate," Lucía suggested.

"I don't think he's done that, señora, because there's no personal interest involved here," Manuel replied.

"The worst of it is that I can't put off the day of our departure. When the train whistles for us . . . ," said Don Fernando, shaking his head.

"You're still planning to leave tomorrow?" asked Manuel.

"Tomorrow, my friend; everything's ready, and if we stayed on we'd have a delay of two weeks. We have to travel five days on horseback; and the train only leaves from the Andes Station, the last on the line, every two weeks. Anyhow, since you're staying . . ."

"Yes, Señor Marín, I'll do all I can."

"Maybe your plan will solve everything, Fernando," said Lucía.

"We'll see. I'm planning to invite everyone to a farewell luncheon tomorrow and talk to everyone there about Isidro, get everyone's support, plead . . ."

"An excellent idea, Señor Marín, and I think we can hope for favorable results."

"I've got an idea, Fernando: send an invitation to Pilate, and if he's here, he's sure to come," said Lucía.

"Well, now, I see you've re-christened the man," Marín answered with a laugh.

Manuel added, "It won't be a waste of effort, because when he gets back he'll see you didn't exclude him, and maybe he'll be prepared to help us."

"Very well, let's get started with the invitations, because I no longer have anything else to do. I'm free, thank God!" said Marín.

"And I'm going to reconnoiter in the kitchen, because an unhurried cook makes the dish tasty and substantial," said Lucía, leaving the room.

"Well, your wife's idea is very much to the point, Señor Marín. Do you know that this invitation for Benites, or Pilate, to use your wife's witty expression, is most important?" Manuel asked Don Fernando.

"Ah, my dear friend, women will always outdo us in insight and imagination. Lucía comes up with things that just delight me! I can assure you I feel more in love with my wife every day; and I hope, Manuel, that when you marry you'll be as happy as I am," said Marín.

Manuel lowered his eyes, his cheeks turned scarlet, and the name of Margarita flashed through his mind, shrouded in the gossamer mist of his dreams; and hiding his emotion, he asked, "How shall we phrase Estéfano's invitation?"

"That's easy. Here's pen and paper," said Don Fernando, seating himself at the table; and after writing a few lines, he held out the sheet to Manuel, who read the following:

Kíllac, the 15th

Señor Don Estéfano Benites
City

My dear friend:

    As I must depart for Lima tomorrow and wish to take a most cordial leave of the leading citizens of Kíllac, I hope to have the pleasure of lunching with all of them tomorrow; and since you are one of those whom I wish to embrace as I leave town, perhaps forever, I beg you to favor me with your presence at the above-mentioned luncheon.

Yours faithfully,
Fernando Marín

"Excellent, Señor Marín! This is one of those cases where, as they say, we shake the hand we'd like to see cut off," said Manuel, folding the sheet.

"Right! Life's full of sham, isn't it?"

"It's nothing we can change, Don Fernando. All right, I'll take charge of sending this note with a servant."

"Thanks, my friend; and tell Don Sebastián and Doña Petronila to be sure to come, won't you?"

"I will, and I'll see you soon," said Manuel, taking his hat and leaving the room.

23

More than twenty horses stood saddled in the courtyard of the white house, for the residents of the town, once they had received Don Fernando's invitation, decided to pay him the customary honor of accompanying him in his departure for the distance of a league. Twelve mules, in full traveling harness, were being loaded with suitcases, trunks, and leather bags for bedding. These were Don Fernando Marín's last hours in Kíllac.

Manuel and his family were among the first guests to arrive and to be courteously received. The table had been set in the ample dining room and bore, as specialties of the season, aromatic strawberries and purple plums, artistically displayed in white china bowls. Next to them, enormous platters stimulated the appetite with pigeons marinated in cider vinegar, bearing sprigs of parsley in their beaks. The parlor was overflowing with people; and the Jew to whom Don Fernando had sold his furnishings was walking from one side to another with a worried face, as though on guard lest his newly acquired property should suffer any damage.

Margarita and Rosalía, dressed in deep mourning, crossed the courtyard with its hubbub of animals and baggage handlers and were led by a servant to the cemetery, there to pray for the last time at their parents' grave and shed a parting tear, precious beyond their childish comprehension. Lucía saw to it that the flame of filial love should ever burn bright in the hearts of the two orphans.

The cemetery of Kíllac is a poor dilapidated place. No mausoleum there trumpets vanity, no inscription tells of virtues. Only small mounds of earth, marked with rough-hewn wooden crosses, tell us that human remains rest in its bosom. But Don Fernando and Lucía, kind and caring even with the grave of Juan and Marcela, had had a cross of white stone placed on it. Margarita knelt at its foot, her heart naturally disposed toward any scene rich in tender sentiments. Her mother's death had left her like the fledgling nightingale, unable as yet to find nourishment and a tree in which to build its nest. Now she came before her mother's ashes with a heart full of consummate love.

"Mother, Father, goodbye!" said Margarita after reciting the Our Father and the Hail Mary, whose words, learned from Lucía, she made Rosalía repeat one by one. Can a child of Rosalía's age know what it means to say farewell forever to a mother's grave, to the sacred urn that holds the ashes of supreme love? Oh endless sorrow! It might be all that henceforth would fill a heart no longer warmed by a parent's love.

While the two orphans are engaged in this visit, let us see what is happening in the white house. Just as the party was about to enter the dining room, Estéfano Benites appeared. Don Fernando, Lucía, and Manuel, on seeing him, exchanged a look worth a whole treatise on moral philosophy; and Lucía smiled in triumph.

"Madam, dear sir," Estéfano quickly said; and to Marín he added, "Just this morning I've come back from a little trip to Saucedo; and when I found your note I came over right away without even changing horses, because I do want to join your party."

"Thank you so much, Don Estéfano; I expected no less from your kindness," replied Don Fernando.

Just then lunch was announced.

"Doña Petronila at the head of the table," Don Fernando decided.

"No, sir, that wouldn't be right while our vicar is here," that lady replied.

"Yes, the father should preside," declared several guests.

"As you wish; I was just thinking that the ladies . . ."

"Yes, my dear Don Fernando, you're quite right; Doña Petronila should sit there, and I'll make myself comfortable right here," the vicar decided.

"Don Sebastián, over here."

"Frankly, I'm fine anyplace."

"Is everybody settled?"

"Yes, everybody," came the general reply.

"Can I offer you a glass of bitters?" Don Fernando asked.

"Whatever you have, sir; one thing's as good as another to whet the appetite," said the vicar.

"For me, frankly, there's nothing like Majes liquor; I'll just have a glass of that," said Don Sebastián, who had replaced his cape with a vicuña poncho with bands of blue silk.

"Gabino, serve everybody," Don Fernando ordered the butler.

"And what will Señora Lucía have?" asked Manuel.

"I'll have a little wine, and your mama will keep me company," Lucía answered.

Once everyone had been served, Don Fernando rose and said, "Ladies and gentlemen! I didn't want to leave this generous town that has received me so hospitably without taking leave of its distinguished good citizens, and so I've taken the liberty of bringing you together for this modest lunch. I raise my first glass to the health and prosperity of the people of Kíllac."

"Hear, hear!" "Bravo, bravo!" was repeated by every male voice; and the banquet proceeded in joyful fellowship and with good and varied dishes, not excluding roast kid. Manuel was seated by the side of Lucía and whispered to her, "What has become of your godchild, señora?"

"Margarita and Rosalía have gone to pay a farewell call; they had an early lunch."

"That's how it had to be since you're leaving today."

"But they'll be back soon."

The level of noise was rising steadily, and of course the atmosphere grew more relaxed. Don Fernando, who was keeping a close eye on everything, rose again and said, "Ladies and gentlemen! I'd like to ask for your attention once more, so I can beg my friends for a token of their affection. I want to carry only pleasant impressions away from Kíllac, and not leave behind any kind of misfortune. I think there's a man in jail now—the sexton, it seems—and I trust all of you will work for his release."

"Bravo!" shouted many of those present, amidst hearty applause lasting several seconds. Once quiet had returned, Don Sebastián, handing the servant the plate he had just cleaned, said, "Let's hear from the vicar. Frankly, he's the one to reply to our host."

The vicar crossed his knife and fork on his plate and wiped his mouth with his napkin.

"Yes, let the padre speak!" shouted some, touching glasses across their plates.

"This really concerns his honor, the judge," said the vicar, turning to Verdejo.

Estéfano and Escobedo exchanged a knowing glance, and Verdejo answered, "As far as I'm concerned I wish I could release every last one o' them prisoners, because they give me more headaches than my wife."

The assembly burst out laughing, amused by Don Hilarión's joke, while Escobedo, in a low voice, said to Estéfano, "Let's see that platter of artichokes over here, my friend."

"If that's what you want, but I can see you're no gourmet," replied Benites, passing him the platter.

"So can we consider the release settled?" asked Manuel as soon as the uproar had subsided.

"As far as I'm concerned, Don Manuelito, how can I say no?" replied the judge.

"Well then, to the release of my sexton!" the vicar proposed.

"Yes, gentlemen, another glass, and . . . time to go," said Don Fernando, addressing the last words to Lucía, who replied, "Yes, dear, let's go; it's after one."

"Gentlemen, your health!"

"Bon voyage, Señor Marín!"

"What a delicious meal! But just the same, I won't skip the chocolate, which is no doubt from Cuzco," said the vicar, setting down the glass he had just drained and wiping his mouth on his napkin.

Margarita and Rosalía, who had just laid a tear and a prayer on the altar of their filial love, returned to the white house, where all was in readiness for departure, as the guests were beginning to leave the dining room. Manuel, as he went to embrace the orphan, was overflowing with happiness, because, with all obstacles now miraculously overcome, dreams as rosy as the shimmering clouds that border the horizon held sway over those youthful hearts, while auguring joyful days to Don Fernando and Lucía, who were eager to weave the garlands of flowers that would forever bind that charming couple.

Manuel! Margarita! God grant that those ruby-colored clouds might never turn leaden and somber!

Virtue, that golden summer sun whose gleaming locks, reaching from the heavens to the earth, make all things beautiful, and which gives warmth and life to all things for the young, presenting a happily smiling universe to those who love and hope, had not folded its wings in Lucía's home, though the harmony of creation, to be complete, also requires man to struggle.

Manuel and his mother had already agreed on their voyage to Lima; but the son would go first to make the necessary arrangements for lodging, investment of their funds, and so forth, and it had been decided that he would take the next train to join Don Fernando and his family, who would be waiting for him in the Gran Hotel so as to go on together until they reached the shores of Callao.

"Goodbye, Señora Lucía."

"Goodbye, my friend."

"Dearest Margarita!"

"All the best, Don Fernando."

"Be sure to come again!"

"Don't forget Kíllac!"

"Oh to be leaving, too!"

"Leaving is forgetting, and staying is regretting."

"Goodbye! Goodbye!"

Those were the expressions, some cursory, others heartfelt, that filled the air.

Lucía, in an elegant riding habit, Russian leather gloves, and a Panama hat with a blue veil, was about to set foot in the stirrup when she dropped her elegant ivory-handled crop. Don Sebastián, who stood close by, hastened to pick it up.

At that moment a detachment of armed men appeared by the front door under the command of a lieutenant of cavalry called José López, who, while his men surrounded the house, addressed Don Sebastián with, "By order of the authorities, you are under arrest, sir."

A bolt of lightning falling in their midst would not have startled the company as did the words of Lieutenant López, who drew a sheet of paper from the pocket of his tunic, unfolded it, and read, "Estéfano Benites, Pedro Escobedo, and Hilarión Verdejo are also under arrest."

"We've been tricked! Don Fernando's trapped us!" Benites shouted angrily.

"A low trick!" Verdejo and Escobedo echoed, shaken.

"And frankly, why am I being arrested?" asked Don Sebastián, while panic spread among the guests, who could not understand the reason for the arrests, having completely forgotten the nocturnal assault of August 5, as well as the right to carry out justice that every newly appointed authority immediately acquires.

Don Fernando, taking no notice of what Benites had said, called Lieutenant López over and asked, "Lieutenant, may I know by whose order these arrests are being made?"

"There's no reason why you shouldn't," López replied, handing Marín the sheet of paper he was still holding.

Don Fernando, as a worried Manuel drew near, learned of a court order, issued at the request of the executive authorities, for the arrest of those named. Thereupon he said to Manuel, "Keep calm like a man, Manuel. Excitement is the worst blindfold for the eyes of reason; deal with the matter dispassionately and directly. Talk to Guzmán, whom I'll write by the next mail."

"Lord, it's as though it were all a plot!" Verdejo was saying.

"This is impossible! What? We should go to jail?" Escobedo and Benites were shouting.

"I suppose this incident will delay your departure," Don Fernando said to Manuel, who, white as a sheet, replied, "I'll manage to get out."

"I beg you all not to be so alarmed; all this will be resolved in a few days, I guarantee it," said Don Fernando, trying to restore calm.

"There's no cause for despair," added Lucía, also anxious to subdue the general excitement.

"Mount your horses; it's time to leave!" Don Fernando ordered in a loud voice, and two groups left the house in very different directions: one, to jail; the other, to the highway.

Manuel stood looking at Margarita, who was shaken and bathed in tears. These tears were a woman's precious pearls that she scattered on the unknown road she was entering on that day, leaving behind her whole world, the world where her cradle had stood and her love been born.

A sad fate, to leave like Margarita!

Sadder still, to stay behind like Manuel, drinking the bitter cup of absence drop by drop with every sigh wrenched from his heart by his soul's tearful yearning for another soul!

24

For the inhabitants of a small town, seeing someone taken to jail is an event comparable to a fire in a larger place. When Don Sebastián, Estéfano, and the rest were led out of Don Fernando's house surrounded by soldiers, the citizens all watched from their doors, an amazing number of boys gathered, and all over town you could hear:

"Jesus, Mary, and Joseph!"

"Lord help me! Can it be?"

"Don Chapaco and Estefito?"

"I can't believe my own eyes!"

"They say Don Fernando tricked 'em, that he asked 'em over so he could have 'em arrested," an old woman informed.

"No, they say he's the one's going to put up bail for them," declared a man as he draped his poncho over his right shoulder.

"Bail, my eye! That's the way these outsiders are: they stir things up and then they take off," said another.

"That's why I ain't had nothin' to do with this one," replied the old woman, turning around and looking about her.

Manuel, employing all his manly fortitude to master the torment in his soul, said to Doña Petronila, "Be brave, Mother. Put your trust in God and don't be frightened." He offered her his arm and led her home through streets as far removed as possible from all the turmoil. Doña Petronila, thoughtful and calm by temperament, shed a few tears and followed her son silently and with a firm step. Once at home, she told him, "Leave me now, Manuel, and go do your duty."

Manuel, who already had some general knowledge of the law, immediately drew up a petition challenging the jurisdiction of the court, arguing his father's innocence, and offering to produce supporting witnesses, a list of whom he attached on a separate sheet, along with the questions they were to answer within the time required by law. Then he went to the office of the judge who was to handle the case and spoke with several persons. He spent that whole night studying the criminal code, marking certain articles with a pencil, and writing lengthy drafts on large sheets of paper. He opened his desk drawer, took out some papers, and began to go through them.

"This is Isidro Champi's defense. Shall I take it up today, too, and thus defend the innocent and the guilty at the same time?" he asked himself. "Life is strange! Good and evil, so mysteriously intertwined! And what with all this, how long till I can leave Kíllac? How many months, which will seem like centuries, will I be separated from my Margarita?" Manuel asked himself over and over, dropping prostrate on the sofa, resting a few brief moments, and then once more taking up his work and his soliloquies. "The main thing is to free Don Sebastián and Isidro. I'll draw up two separate petitions asking for release under recognizance. Yes, but who will give surety for Isidro? I have to find someone, and tomorrow I will. I can give the necessary guarantees for Don Sebastián myself. Now that I think of it, Don Fernando's told me to arrange things with Señor Guzmán. I'll go see Guzmán and I won't rest till everything's been straightened out and my heart can fly away to its true home . . . Margarita! Margarita!"

Such was Manuel's invocation, raised to the god of slumber and received by the angel of the night, who beat his ethereal wings above the budding lawyer's burning forehead until he fell sound asleep on the sofa of his room, still holding a book in his hand.

Doña Petronila wept and prayed, offering her concern for husband and son to Heaven. She seemed resigned to every disaster, with that Christian resignation that carries man beyond misfortune to the highest peaks of heroism. "I must have faith and hope!" Doña Petronila said to herself, and she waited for the dawning of calm after the dreadful hours of the storm.

25

As the travelers proceeded on their way, they left the raging tempest behind them. Indifferent to the painful scenes in Kíllac, nature displayed her cheerful and varied panoramas, untroubled by their discord with the sadness of certain hearts.

Don Fernando's party trotted over endless pampas teeming with cattle; it crossed hills shaded by mighty trees; it climbed steep rocks whose baldness, like that of the thinker's brow, speaks to us of time and invites us to meditate. During the five days' journey from Kíllac to the railroad station, the traveler treads on wild flowers whose aroma perfumes the air he breathes; then he comes upon the sheer peaks of the Andes, covered with the "combed cotton" of the snows that reflect the sun as it melts them to plunge down in crystal-clear streams; then he descends once more onto the plain, where the grasses wave in the wind and echo its whisperings.

"Fernando, what do you say to what's been happening?" Lucía asked her husband, after riding in silence for some time.

"When I think about the sequence of these events, my dear, I'm overwhelmed. Ah, life seems like a novel!" Don Fernando answered, holding his horse back a little.

"God didn't want us to leave Killac without seeing the guilty punished," said Lucía.

"No, He didn't, sweetheart; we must never doubt that Providence will mete out justice—slowly at times, but surely."

"And so it does, Fernando. People are right when they say, time will bring truth and God will bring justice. What will become of Isidro Champi?"

"I hope he'll be all right. That Indian is innocent, don't you doubt it."

"Me? I've never doubted it. I know that when an unfortunate Peruvian Indian does wrong, it's because oppression forces him into it and mistreatment makes him despair . . ."

"Look out for that ditch! Pull your reins to the right!" Marín warned her.

"Good Lord! If you hadn't warned me I'd have gotten a good scare when my horse jumped."

"That's if you hadn't tumbled right off to stake out your squatter's rights on the ground."

"Well, now, it wouldn't have come to that; I'm not that clumsy a rider. How far is it to the post-station?"

"It's still a way. We'll be settling into lodgings at seven, if we step lively and don't stop to chat."

"In that case, my lips are sealed. Let's go!" said Lucía, applying the whip to her horse.

· · · ·

On those boundless plains the jagged lightning sometimes descends in frightful bands of fire, bringing destruction to the hut and death to the cattle, which flee in terror in search of a sheltered refuge. And in the midst of that imposing solitude, all at once there appear two vibrating serpents of steel, stretched out over the yellowish grass; and above them rise the smoke and steam that, like the powerful breath of a giant, impart life and movement to massive railroad cars. The puffing of the locomotive is suddenly heard, and the whistle that announces progress, brought by the rails to the place where Manco Capac stopped to found the empire of the Incas.

"The train!" shouted those who first saw it. And it was indeed the train pulling into the southernmost station on the line, located in a little town whose straw-thatched and unpainted adobe farmhouses present a melancholy sight to the traveler.

A few hours after they had first glimpsed the train, our travelers had dismounted and were heading for a small room inside the station: Lucía on her husband's arm, lifting the long skirt of her riding habit, the whip hanging from her waist; preceding her, the two girls; and following her, several servants.

"You can all go in here to get ready; I'm going to pay for our tickets and see to the loading of the baggage and the return of the horses," said Don Fernando, releasing his wife's arm and pointing toward the room.

"You, Gabino, bring that green suitcase over here," said Lucía, addressing the servant who was handling their baggage.

"Are we going to change clothes, Godmother?" asked Margarita, loosening the ribbons of her hat.

"Of course, dear; from here on we can't wear riding habits," Lucía replied, drawing a bunch of keys from her pocket, unlocking the suitcase, and adding, "Put on your gray dress with blue ribbons, Margarita. It looks nice on you, and it's a good color for traveling."

"Yes, Godmother. And which one will you wear?" the orphan asked.

"A black one, of course; that's the most elegant color for a lady."

"And it looks so pretty on you!"

"Flatterer! Let's see that hat."

At that moment a freight train was arriving, its bell warning everyone to "clear the way!"

Gabino, when he saw it, began to cross himself, saying, "Lord Almighty! It's the devil! Who else could move all that? *Supay!*[32] *Supay!*"

Just then Don Fernando returned, knocked on the door, and said, "Hurry, hurry! The train waits for no one, madame!"

"Good Heavens! I hope they don't leave us behind!" Lucía exclaimed, tossing into the suitcase the clothes they had just taken off, now lying scattered on the floor.

"Where's the coca extract? You've got to keep it handy because it's good protection against nausea and altitude sickness," said Don Fernando, entering the room.

"Right you are; here's the coca," Lucía replied after searching the suitcase, as she handed her husband a flask carefully wrapped in a sheet of pink paper with the green lettering favored by the press of *La Bolsa* in Arequipa.

32. *Supay*, "The devil!"

"Don't forget the books, either, Lucía; train travel without reading matter is pure torture, you'll see," Don Fernando warned; and when Margarita heard him, she pulled out a package wrapped in an issue of *El Comercio* and tied with coffee-colored cotton ribbons, handed it to Don Fernando, and said, "Here are the books, Godfather. You take them, because I'll take my little sister by the hand."

Don Fernando took the parcel from the girl, put it under his arm, and said, "Here's our food for thought. Gabino, take the suitcase." And they all headed for the carriage in which the women of the group were to take their first journey by rail.

26

In spite of the weighty tasks that Manuel had before him and that might have served him as distraction, sadness marked his face and silence sealed his once talkative lips, which now uttered nothing but sighs of deep sorrow. Waves of blood such as he had never known surged in his heart, waves in which a woman's heart would have seen an omen of misfortune. Manuel was beginning to lose confidence in the future. He questioned the possibility of seeing Margarita again, but he adhered to his plan of settling the cases of Don Sebastián and Isidro and then leaving at any cost.

His meetings with the judge, with the new subprefect, and with Guzmán finally bore fruit, along with the efforts made by the families of Estéfano, Verdejo, and Escobedo. One day he came home and told Doña Petronila, "Mother, I've succeeded in getting Don Sebastián released under my recognizance, and he'll be home today."

"Has the judge already given the order?" she asked eagerly.

"Yes, Mother; we've taken every necessary step, and he'll be here by noon."

"Bless you, my darling son. And what about the others?"

"I don't know anything about the others and I don't care about them. The only one for whom I've done something is Isidro; and he'll be out soon, too. I'd have him out by now if it weren't for the committal and attachment that have to be quashed, and that takes patience."

Doña Petronila had been deeply saddened as she observed her son's mood day after day. Now, after receiving the news of Don Sebastián's impending release, she drew him to her and said, "Quite apart from all this legal business, you're suffering, Manuelito. There's a worm gnawing at your heart that will bring you sorrow and death," and great tears rolled down her cheeks.

"Mother, Mother dearest, why are you crying?"

"And why won't you tell me what's troubling you? My heart is a mother's heart, your mother's heart. Don't ever forget, Manuelito: I only live for you!"

Manuel could resist no longer. He was as weak as a woman. He had suffered so! He threw himself into his mother's arms, hiding the tears of his manhood as in another time he had hidden the toys of his childhood. "Mother! Dearest Mother! God bless you! But . . . it's more than I can bear!" was the reply, interrupted by sobs, of that young man so timid when it came to home and heart, yet so heroic in times of struggle.

"Yes, Manuelito, my boy, I know, I've guessed what worm is gnawing at your soul. Yes, you love Margarita, and you're weeping because you've been separated from her and because you're afraid you'll never see her again."

"Dearest Mother! Forgive me if my heart is no longer yours alone, but that angel whose name you've spoken is the angel of my happiness. Yes, I love her, and perhaps . . ."

"Why are you so downcast, Manuel? Why shouldn't you marry her? Why shouldn't I be happy having two children instead of one?"

"You're my guardian angel, Mother! But remember that Margarita will see me as the son of her parents' murderer, and refuse me her hand and cast me out of her heart."

"What nonsense you're talking, good Heavens! Cast you out?" replied Doña Petronila, raising her folded hands to heaven and sinking for a moment into fretful silence while her son gazed at her lovingly. And as though returning from the intoxication of battle she added, "That's easy to overcome. Talk to Don Fernando, and . . . tell him the name of your real father."

"Mother!"

"Yes. Are we to blame? I was unfortunate then; why shouldn't I suffer a moment of shame now for the eternal happiness of my dear son, for your happiness, Manuelito?" At that moment Doña Petronila was making the supreme sacrifice of a loving mother and a deceived woman.

"Go," she continued, "catch up with them. You can do it; you've got horses and money. Settle your marriage and then come back reassured, so you can devote your full attention to our family affairs and our own journey. You can't think clearly now."

Over and over again, Manuel kissed the forehead and the hands of Doña Petronila, so deeply moved that for many a second no sound was heard but that made by his lips as they touched his mother, down whose glowing cheeks ran copious tears, the purifying water that was to bless the future union of Manuel and Margarita.

Breaking that silence of sublime joy, Doña Petronila said, "That's enough, my dear."

The young man raised his head with manly pride and replied, "This day I swear to you, dearest Mother, that I'll sacrifice my last breath of life for your happiness and that of my Margarita. I'm going right now to make all the arrangements; and tomorrow at the break of dawn I'll set off to catch up with Don Fernando, whose withdrawal of charges and formal reconciliation are no longer so urgent, and I'll ask him for the hand of his godchild."

And having said that, he rushed out, leaving his mother sunk in tender thoughts, which she interrupted with the exclamation, "Oh compassionate Mother of God, pray for him, who is so good, and ask for pardon for me! Manuel! And myself! Can we be guilty, either of us? Was it not the power of dark fate, as dark as a moonless night, that led me into the forbidden arms of a man without faith?" Doña Petronila fell to her knees bathed in tears, repeating a name amid sobs and covering her face with both hands. Her heart and soul bled as she recalled the scenes of twenty years before.

27

An elegant carriage was ready for departure as soon as the train whistle might give the signal to the locomotive, which had been baptized *Socabón*[33] with champagne. Meanwhile, the first-class passengers

---

33. *Socabón,* a town in central Peru.

were looking over the merchandise displayed on both sides of the tracks, where Indian women were offering vicuña gloves, preserved peaches, butter, cheese, and cracklings from the renowned mountain ranches of Peru's interior.

After helping Lucía and the girls to their seats, Don Fernando settled comfortably next to his wife on a bench for two upholstered in red plush. He drew out a cigarette, silently readied it for smoking, and, after lighting it, put away his box of matches, blew out a few puffs of smoke, held the cigarette in his lips, and untied the package of books. Two more times he drew on his cigarette and then said to his wife, "Which one do you want to read, Lucía dear?"

"Give me the poetry of Salaverry,"[34] she answered with a smile of contentment.

"All right; I'll enjoy myself with Palma's *Tradiciones*,[35] which are distinctively Peruvian stories that I find absolutely delightful," said Don Fernando as he handed a volume to his wife. Then he crossed his legs, propping them against the footrest of the neighboring seat, leaned back in his own, and opened his book, which was the second series of *Tradiciones*, just as the train was beginning to travel at fifteen miles an hour, rushing along the track and leaving plains, huts, stables, and meadows behind with dizzying speed.

As Lucía's curious glances fell on them, the various passengers placed near her were also beginning to look for entertainment. A thin, swarthy, bearded officer sat near two elderly civilians, former dealers in cochineal and sugar, to whom he offered the following invitation:

"Should we play a little hand of ombre just to kill the time?"

"Not a bad idea, captain; but where the deuce are we going to find a pack of cards around here?" answered one of the civilians, wrapped in a vicuña muffler. The captain, drawing a pack from his pocket, said, "Lo and behold, Don Prudencio! A soldier who doesn't play, drink, and flirt might as well turn friar."

A Mercenarian friar was sitting across from these three; and suspecting in the captain's remark an allusion to himself, he glared defiantly at the card-players, who, without noticing him in the slightest, flipped over the back of an adjoining seat and thus set up their card table. The friar then took out a book; and three women who were sitting nearby started

---

34. Carlos Augusto Salaverry (1830-91), Peruvian poet.
35. The *Tradiciones peruanas* of Ricardo Palma (1833-1919), a friend of the author's.

to chat with Margarita and Rosalía, offering them apples that they peeled with a pocket knife.

Half an hour later, the girls and the women were sleeping like doves huddled together on a single bench and the friar was snoring away peacefully, his sound slumber undisturbed by the enthusiastic exclamations that came from the card players, when the carriage door opened to admit an individual some thirty years old, tall, thickset, tanned from the cold mountain air, with a neatly trimmed mustache and a fleshy mole on his right ear. He wore gray trousers and jacket and, on his head, a black oilcloth cap; and he carried a ticket punch in his hand. "Your ticket, Reverend?" he said, coming close and raising his contralto voice, whereupon the friar opened his sleepy eyes and indolently drawing a yellow ticket from between the pages of his book, handed it to his interlocutor without saying a word. The conductor punched the piece of cardboard and returned it before going on to the card players.

The two civilians handed over their tickets; and the officer, unbuttoning his tunic, took a piece of paper from his pocket and showed it to the conductor, who, after examining the signatures, returned it while mumbling to himself, "These guys always have some special document." When he got to Don Fernando, and as he was punching their tickets, Lucía asked him, "Could you please tell me how far we've gone?"

"Four hours, ma'am, meaning sixteen leagues; and we've got that much farther to go," the conductor answered, and went on.

"Isn't this a marvelous way to travel? And with no strain or bother, we'll soon be in the city," Don Fernando said to his wife, closing his book.

Lucía, who was looking at the girls, replied, "Marvelous indeed, sweetheart! Look, Fernando, look how cute they are, sleeping there. They're like two angels of peace."

"They must be New World angels, what with all that Peruvian blood that gives color to their cheeks."

"Do you suppose Margarita's dreaming of Manuel? Not yet, I think." And at that moment her godchild's large eyes raised their curved lashes and fixed their gaze on her.

That stretch of the route included an iron and wooden bridge, elegantly spanning a shallow river. More than once the train's whistle sounded the alarm, for a herd of cows occupied the very midpoint of the bridge, unnoticed by the engineers until the animals began to flee in terror, though not quickly enough for the speed of the train. The efforts of the chief engineer and brakemen and the gallop of the herd did not suffice to avoid a collision, and an accident became inevitable. The animal on wheels snorted like a wild beast, sowing first confusion and then consternation among the passengers, whose death was almost certain.

"Lord have mercy!"

"God help us!"

"Dearest husband!"

"Lucía! Girls!"

"Godmother!"

"Godfather!"

"What's going to happen to us?"

"Brutes!"

"Lord have mercy!"

All this sounded in a variety of tones amidst the confusion and frightful shouts that filled the carriages; but, cooped up as they were, what chance was there of flight? The whole train was traveling with the destructive speed of lightning. It reached the cattle and ran over them, crushing their bones and jumping its track. It was about to fall into the river!

Mr. Smith, the brave engineer, preferred to sacrifice his own life rather than all those others entrusted to his care, and tried to pierce the boilers with bullets from his revolver; but it was too late, and the first-class carriage, uncoupled by a brakeman, came to rest on the wet sands of the left bank of the river.

28

Manuel's efforts had increased a hundredfold in the course of the day. He came home and told his mother, "Everything's going well, Mother; it seems as though God is watching over my hopes. Don Sebastián and Champi are getting out of jail. The order's just been sent to the warden, and when the time comes I'll go for Don Sebastián myself."

"So the judge has agreed . . . And what conditions did he impose?" asked Doña Petronila.

"Just that he keep himself available and not leave town."

"And so we won't be able to go away?"

"You two won't, but I'm leaving tomorrow so I can take the Thursday train and catch up with Don Fernando and my Margarita."

"But the case is still going on, son, and your father won't know how to deal with it."

"I've taken care of everything for the few days I'll be gone; and besides that, when I come back I'll bring Don Fernando's written withdrawal of the charges, so it wouldn't matter if I hadn't," Manuel replied, walking about the room.

"Or would it be better if you wrote to ask for those papers and for Margarita's hand?" said Doña Petronila, as though regretting that she had agreed to her son's immediate departure.

"Mother, Mother! Under other circumstances writing would be the proper thing to do, but remember that I have to explain something . . . ," Manuel reminded her.

"Yes, yes, I understand, but . . ."

"Mother! A twenty-year-old heart, fiery and passionate, does not shrink from danger; it's delay that kills it. I'm going. I'll settle my engagement and then come straight back to you."

"What can I say?" she replied, shaking her head.

"Do you have confidence in me, Mother?"

"Absolutely, son. Why do you ask?"

"Because I see you're not sure, and because you've got to understand that apart from my love for Margarita, there's always my duty toward you and my concern for Don Sebastián, even though he treated me like a true stepfather when I was a boy."

"Why bring up all that? Now he treats you well . . . ," said Doña Petronila, just as Don Sebastián appeared, accompanied by one of the servants.

"Chapaco!" said Doña Petronila, running to embrace her husband.

"You beat me to it!" Manuel exclaimed.

"Petruca!" said Don Sebastián, returning his wife's embrace and adding, to Manuel, "So you didn't come back? Frankly, I thought you'd come for me."

"You got ahead of me, Don Sebastián, because I came to give the news to Mother so she wouldn't be startled at seeing you all of a sudden, and I was just about to go for you."

"Well, fine. What do you have to drink, Petruca? Frankly, I'm thirsty enough to . . ."

"I'll make you a *chabela*.[36] We've got some good **chicha** and good wine."

"Bring it on!"

"Since you're home now, I'll ask you for your blessing and your permission, Don Sebastián."

"How's that? Frankly, I don't understand you."

"You are my second father. I plan to ask for the hand of Margarita, and that will really put an end to all these quarrels," said Manuel, carefully measuring his words.

"I don't disapprove of your intentions, Manuelito; frankly, that girl is a jewel, but she's still a baby, and in these times . . . Frankly, it's no time to be getting hitched," Don Sebastián replied.

"I'm not talking about marrying right away, Don Sebastián; I want to ask for her hand, and once we're engaged, go on with my studies, become a lawyer, and fulfill . . ."

"That's different, son; frankly, I'm delighted."

"He wants to go and catch up with Don Fernando," said Doña Petronila from the other side of the room, where she was preparing the *chabela* on the table.

"That's nonsense! Frankly, Manuel, I must tell you that that's ridiculous, a schoolboy's caper, do you understand?"

"Don Sebastián, I absolutely have to go. I'm not needed here, and I have to get the withdrawal of charges from Don Fernando so that this case will be closed and we're not bothered with it any more. Otherwise we'll be in court till Judgment Day."

"Now that's another story, frankly. I don't mind if Manuel goes, so give him my gold watch and my vicuña poncho with the blue bands," Don Sebastián announced, addressing Doña Petronila, who was bringing him a glass containing a curious mixture, yellow on the bottom and red on top.

"Obviously it's all a question of whom we're talking about, Chapaco," said Doña Petronila, handing her husband the glass.

"Aha! Well, there's a difference between a bellyache and a toothache, frankly," said Don Sebastián, coughing and taking hold of the glass.

"Heavens, what a cough! You must have caught cold in jail, poor dear."

Don Sebastián drank his *chabela* to the last drop, savoring it with a sound that resembled that of a kiss, wiped his mouth, and declared, "A

36. *Chabela,* a mixed drink of the Andean region.

delicious *chabela!* Frankly, Petruca, it puts hair on a man's chest," and then he asked Manuel, "How and when do you plan to go?"

"Early tomorrow morning, sir."

"All right. Give him all he needs, Petruca; and let him choose some horses and so on, because, frankly, how they treat you out there depends on the impression you make."

"Thank you, sir. You're very kind," Manuel replied, and he left to attend to his preparations.

It was nine o'clock in the evening when Manuel returned and entered his mother's room, where he found Don Sebastián in intimate conversation with Doña Petronila.

"Good evening, Don Sebastián. Mother dear, I've come to say goodbye. With God's help, everything's settled," said Manuel.

"Darling son! May the Blessed Virgin watch over your life and health and bring you back to me," Doña Petronila answered, taking a scapulary of the Virgin of Mount Carmel from around her neck and placing it on Manuel's chest as she tenderly embraced him.

"Don Sebastián, watch your step . . . keep to yourself . . . don't talk. No one will bother you. And don't worry about me. And now another hug. Goodbye!"

"Hurry back. Frankly, I have great hopes for your trip. Do you have the watch?" were Don Sebastián's parting words to Manuel, who left to rest in his room, for at daybreak, buoyed by his hopes and spurred by the vigor of his youth, he was to set out on the same road where only a few days before he had seen his fair Margarita disappear.

Isidro Champi, accompanied by his faithful Martina and followed by Zambito and Desertor, also came home that day, pale and dejected. As soon as his children saw him, they ran toward him, like partridge chicks that espy their mother. The sexton's heart, gloomy as the cave we hear about in tales of witchcraft, received light and warmth from the kisses of his children, whom he embraced without a word.

Martina walked slowly into the hut and knelt in the middle of the room, raising her folded hands to heaven. *"Allpa mama!"*[37] she exclaimed; and with that exclamation she buried in her breast all the accusations that her wounded soul might have brought against the unjust race of men, as represented by the gentry of Kíllac, and her eyes shed copious tears.

---

37. *Allpa mama,* "Mother Earth!"

"Are you crying, Martinacu? Is it still raining in your heart?" asked Isidro as he watched his wife.

"Ay, husband," replied Martina, getting to her feet, "sorrow floats on tears as the gull floats on the still waters of our ponds, and like the gull it revives its breast even as it wets its feathers. Ay, ay!"

The company of his children seemed to console Isidro; but as he took pleasure in calling out their names, he came to remember his lost heifers and said with a sigh, "The little brown one! The black one . . ."

"Ay, Isidro! In the stormy night, when the lightning falls and the thunder echoes from the rocks, people hide in their huts and the puma and the foxes come out of their lairs to steal the lambs. We've gone through a fierce storm," said Martina, setting her littlest daughter on the bed.

"You're right, and what can we do about it? These foxes in white shirts have stolen our cattle, just as they stole my freedom and as they steal the fruits of our daily labor," said Isidro, agreeing, even enthusiastically, with his wife's words, and lying down on the bed next to his little girl.

"We have ways of defending ourselves against the puma and the fox, but there's no way to get rid of these others. Be patient, Isidro, be patient; death is sweet for those in sorrow," Martina went on, sinking once more into melancholy.

"The grave must be as restful as a moonlit night when you hear the shepherd playing his *quena*. Ay, if we didn't have these little chicks, we'd be so glad to die, wouldn't we?" asked Isidro, pointing to the children running and jumping around Miguel, the eldest; and Martina answered, "We were born Indians, the slaves of the priest, slaves of the governor, slaves of the headman, slaves of all those who manage to get the whip hand."

Isidro Champi, placing a folded poncho under his head as a pillow, repeated, "Indians! Yes, only death offers us the sweet hope of freedom."

Martina had lain down next to her husband; and to distract him from his sorrows, she ran her fingers through his hair and asked, "Will you go up in the tower again?"

"Maybe," he replied, "I'll ring those cursed bells again tomorrow, much as I loathe them now."

29

The first to jump onto the ground, sinking into mud up to his knees, was Mr. Smith, who at the top of his lungs and in his broken Spanish shouted, "Don't anybody move, all right? Everybody just stay put!"

Numerous heads immediately peered out of the carriage's windows, now bereft of all glass. The collision that had caused the derailment had also produced some fortunately slight wounds.

"What a scare! Enough to make our hearts stand still! Were you very frightened, my love?" Don Fernando said to Lucía.

"Terrified, darling! It's a miracle we're alive."

"You're very pale. I wonder whether the bottle of coca broke," said Marín, looking for a small bag.

"Good Lord!" Lucía exclaimed again, peering through the window to see what sort of place they were in and paying no attention to the cries of Margarita, who was holding a Rosalía drenched in blood, nor to the commentaries of the other passengers.

"Damn, that was a close one!" said the officer.

"We've been given a new lease on life, praise God," the friar declared.

"You know, these dumb gringos are capable of taking us down into the bowels of the earth," said one of the card players, to which the other added, "I was afraid of something like this ever since I saw the reverend get on."

"Hush! There are ladies present," his partner urged.

"Well, and how do we get out of here?"

"The coca extract made it, so I'm going to give you a little, darling," said Don Fernando, searching his pocket for a knife with a corkscrew.

"Fortunately we were derailed after we passed the bridge, so we can fix everything," said a brakeman running from one end of the carriage to the other with a roll of rope while various voices bombarded him with questions.

"What do we do now?"

"It's all right, boss, everything's all right, it's all over," the brakeman replied.

While all this was happening in the first-class carriage, the second-class passengers, who were at the other end of the train and whose car had been uncoupled in time, ran toward the one stuck in the mud, shouting, "Paulino!" "Is that you, Indalecio?" "Over here!" "What the devil!"

"Stay calm, ladies and gentlemen; this isn't my fault, do you understand that? It's the fault of those cows, and we'll soon fix things up," said Smith, the engineer, embellishing the language of Castile with his Yankee tongue and instilling confidence in the shaken spirits of the first-class passengers.

"When will we get there, Mr. Smith? We almost didn't make it," Don Fernando asked of the engineer, with whom he was acquainted.

"Oh, Señor Marín, it's bad luck I've had! But we'll get there tomorrow morning; just be patient," replied Mr. Smith, as he supervised the operations he had already got under way. And with characteristic Yankee energy, wheels and bearings were set in motion that after two hours' constant effort freed the mired carriage and replaced it on the rails, ready to continue on its way.

"We really have been given a new lease on life. Poor little dears!" said Lucía, using her handkerchief to wipe away the blood that issued from Rosalía's lips as the result of something hitting her mouth.

"Good Heavens! Hush, dear! Poor child!" added Don Fernando, bringing the little girl a package of Arturo Field cookies and placing it in her hands.

"It'll still take us five hours," said the captain of artillery.

"These things can only happen in Peru; anywhere else they'd skin the gringo alive," remarked the dealer in cochineal.

"I'm still scared out of my wits."

"Me, too—Lord!" said the two women.

And the train went on its way, speeding along steadily as though the disaster had never occurred.

Once again the whistle sounded insistently.

"Another accident?" several passengers asked in surprise.

"No; this is the second station of the city. They're signaling our arrival," the officer explained.

"Lord, how a scare like that puts our nerves on edge," observed Lucía.

"It really was pretty serious," Don Fernando answered.

Soon the voyagers were pointing through the broken windows at a white spot in the middle of a cheerful bright green panorama.

"Arequipa!" some exclaimed. And the whistle screamed again, like an animal goaded by a sharp instrument.

"What a beautiful countryside! What a pretty city!" said Lucía, drawing closer to the windows.

"It looks like a white dove slumbering in its nest of willows and mulberry trees," added Marín, whom his wife asked, "Fernando, is this our second largest city? What are the people like?"

"Yes, dear, the second largest; and its beauty can only be compared with the goodness of its daughters. You'll really enjoy the days we stay here," Don Fernando replied; and the sound of the bell announced that the train was pulling into the main station, where a good crowd was waiting, since the telegraph had already brought the news of the accident, and curiosity had mobilized hundreds of persons.

Once the carriage doors had opened, swarms of urchins descended on the baggage, and the passengers of the train mingled with those of the horse cars, which ran along a convenient route and brought Don Fernando Marín and his family right to the door of the Gran Hotel Imperial, where they all got off.

30

They entered a spacious room papered in deep red with gold trim; gold pilasters marked the corners; curtains, white as ermine, screened the doors and windows, beneath a valance of scarlet silk bordered in gold and secured with silken cords. The floor, covered with fine Belgian carpets, made a pleasant contrast with the Louis XV furniture, upholstered in dark blue napped silk and reflected in two enormous mirrors that occupied almost the entire right-hand wall.

"This is the parlor. Is it to madame's liking?" said Monsieur Petit, making an exaggerated bow.

"Yes; blue is my favorite color. I'll be happy here," Lucía replied to the hotel-keeper, which is who Monsieur Petit was.

"This must be a bedroom," said Don Fernando, pointing to a door.

"Precisely, sir. We offer every comfort and excellent service to the travelers who are kind enough to honor the Hotel Imperial with their presence," answered Monsieur Petit, with all the courtliness of a Frenchman recommending his establishment.

"We expected no less."

"If there's anything you need, monsieur, madame, you can ring for it with this cord," Monsieur Petit informed them. Then he bowed and left the room.

Margarita, who was examining everything around her, asked with innocent simplicity, "What would Manuel have said to all this, Godmother?"

Lucía smiled the smile of a mother who delights in powerful feelings. In that question she read the poem of a virginal heart's memories, and she answered, "He'll tell you himself when he gets here."

"Are we waiting for him here?"

"Yes, we are, dear," Don Fernando assured her, taking part in the exchange between godmother and godchild.

Rosalía came over to Marín and, putting her arms around his legs, said, "Another cookie!"

The door opened to admit the servant who was leading the porter with their baggage.

• • • •

A week was enough to make the travelers acquainted with the great city. They observed everything and inquired into its ways and customs with the thoroughness of those who travel with limited but first-hand knowledge that will expand as they peruse the open textbook that the practical school of the great world offers them. Straight and broad, though badly paved, streets; churches built in Moorish and other styles, their asphalt and trachyte rock grown cold and hard with the passing of the years; women of legendary beauty; robust peasant women, the purity of their souls reflected on their faces; Jewish shops offering to buy and sell; theaters spreading civilization as they grew in number—they saw it all and formed opinions about it all.

Nothing escaped Lucía's microscopic scrutiny, ever guided by the informed comments of Don Fernando, to whom she said, "I assure you, Fernando dear, that this place would be heaven if it weren't for an objection that occurs to me from simple experience and that has nothing to do with material conditions."

"I know, dear; I foresaw those objections: impatience at being delayed here, eagerness to reach Lima, the bright light that captivates every moth in Peru. It really is irresistible."

"Very logical, Fernando, but wide of the mark," replied Lucía, laughing and patting him on the shoulder.

"Is it? Well then, tell me, what has most drawn your attention?"

"Two things have drawn my attention," Lucía replied simply, using her handkerchief to wipe her lips, slightly moistened by her laughter.

"Ah, I know, you scamp!" Don Fernando answered, returning her affectionate pat.

"What do you know? I'll bet you never guess."

"It must be all the friars of every kind that you see on the streets."

"Cold, cold, my love!"

"So what is it?"

Lucía turned serious, collected her thoughts as though recalling something distant, sighed deeply from the bottom of her heart, and said, "What has most drawn my attention is the surprising number of children in the foundling home. Ah, Fernando dearest! I know that a woman of the people does not cast her flesh and blood away like that. I know she has no need to cast them away, because those social conventions that wear the mask of a feigned virtue mean nothing to a mother of that class and to her child, the fruit of chance, or perhaps of crime. May God forgive me for thinking ill of anyone, Fernando; but these thoughts have led me to others, sad ones, very sad, and reminded me, not that I wanted it, of Marcela's secret."

Don Fernando was surprised as he attentively listened to that discourse on morality. He was stunned by the lucidity of a great soul, of whose greatness he had perhaps been unaware until that moment. Silence fell between husband and wife, until he sighed with as deep a sorrow as Lucía's and said, "At times the poor also have recourse to the foundling home." And with that he approached his wife and placed a kiss on the forehead of the woman who would soon be the mother of his first-born child.

31

Manuel's journey was a happy one. It seemed as though the winged gods of Love and Marriage had allowed their balsam breath to fall on the snowy peaks and the prairies that he crossed on the train, unaware of the dangers that only days before had threatened the

Marín family and with it his Margarita, that hymn of tenderness rising from the most delicate cords of his heart as from the Aeolian harp played by the angels of Happiness as they beat their ethereal wings over the immense plain.

He, too, glimpsed the longed-for city in the Andean valley, which for him was the empress of the world because it sheltered the queen of his heart. He arrived; he took a room in the Casino Rosado, hurried through the necessary grooming, changed his clothes, and dashed off to the Imperial, saying to himself, "Thank you, Lord! I'm going to see her! How true it is that at the age of twenty our blood is hot and can bear no delay! Not one more day can I put off turning my dreams of happiness into reality . . . but . . . should I speak to Don Fernando right away? Ah, this need for prudence that holds back the impulses of our soul! During these days of her absence jealousy has already stung me with its poisoned barb. Oh, how could her loveliness, so authentically Peruvian, the beauty of her soul so innocent of worldly chatter, fail to surround her with admirers who will dizzy her with their polished phrases and taint the heart of the woman I love!"

Manuel walked as though drunk, noticing nothing in the unfamiliar streets, mechanically following the directions the porter of the Casino had given him. "Jealousy is both a low and a noble sentiment," he told himself. "Coiled like a snake it sleeps deep within a lofty happy love; it crawls on the surface of a lower sort of love and bites us with its poisonous fangs. No jealousy for me, no! I love Margarita so much!"

Manuel's footsteps resounded in the courtyard of the Hotel Imperial, and that sound caused Margarita's soul to tremble. Why is it that a woman in love not only recognizes the footsteps of her lover but can sense his perfumed breath from far off and distinguish the vibration of his voice among the echoes of countless voices? Mysteries of that magnetic current that unites our souls even as it makes our bodies tremble!

The door turned on its hinges, a slight breeze moved the delicate curtains, and Manuel appeared in the blue parlor, looking as distinguished and engaging as could be.

"Yes, it was he!" Margarita said to herself, standing next to a marble-topped table that held an enormous Chinese porcelain vase filled with daffodils and aromatic jasmine.

"Señora, Señor!" said Manuel, offering his hand to his interlocutors.

"Don Manuel!" husband and wife answered almost simultaneously, shaking his hand.

"My dear Margarita!"

"Have you really come, Manuel?"

The two young people were on the verge of an embrace, but something held them back. Yet from their eyes shone the embrace of two souls that dream of an eternal union.

"Please sit down. And . . . how are folks back in Kíllac?" Marín asked.

"Fine, sir."

"Has your father's problem been cleared up? Did that poor sexton, Isidro, get out of jail?"

"It wasn't hard to get Don Sebastián out; but in Isidro's case I had to take some additional steps because there'd been a committal, an attachment of his property, and who knows what else. And so I come with a light heart after carrying out your instructions, Don Fernando," Manuel answered.

"Ah, you're a perfect gentleman. I couldn't send you the letter for Guzmán because there wasn't a single mail carrier to be found at the post-stations where we stopped. And what about our latest subprefect?"

"A disaster, Don Fernando. Clean as a whistle the first days; but after that, I know he got some heifers so he'd free Estéfano, Escobedo, and Verdejo."

"Obviously there's no solution, my friend," Don Fernando said, getting up.

"And what do you say to my seeing through that bogus trip of Estéfano's?" Lucía asked Manuel.

"Ah, señora, when it comes to shrewdness and being judges of character, you ladies will always have the better of us. I can't stand the fellow," Manuel replied.

"These pettifogging scribblers, half-educated and with no clear aim in life, are a true plague in those unfortunate towns," said Don Fernando.

"They're Pontius Pilates, as madam baptized Estéfano," Manuel added with a smile.

"Heavens, this is the first time I've laughed since that scare," Lucía remarked, looking at Margarita, who was also smiling.

"You don't know about our misadventure on the train?" Don Fernando asked Manuel.

"No, sir. What happened?"

"Well, we came within a hair's breadth of being smashed to pieces."

"How was that?" Manuel asked with a shudder, looking at Margarita.

"The train derailed. Didn't they tell you when you were coming?"

"Yes, now that I think of it, I heard two passengers talking; but I thought it was about something that happened long ago."

"Lord, what we went through!" Lucía interrupted.

"Rosalía was hurt," Margarita said.

"And how about the rest of you?"

"Quite undamaged, fortunately, and that was the end of it. Let's not talk about it any more because Lucía's nerves can't bear it," Don Fernando suggested.

"Small wonder, Señor Marín."

"And what do you say the judge wanted for letting Isidro go free?" Don Fernando asked.

"For him to dismiss the case, you have to submit a declaration that the attack on your house was a misguided attempt to catch some bandits who were believed to have taken refuge there, and that it was simply a civil commotion, and so forth. I'm going to go right back to settle everything, see to it that Don Sebastián is all right, and arrange my definitive journey to Lima," Manuel informed him.

"Well, I'm going to draw up this declaration in no uncertain terms, my friend. I'm not going back to Kíllac, and I want to protect that poor Indian whom some day they might harass on this account. Do you think my declaration will put an end to it all?" Marín said.

"Yes, Don Fernando, although without the declaration the case would go to the attorney general's office and . . . still eventually come to nothing."

"And so you've freed Isidro Champi. Ah, but who will free that whole hapless race?"

"That's a question for every man in Peru, my dear friend!"

"And so you're going back to Kíllac?" Lucía asked.

"Yes, ma'am."

"And aren't we going on to Lima?" Margarita said, crushing a jasmine blossom that she had torn from the bouquet.

"Yes, Margarita; I'm going and then I'm coming back. Traveling is simple for a man," Manuel replied.

"And how's Doña Petronila?" Lucía asked.

"You can imagine how she is with me gone."

"Well, since there's mail going out tomorrow, I'll have the declaration for Guzmán ready so it will get there before you do. Now I have some errands in town, so if you'll excuse me . . ."

"Of course, Señor Marín. I think you're saving time by sending the declaration to Señor Guzmán, but . . . I also have to talk to you about something else, something very important. When would you have some free time?" Manuel asked, clearly agitated, and picking up his hat.

"I'd be glad to see you this evening, any time after eight."

"Come have a cup of chocolate with us," Lucía invited Manuel.

"Thank you, ma'am; I'll be sure to come," the young man answered, politely taking his leave; and the door closed after him, separating him from the queen of all his being.

On leaving the hotel, Manuel set to walking around the city; and as he passed by a jeweler's shop he saw a lovely cross of agate delicately mounted in gold and displayed in a purple velvet case. "What a fine gem! How pretty it would look on Margarita's breast!" he thought, and stopped to look at it more closely. "I'll buy it!" he decided. He stepped inside the shop, settled on a price, and paid with three large bills issued by the Bank of Arequipa; and putting the case in his pocket, he continued on his way, lost in thoughts that fluttered through his mind like glowing sparks or like swallows that dip to brush the ground with their sable wings.

32

Hanging in a cloudless sky, the moon, no longer quite full, was shedding its silvery light, which, though it neither heats nor strikes the eye like the rays of the sun, envelops nature in a sweet and serene melancholy and sheds a warm and perfumed air on those December nights made for lovers' meetings.

Manuel kept looking at his gold watch, restless and lost in thought. Finally the hands showed the appointed time, and he took his hat and rushed out.

In the blue parlor of the Imperial, brilliantly lit by elegant crystal chandeliers, the door stood wide open. Margarita, leaning back in one of the chairs next to the table with the flowers, was playing with the hem of a white handkerchief, her mind off among the clouds of her dreams. All around her was deepest silence.

When Manuel reached the door, she quickly changed her position; and her first glance went toward the bedroom, to which Lucía had no doubt withdrawn.

"Margarita, my dearest darling! I've come for you!" said Manuel, taking the girl's hand and sitting down by her side.

"You have? But you're going away again," she answered, without withdrawing the hand that Manuel's was softly pressing.

"Put aside all your doubts, dear Margarita: I'm going to ask Don Fernando for your hand in marriage."

"And will my godmother know about it?" the girl interrupted him.

"I'll ask both of them. You . . . are going to be mine!" the young man said, his eyes fixed on Margarita's while he raised her hand to his lips.

"And what if they don't want that?" Margarita asked innocently, lowering her bashful glance.

"But do you love me, Margarita? Do you love me? For God's sake answer me!" Manuel pressed her, urged on by the frenzy of his all-devouring eyes.

"Yes," Marcela's daughter said in a timid voice; and Manuel, reeling in his elation, touched his lips to the lips of his beloved and drew in her breath, drank the pure dewdrop of her soul in the chalice of happiness, only to be left thirstier than before. Trembling with emotion, Margarita sighed, "Manuel!"

Just then, as though on cue, Manuel remembered something. He put his hand in his pocket, brought out the velvet case, opened it, and handing its contents to Margarita, said, "By this cross I swear to you, Margarita, that my first lover's kiss shall be as chaste as you! Take this cross, my love; agate gives strength to the heart." Almost mechanically Margarita took the cross, closed the case, and hid it in her bosom with the speed of a thief, for the sound of the bedroom doors announced the entrance of Lucía and Don Fernando.

Manuel could barely control his agitation. His face was the color of the pomegranate blossom, and all his body trembled slightly. Had we been able to take his hand, we should have found it damp with a cold perspiration; had we penetrated into his mind, we should have seen a hundred ideas swarming like bees, struggling to see which would be the first to spring forth clothed in words.

Margarita, stunned by the novel feelings in her heart, could ill conceal her condition.

"There's something serious on your mind, Manuel," said Don Fernando as he looked at the young man.

"Señor Marín," Manuel answered in a tremulous voice and broken sentences, "it's the most serious thing . . . I expect to feel . . . in my life. I love Margarita and I've come . . . to ask you for her hand . . . in three years' time."

"Manuel, I'd be delighted, but Don Sebastián . . ."

"I know what objection you're going to raise, sir, and I have to begin by demolishing it. I am not the son of Don Sebastián Pancorbo. I owe my being to a misfortune, to a man's taking advantage of my mother's weakness. Between me and Don Sebastián there is a bond of gratitude, because when he married my mother while she was carrying me in her womb, he saved her honor and gave me his name."

"Bless him!" said Margarita, raising her hands to heaven and unable to remain silent.

"My dear!" said Lucía.

"Your noble conduct obliges us to make use of the right that Marcela, before she died, bequeathed to us along with the secret she entrusted to Lucía," Don Fernando answered gravely.

"By all means, Don Fernando; the child is not responsible in these cases, and we must place the blame on the laws of men, and never on God."

"You're quite right."

Manuel, lowering his voice a little, and even his mortified glance, said, "Don Fernando, my father was Bishop Don Pedro Miranda y Claro, the former parish priest of Kíllac."

Don Fernando and Lucía turned pale as though jolted by a single electric discharge. Surprise froze the words in their throats, and for some moments the room was plunged into total silence, which Lucía broke by exclaiming, "My God!"; and the joints of her hands cracked from the force with which her emotion pressed them together.

With lightning speed the name and life of Father Pascual flashed through Don Fernando's mind, and he said to himself, "Shall the father's sin crush the happiness of two angels of goodness?" and as though still doubting what he had heard, he asked anew, "Who did you say?"

Manuel, regaining some of his composure, hastened to reply, "Bishop Claro, sir."

Don Fernando came up to the young man and drew him to his breast, saying, "You were right, Don Manuel: let us not lay the blame on God but on the inhumane laws of men that deprive the child of its father, the bird of its nest, the flower of its stem . . ."

"Manuel! Margarita! Poor birds torn from the nest!" Lucía interrupted, pale as the almond blossom, distraught, with tears coursing down her cheeks.

Manuel could not understand this scene in which Margarita trembled in silence like the lily buffeted by the storm.

Don Fernando's words had to put an end to the painful situation; but his manly voice, ever firm and frank, quavered like a child's. His noble high forehead was bathed in perspiration, and he shook his head in doubt and astonishment. Finally, pointing to Margarita as though entrusting her to his wife's care, and turning to Manuel, he went on, "There are some things in life that crush us completely. Be brave, young man . . . unfortunate young man! On the very threshold of the grave Marcela confided to Lucía the secret of Margarita's birth. She is not the daughter of the Indian Juan Yupanqui, but of . . . Bishop Claro."

"My sister!"

"My brother!"

So exclaimed Manuel and Margarita with a single breath; and the girl fell into the arms of her godmother, whose sobs accompanied the anguish of those fledgling birds *torn from the nest.*

Printed in the United States
135353LV00002B/105/A

Made in the USA
Lexington, KY
16 October 2015